"ON TO THE ALAMO"

COL. CROCKETT'S EXPLOITS AND ADVENTURES IN TEXAS

DAVID (a.k.a Davy) CROCKETT was born in Tennessee in 1786 and was raised in frontier country, suffering much hardship during his early years. As a young man he served under Andrew Jackson during the Creek War (1814) and soon began establishing a reputation as a mighty hunter and a teller of even mightier tales. These qualities, along with quick wit and considerable charisma, led to his election to the Tennessee legislature (1821) and then in 1827 to the U.S. House of Representatives, where he was an advocate for the frontiersmen of western Tennessee until defeated for reelection in 1835. Elected as a Jacksonian Democrat, he soon began to differ with the president on a number of issues and by the end of his career had drifted toward positions held by the Whig Party. Early on, the rough-hewn congressman began to call public attention to himself through his humorous remarks and tall tales; by 1830 he had inspired a popular theatrical farce and shortly thereafter collaborated on several autobiographical works, including the well-known *A Narrative of the Life of David Crockett* (1834).

Out of office and suffering from financial reverses, Crockett headed for Texas in 1836, hoping to buy land to which he could relocate his wife and children. But his plans were changed by the armed revolt of other American emigrants who hoped to throw off Mexican rule and establish an independent republic. Crockett joined the small garrison at the Alamo in San Antonio, where he gained a further measure of fame as a martyr to the cause of Texan freedom, dying a heroic death at the hands of the attacking Mexican Army led by President Santa Anna.

JOHN SEELYE is a Graduate Research Professor of American Literature at the University of Florida. He is the author of two novels and a number of books dealing with American culture from the colonial period to the twentieth century. He has written several essays on the mythic Davy Crockett, devoted to separating fact from fiction. He serves as consulting editor of the Penguin Classics.

RICHARD PENN SMITH

"On to the Alamo"

COL. CROCKETT'S EXPLOITS AND ADVENTURES IN TEXAS

Edited with an Introduction and Notes by
JOHN SEELYE

PENGUIN CLASSICS

PENGUIN BOOKS

Published by the Penguin Group
Penguin Group (USA) Inc., 375 Hudson Street,
New York, New York 10014, U.S.A.
Penguin Books Ltd, 80 Strand,
London WC2R 0RL, England
Penguin Books Australia Ltd, 250 Camberwell Road, Camberwell,
Victoria 3124, Australia
Penguin Books Canada Ltd, 10 Alcorn Avenue,
Toronto, Ontario, Canada M4V 3B2
Penguin Books India (P) Ltd, 11 Community Centre, Panchsheel Park,
New Delhi – 110 017, India
Penguin Books (N.Z.) Ltd, Cnr Rosedale and Airborne Roads, Albany,
Auckland, New Zealand
Penguin Books (South Africa) (Pty) Ltd, 24 Sturdee Avenue,
Rosebank, Johannesburg 2196, South Africa

Penguin Books Ltd, Registered Offices:
80 Strand, London WC2R 0RL, England

Col. Crockett's Exploits and Adventures in Texas first published in the
United States of America 1836
This edition with an introduction and notes by John Seelye published in
Penguin Books 2003

1   3   5   7   9   10   8   6   4   2

Introduction and notes copyright © John Seelye, 2003
All rights reserved

LIBRARY OF CONGRESS CATALOGING IN PUBLICATION DATA
Smith, Richard Penn, 1799–1854.
[Col. Crockett's exploits and adventures in Texas]
On to the Alamo : Col. Crockett's exploits and adventures in Texas / Richard Penn
Smith ; edited with an introduction and notes by John Seelye.
p.   cm.—(Penguin classics)
Includes bibliographical references (p.).
ISBN 0 14 24 3764 6
1. Crockett, Davy, 1786–1836.   2. Texas—History—Revolution, 1835–1836.   3. Alamo
(San Antonio, Tex.)—Siege, 1836.   4. Pioneers—Tennessee—Biography.   I. Seelye, John D.
II. Title.   III. Series.
F436.C96136 2004
976.4'03—dc21   2003053598

Printed in the United States of America
Set in Sabon

Contents

For Ham Hill

Introduction

I.

It has been more than sixty years since Walter Blair, the distinguished scholar of American humor and folklore, established that there were at least "six Davy Crocketts." They ranged from the Democratic congressman from Tennessee who set himself in opposition to the policies of President Andrew Jackson to the "mythic" hero of comic almanacs published in the 1830s and '40s, a figure essential to the tradition of southwestern humor that was brought to a fine art by Mark Twain. But perhaps the most enduring of the Crocketts has been the martyr-hero of the Alamo, who, with the other defenders of the fort in San Antonio, was killed in 1836 by the army commanded by General Santa Anna, president of Mexico. Texas was then Mexican territory, and Santa Anna was attempting to drive out American colonists because they were planning to establish a republic independent of his tyrannical rule.

And if there were six Crocketts then it must be said that five died defending the Alamo: the one who was shot and killed early in the battle as he crossed the fort's parade ground, the one who fell surrounded by the bodies of the Mexican soldiers he had killed, the one captured and executed with four other Americans on the orders of Santa Anna, the one who tried to escape that fate by claiming immunity through virtue of his status as a U.S. congressman, and the one who, on being sentenced to die, attempted to assassinate Santa Anna before being killed by the general's men.

The preferred version deep in the hearts of Texans is the second, and indeed it was the one reported firsthand by the two survivors of the massacre at the Alamo: Mrs. Susanna Dickinson, widow of a gunnery officer slain in the battle, and a slave named Joe, the servant of Colonel William B. Travis, who died while commanding the defense of the fort. The alternative versions may be traced to Mexican and other sources, some of dubious authority, many recounted well after the fact. Moreover, it must be said that the stories told by Mrs. Dickinson and Joe were filtered through a journalistic sieve. In short, the manner of Colonel Crockett's death will never be known, but none of the contradictory accounts deny him his heroic stature, not even the story of his attempt to bluff his way to freedom, which is the kind of brass that passes for gold in Texas.

The point to be made is that the fame of Davy Crockett is inseparable from the name of the Alamo, and will last so long as the other endures in the national memory. "The Alamo," wrote the journalist Richard Harding Davis in 1892, "is to the Southwest what Independence Hall is to the United States, and Bunker Hill to the East; but the pride of it belongs to every American, whether he lives in Texas or in Maine" (Davis: 17). The occasion of this remark was Davis's visit to San Antonio, and the irony of it is that, according to Davis's biographer, Arthur Lubow, the reporter had only recently learned about the Alamo. At a dinner party in New York given by Theodore Roosevelt, then a young civil service commissioner, the host was politely but firmly indignant when his guest admitted his ignorance regarding that sacred site in Texas. TR forthwith informed Davis of the history of the Alamo, which the reporter dutifully included early in his account of his western travels.

Roosevelt in 1892 had only just begun his political career, which would be given a considerable boost by his role in the Spanish-American War, thanks in large part to the account of the fight for San Juan Hill written by Richard Harding Davis, but he was already associated with the American West in the minds, if not the hearts, of his fellow Americans. Roosevelt had written books about his adventures as a ranchman in North Dakota and the first two volumes of his *Winning of the West* had been published in 1889. More to the point, in 1895 he would write, in collaboration with his friend Henry Cabot Lodge, *Hero Tales from American History*.

This was a book intended for "young Americans," containing the stories of "some Americans who showed that they knew how to live and how to die; who proved their truth by their endeavor, and who joined to the stern and manly qualities which are essential to the well being of a masterful race the virtues of gentleness, of patriotism, and of lofty adherence to an ideal" (xxiii). This jingoistic, chauvinistic collection was in many ways a prolegomenon to the forthcoming war with Spain, and among Roosevelt's contributions was an essay titled "Remember the Alamo," the famous slogan that soon enough would be updated to "Remember the *Maine*."

The hero who emerges from Roosevelt's account of the Alamo siege was predictably Davy Crockett, who "was the last man" left standing: "wounded in a dozen places, he faced his foes with his back to the wall, ringed around by the bodies of the men he had slain" (86). But as Mexican lancers held him at bay, "weakened by wounds and loss of blood," he was helpless against soldiers with carbines who "shot him down." "Some say," added Roosevelt, "that when Crockett fell from his wounds, he was taken alive and was then shot by Santa Anna's order; but his fate cannot be told with certainty, for not a single American was left alive. At any rate, after Crockett fell the fight was over. Every one of the hardy men who had held the Alamo lay still in death. Yet they died well avenged, four times their number fell at their hands in the battle" (87).

In *Hero Tales*, Crockett keeps company with, among other notable Americans, Daniel Boone and George Rogers Clark, whose stories were also told by Roosevelt, a man drawn to soldiers who were also frontiersmen and mighty hunters. As the revisionist historian Richard Slotkin has maintained, Roosevelt regarded Boone and Crockett as "feasible role models as well as heroic ideals," and his "veneration of archetypal frontiersman . . . was an American equivalent of the Victorian gentleman's playing at medieval chivalry" (*Gunfighter Nation*: 37). In 1888, Roosevelt and Lodge founded the Boone and Crockett Club, an organization whose members were devoted to "manly sport with the rifle" and who were dedicated to the preservation of large game animals through legislation (Morris: 383–84). In that same year Roosevelt published *Ranch Life and the Hunting-Trail*, which with his earlier *Hunting Trips of a Ranchman* (1885) established his fame as a man in whose arms a rifle sat easy and whose walls were covered by trophy heads of formidable beasts he had killed.

David Crockett's autobiographical *Narrative of the Life of David Crockett of the State of Tennessee* (1834) contains several accounts of his encounters with large bears, the pioneer's most ferocious four-legged adversary, from which he invariably emerged victorious. But in *Hero Tales* it was Crockett's slaughter of Mexicans that Roosevelt celebrated in the name of "the freedom of Texas," for the courageous Tennessean was representative of the other frontiersmen killed at the Alamo. They were "a wild and ill-disciplined band, little used to restraint or control, but they were men of iron courage and great bodily powers, skilled in the use of their weapons, and ready to meet with stern and uncomplaining indifference whatever doom fate might have in store for them" (85).

Slotkin notes that the battle for the Alamo occurred too late for inclusion in TR's *Winning of the West* (1889–96), the chronology of which ends early in the nineteenth century. But drawing on Roosevelt's account in *Hero Tales,* he observes that "Crockett's death at the Alamo would have symbolized the transfer of all those qualities that the hunter personified to a new field of struggle in which the primary enemy is not a 'savage' race but a civilized (or 'semicivilized') nation formed by an inferior race in which Indian and Latin stocks are mixed" (51). Certainly, Roosevelt's description of the defenders of the Alamo suggests the qualities of the western men he would bring together as the Rough Riders in 1898, warranting Slotkin's assertion that the Alamo signified "the shift from one form of Frontier expansion to another . . . provid[ing] a metaphoric anticipation of Roosevelt's polemic on behalf of overseas imperialism, which he saw as the necessary continuation of the 'Winning of the West.'"

Roosevelt's account of the Alamo drew in part on a book

published in 1836, *Col. Crockett's Exploits and Adventures in Texas,* a first-person narrative supposedly based on a diary written by Crockett that was recovered by a Mexican general after the battle for the Alamo. Later found on the general's body by an American after the subsequent battle of San Jacinto, in which an army led by Sam Houston defeated Santa Anna and took the Mexican president prisoner, the "diary" was rushed into print and was regarded as genuine for many years. Eventually the book was declared spurious and identified as a work of virtual fiction, but it was so vivid an account of Crockett's last adventure that it continued to influence other writers. Thus the Walt Disney version of the Crockett story, filmed in the 1950s, starring Fess Parker as the "King of the Wild Frontier," relied on *Exploits and Adventures* for its account of the hero's journey across Texas toward the Alamo and immortality.

Most recently, a lengthy excerpt from *Exploits and Adventures* appeared in a collection of documents, *Eyewitness to the Alamo,* edited by Bill Groneman, with the explanation that although the book was "not written by Crockett," it was accepted for years as authentic, and "has served as an eyewitness account of the Alamo in the past" (43). After all, Groneman argues, so many "other accounts are phoney, or at least suspect, there is enough reason to include this one." The thesis underlying Groneman's collection, borrowed from Thucydides, is that the historic record is made up of such a multiplicity of contradictory accounts of events, most of which are dictated by self (or other) interests, that the truth can never be known. Since the historical record is mostly fiction, why not include fiction presented as fact?

By 1884 the author of *Exploits and Adventures* had been identified as Richard Penn Smith, a Philadelphia author hired by the publishers Carey and Hart in 1836 to produce a book attributed to Crockett that would exploit his recent martyrdom. The hope was that its popularity might help the sales of another book credited to the famous Tennessee congressman, *An Account of Colonel Crockett's Tour of the North and Down East,* issued by Carey and Hart the year before. It must be said that by 1836 ghostwritten autobiographical books credited to Crockett were not uncommon, starting with *Life and Adventures of Colonel David Crockett of West Tennessee* (1833), a popular collection of hunting tales and humorous stories rendered in the first person that appeared later that same year as *Sketches and Eccentricities of Colonel Crockett of West Tennessee.*

There is evidence that Crockett contributed to this book, which he later disavowed as his own work because he emerged from it as something of a backwoods buffoon. He attempted to correct this comic image with his *Narrative of the Life of David Crockett,* a text heavily revised by another hand, for the simple reason that Crockett was strategically unlettered. Though he became a congressman, his correspondence has the orthographic and syntactical resonance of the tall tales issued under his name as the "Davy Crockett" almanacs, the first of which was published the year of his death. Inspired by the boastful hunter and Indian slayer of *The Life and Adventures of Colonel David Crockett,* the almanac anecdotes were entirely spurious, though they contributed greatly to Crockett's subsequent stature as a folk figure.

Constance Rourke may be credited with Crockett's twentieth-century elevation to mythic status, thanks to her biography that first appeared in 1934. In keeping with the nativist spirit of the times, her book is a melange of elements taken from the autobiographical narratives and the almanacs, and in the latter instance Rourke suggested that the fictional tall tales had parallels with traditional mythology. Rourke believed that the almanac stories were derived from authentic oral sources, originating in the backwoods and the frontier, and should be acknowledged as genuine American folklore. This uncritical stance was forwarded by Walter Blair, who also compiled material from the almanacs about the famous and soon fabulous Mississippi boatman Mike Fink, portrayed as Crockett's boon companion. Blair conjoined them both with other "folk" figures like Paul Bunyan, the giant lumberjack; Mose, the courageous New York fireman; and Pecos Bill, the storied cowboy.

In time, the heroes of this pantheon were shown to be the creation of relatively sophisticated eastern writers, print-shop hacks for the most part who may have borrowed from European mythological sources but whose stories had nothing to do with any backwoods oral tradition. Indeed, the "heroes" they created were for the most part crude, violent, racist, and misogynistic braggarts and buffoons. These savage caricatures of primarily frontier types were satiric representatives of the democratic masses whose power was associated with the emergence of President Andrew Jackson. "Fakelore," not folklore, as Richard Dorson came to style them, the comic almanacs were expressions of eastern elitism, uneasiness regarding the threat of Jacksonian democracy. This anxiety came to full flower a half-century later during the presidential contest between William McKinley, a Republican identified as the candidate of moneyed eastern elites, and William Jennings Bryan, a Democrat with a large western agrarian constituency, the heart and soul of Populism.

We may find the roots of the antipathy between East and West buried in the politics of the early 1830s, specifically with the emergence of the Whig party in reaction to the ascendancy of Jacksonian democracy. And it was out of the political broils of this decade that the mythic Davy Crockett first emerged, as a "hero" whose self-creation and self-contradictoriness are a register of the complex discontent that was sown by the ultra-democratic yet dictatorial policies of Andrew Jackson. As V. L. Parrington wrote, Crockett provides "a full-length portrait of the Jacksonian leveler, in the days when the great social revolution was establishing the principles of an equalitarian democracy" (II, 390–91).

Yet David Crockett, as he always styled himself, was a single-minded congressional advocate of an increasingly anti-Jackson policy; indeed his fame rose because it was fueled by his antipathy toward "Old Hickory." Without that anger there would have been no legendary Davy Crockett and most definitely no hero of the Alamo, never mind of the book titled *Col. Crockett's Exploits and Adventures in Texas*. That is, to understand Davy Crockett of Texas fame we must start with David Crockett of Tennessee.

II.

The son of Rebeckah Hawkins Crockett and her husband, John, David was born in 1786 in eastern Tennessee, his parents having moved there from North Carolina, fleeing those familiar frontier specters, poverty and debt. John Crockett's own parents had been slaughtered by Native Americans in 1777, shortly after they had relocated from North Carolina to land that would soon become Tennessee. John was married by 1780, and settled in Washington County, North Carolina. Court records supply the material of his early biography, which was typical of his generation, for like many he was the son of an immigrant Irishman who had sought prosperity in the West but found only hardship and sudden death. The son shared the familial (and generational) propensity for misfortune: with a partner John built a mill in 1794 that was subsequently destroyed by a flood. He also speculated in land, one parcel of which he sold for a profit, but another parcel in eastern Tennessee, to which he moved his family from North Carolina after losing his mill, was auctioned off in 1795 to satisfy his debts.

On a remnant of this land John built a tavern, and it was there, in Greene County, Tennessee, that David—namesake of his late grandfather Crockett—was born, a fifth son, well short of the blessed seventh, and with no great expectations. His youth, chronicled by himself in the *Narrative* of his life published in 1834, was a series of hardships and feats of endurance. At the age of eleven or twelve he was hired out by his father to a man driving a herd of cattle to Virginia who attempted to keep him on afterward as his employee, against the boy's will. David escaped on a snowy evening, hiking through knee-deep snow for seven hours until he was rescued by travelers who, knowing his father, came to his aid.

Once again, one of the party tried to keep the boy with him, but David continued on by foot until he reached home. Then, in the fall of 1799, he ran away, fearing retribution by his father or his teacher (or both) for having fought with a schoolmate, and hired himself out to a drover taking cattle to Virginia. David's later attempts to return were balked by this and subsequent employers, who often swindled him out of his pay, and it was 1802 before he was able to reach his father's tavern, with nothing to show for his experience save a greater awareness of the frequent meanness and occasional generosity of strangers.

The schoolyard episode had been forgotten, but, having been gone for more than two years, David had missed a critical period in his education. He was in effect illiterate, not even knowing the alphabet. For the next year he worked for hire, earning money to pay his father's debts, but he later managed to acquire six months of further schooling by hiring himself out to a teacher in return for instruction. He could then read, write, and "cipher," on a very basic level, sufficient for frontier conditions. Despite David's poor prospects, he determined in 1805 to get married, again encountering obstacles, as the first young woman he courted married suddenly out from under him. But the second venture was successful.

In 1806, he married Mary Finley, called Polly, over her mother's objections, and the couple rented a small farm that yielded a meager income. Two sons were born to them before David set out in 1811 with his father-in-law for central Tennessee to claim land in Lincoln County. Crockett supported himself by hunting (game in new country being plentiful), a skill at which he became adept over the next two years, but in 1813 he left the Finleys for Franklin County in western Tennessee, the frontier region with which he would be identified for the rest of his short life.

The War of 1812 was identified in the Southwest as a conflict with hostile Native Americans who were in league with the British. In Tennessee it was called the Creek War, during which Andrew Jackson first distinguished himself as a military leader before marching on to New Orleans and fame. It was during this war, also, that Crockett as an enlisted mounted volunteer first crossed paths with "the old general" while serving under his command during several important battles, service that took him as far as Tallahassee in Florida but not on to New Orleans. According to an early biographer, Crockett was present when the captain commanding his troop, which had been repeatedly insubordinate, went to Jackson for advice, that Crockett, upon returning to camp, distilled as "Be sure you are right, then go ahead," a motto which he would famously make his own in future years (Shackford: 26).

In his "authorized" autobiography, Crockett claimed to have been involved in a mutiny against Jackson, identifying himself with those soldiers whose term of enlistment had expired, and who attempted to return home against the general's orders but were turned back by Jackson himself. The facts were otherwise, David having been with his family on an approximate furlough at the time, and as his best biographer, James Atkins Shackford, observes, his claim that he had participated in the mutiny was inspired by his subsequent quarrels with President Jackson during his years in Congress.

Shackford also notes that Crockett's account of his brief military career was somewhat exaggerated for political effect, but by all accounts, including his own, Crockett was a brave and diligent soldier. He underwent great hardship from hunger and cold while improving his hunting abilities by supplying his fellow militiamen with meat. He left the army somewhat short of his ninety days of contracted service, but he paid another man to serve out the remainder of his time. No deserter, despite his subsequent claim, David ended his enlistment with the rank of fourth sergeant.

Crockett returned home early in 1815, about the time that Mary gave birth to their third child, a daughter. In the summer of that same year Mary died, and David, now responsible for a growing family, soon remarried. His new wife, Elizabeth ("Betsey") Patton, was herself a young widow with children, well-born in frontier terms and a woman of strong character who would be of great help to David, who was not much gifted with "managerial abilities" (Shackford: 34). His gifts were, like those of Cooper's Leatherstocking, suited for the wilderness life and the hunting trail, and in subsequent years he had frequent opportunity for displaying them.

After an initial foray into Alabama in 1816, he took his family west the following year, to Lawrence County in Tennessee, newly created from land ceded by the Chickasaws, hence filled with wild game. There he became a justice of the peace and was elected colonel of the local militia, warranting the title by which he was thenceforth known, not an honorary but a genuine rank. It was also an indication of Crockett's popularity, which was further testified to by his election to the state legislature in 1821 as a representative from his county.

Colonel Crockett's military rank and elevation to political power are associated by Shackford with the same "squatter democracy" that swept Andrew Jackson into office in 1828. The reference is to Crockett's frontier constituency, which in western Tennessee was often identified with settlers who had taken up lands without authentic claims. But in Jackson's case it overlooks the support the president received from northeastern Democrats, not only workers but elites represented by the historian George Bancroft and the author Nathaniel Hawthorne. Nonetheless, it is undeniable that Crockett's style of political campaigning was very different from that found in long-established communities in the Northeast and the South and resembles the depictions of stump speaking and election days in Missouri painted by George Caleb Bingham.

It was by Crockett's account something of a game, staged between friendly adversaries who took pride in verbal athletics and pranks. It involved (as Bingham's paintings suggest) the dispensation by candidates of free liquor to the electorate, and required a sense of humor and a fund of anecdotes. Elections, like camp meetings, were social affairs, providing relief from the isolation and tedium of life on the frontier. Democrats being virtually without competition in southwestern Tennessee, party was not the issue, and candidates vied with each other in promising prosperity for their people, whether by building roads or opening new lands for settlement. Crockett became as adept at electioneering as at hunting—nor were the two talents unrelated, the reputation as a skillful man with a rifle being highly valued by his frontier constituents—and he undoubtedly drew on his wilderness exploits for the stories he told during political campaigns.

During his first term of legislative office, moreover, Crockett became acutely aware that the interests of voters in western Tennessee were quite distinct from those in the east. Thus representatives from the eastern and middle sections of the state differed from representatives from the west over the matter of land warrants, made complex by Tennessee having been carved out of the western part of North Carolina. As in the similar creation of Kentucky from part of Virginia, a situation emerged in which a man might unknowingly claim land actually owned by another; then, having set up a cabin and made improvements, he could lose all to the original claimant. Daniel Boone, the grand original for hunter-pioneers like Crockett, had lost his Kentucky lands to absentee owners in Virginia, speculators who had bought large tracts with the intention of selling them after their value increased.

Shackford tells us that David, while serving as an enlisted man in the army, had come to resent the privilege and power engendered by mere rank. As a legislator representing western interests, it was easy to translate this inequity into the conflict between propertied elites in east and middle Tennessee and the poor settlers in his own region. Men like Andrew Jackson of Nashville not only lived on large plantations, they aped the manners of the southern aristocracy, including the assertion of personal honor by fighting duels, whereas differences on the Tennessee frontier, a region of struggling farmers rather than wealthy planters, were settled by the exercise of wits or fists.

It was during Crockett's first term as a member of the state legislature that he was styled "the gentleman from the cane" (a reference to the unsettled regions where the tall stalks of wild cane grew in abundance, forming thickets called "brakes") by an opponent during a debate, an epithet which he first found offensive but then turned into a joke against the other man. He subsequently made it a part of his emerging identity as a champion of the underprivileged settlers in the west, those other "gentlemen from the cane" who had elected him to office.

That is, Crockett had begun to form the backwoods persona that would make him famous, yet had he ended his political career in 1824 he would have followed a mute and inglorious ca-

reer not much different from that of his constituents. Frontier
life was often marked by financial failures inspiring a move farther west, an experience involving considerable hardship that
could well be followed by subsequent failures. During the first
legislative session in which he served, Crockett was called
home because a grist-and-powder mill he had built had been
destroyed by a flood along the very waters that were to turn the
mill wheel and that also swept away a distillery connected with
the operation. This disaster was similar to the one experienced
by his father in 1794 and likewise inspired Crockett to plan a
move with his family to lands newly opened west of the Tennessee River.

Before Crockett left for home, the legislature met in joint session to consider an issue of serious interest to settlers in western
regions, a call for a convention to revise the state constitution,
necessary to give due representation in the legislature of the
rapidly settled districts in west Tennessee. A convention would
also correct inequities in property taxes, which being uniform
throughout the state, bore heavily on western settlers. Favored
by the newly elected Governor William Carroll (and Colonel
Crockett, soon to be of west Tennessee) the call for a convention was opposed by wealthy landowners in central Tennessee,
and was tabled for the time.

No sooner had the state legislature adjourned in November
than David headed out in search of a suitable site to which he
could relocate his family. This he found on a branch of the
Obion River, in a region that had experienced both hurricanes
and earthquakes in 1812–13, resulting in tangled windfalls,
large crevices in the ground, and a change in lakes and river
courses that left great swamps behind. Though apparently hostile to the needs of settlers, the region was friendly to wildlife,
which made it very attractive to men with Crockett's talents.

On the other hand, his penetration of this wilderness involved wading and swimming through flood waters in order to
bypass heavy thickets and windfalls, this in the winter months.
David demonstrated the qualities of courage and hardihood
shown by him as a boy and an enlisted man, but having staked
out his new home, he returned to the old one to be confronted

by lawsuits for the debts occasioned by the loss of his mill, along with other claims against him that required the sale of his house and land to satisfy. He moved his family to the cabin he had built on a branch of the Obion in September 1822, but in the meantime he responded to the newly elected governor's call reconvening the General Assembly for a special session in July.

The Tennessee legislature met to vote on issues of serious interest to Crockett and his constituents, including a proposal to extend the date terminating the land warrants issued by North Carolina—which Crockett opposed—and a resolution to be sent to the United States Congress asking that a bill be passed that would allow Tennessee to sell off vacant lands, thereby acquiring funds to be used for fostering education in the state. Crockett voted for this resolution, apparently under the assumption that it would deal fairly with settlers already living on "vacant lands." He likewise voted once again to issue a call for a convention to revise the state constitution, which he would continue to support during his career in the state legislature.

Crockett returned home to move his family across the Tennessee River to their new place of residence, where he began to kill game in such large quantities as to earn him a considerable local reputation as a great hunter in the tradition of Daniel Boone. Where before Crockett had lived in regions where bears had become scarce, this region of windfalls and deep holes in the earth was a virtual haven for the animals settlers greatly valued for meat and fur. In one year he claimed to have killed 105 bears, a figure that Shackford questions, but he accepts as probable Crockett's story about crawling into a crevice left by an earthquake to kill a bear with a hunting knife as well as another tale about shooting a bear that was as large as a bull.

In the election of 1823, Crockett was returned to the Tennessee house of representatives, as before voting for bills favorable to "gentlemen from the cane," especially those who had settled on lands still subject to North Carolina warrants, and he introduced a bill mandating the improvement of navigation in the western part of the state. He increasingly found himself at odds with representatives loyal to General Andrew Jackson, who had been nominated by the legislature in 1822 as their presidential candidate for the election of 1824, but who was identified by Crockett with eastern elites. In October of 1824 Crockett returned home, the second session of his term having ended, thus closing his career as a state representative.

The very next year, he offered himself as a candidate for the U.S. House of Representatives but was defeated and, seeking to augment his income, he set about building two flatboats loaded with a cargo of barrel staves intended for New Orleans. His skill as a frontiersman and hunter did not translate well into river navigation, and he was nearly drowned when the boats, lashed together and floating sideways down the Mississippi, grounded on an island of tangled logs. The boat on which Crockett was aboard began to sink, and being below decks, he barely escaped through a small hatch with the help of his friends, parting with his clothes and considerable skin in the process. Both boats and their cargoes were lost, along with the time and money invested in the venture, and he returned to hunting bears for a living, a hazardous but familiar trade.

In 1827 Crockett again ran for Congress, trailing the usual cloud of humorous anecdotes, dispensing free liquor to voters, and outwitting (and outlying) his opponents. This time he was successful, heralding his appearance on a much more prominent platform, which for Crockett was tantamount to a stage. By then he had mastered his public persona as something of a self-parodying backwoodsman; he was not in Washington long before he was discovered by newspapers, and anecdotes describing his eccentric behavior began to circulate, resulting in Crockett's becoming what we now call a celebrity. Like many such, Crockett confused notoriety with true fame, at least for a time, and it was during this period, of about five years' duration, that the mythic "Davy" began to cohere.

III.

Crockett's emergence as a national figure came at a time when great changes were occurring in American politics: Thomas Jefferson and John Adams had died in 1826, and for all intents and purposes the Republican and Federalist parties were extinct. Monroe had been succeeded in 1825 by John Quincy Adams, a former Federalist who espoused many of the positions associated with Jeffersonian Republicans, including government funding of internal improvements. The popular vote in that election was won by Tennessee's favorite son, Andrew Jackson, but the story was that Adams had cut a deal with Henry Clay, offering him the position of secretary of state in return for his support in the House of Representatives, where the close election was determined in Adams's favor. Whether true or not, the story cast a shadow over Adams's presidency, and in 1828 Jackson famously won.

From the wreck of the Adams administration emerged two great statesmen who would dominate American politics for twenty years: Henry Clay of Kentucky and Daniel Webster of Massachusetts. Both were eminently qualified for the presidency, which both coveted mightily; both were identified with the rise of the Whig party, which emerged in 1834, but neither man was able to convince the voters that he was a viable candidate. Moreover, the Whigs, taking their cue from General Jackson's success in using his western origins and military fame as political capital, were forever searching for a like champion. In 1840 they were successful in their choice of General William Henry Harrison, celebrated as the hero of the Battle of Tippecanoe, a minor and indecisive skirmish preceding the War of 1812.

I rehearse what may be familiar facts to clarify the otherwise puzzling course of Crockett's career in Congress. When he was first elected, Crockett maintained that despite his earlier differences with the general he was a Jacksonian Democrat but he ended his congressional career five years later a champion of the Whigs. It was Crockett's claim that he had remained a true Democrat while Jackson had become a dictator, a familiar enough charge at the time, thanks to the old general's aggressive and authoritarian personality. But as James Shackford maintains, Crockett's defection was chiefly inspired by the same old issue of squatters' rights, on which he and Jackson had taken opposing positions early in the 1820s. The matter of the disposition of vacant lands in Tennessee was made a national issue by James K. Polk, who had been elected to the state legislature during Crockett's tenure and who in 1825 was elected ahead of Crockett to the U.S. House of Representatives. Polk was a powerful member of Congress by the time Crockett arrived and became even more powerful after the election of 1828, thanks to his friendship with and loyalty to Jackson.

As a representative from Tennessee, Polk heeded the resolution of 1822 and sought the sale of hitherto vacant lands there for the purpose of funding public education in his state; Crockett at first supported Polk's Vacant Land Bill, operating as before under the assumption that the tracts already settled by farmers would be ceded to them without cost. But things turned out differently, and when Crockett learned that all of Tennessee's vacant lands would be offered for sale, thereby shutting out impoverished squatters while opening up opportunities for speculation, he opposed Polk's bill, which had the approval of President Jackson.

Throughout his subsequent career in Congress Crockett tried to advance substitute bills and proposed amendments to Polk's bill that favored those who had already settled on the "vacant lands," but to no avail, and his failure was increasingly a source of frustration and anger, increasingly aimed at Jackson and his supporters in the Democratic party. The congressman was undoubtedly sincere in his loyalty to the poor farmers of western Tennessee, but he also knew that his reelection depended on his success in protecting their rights to the land on which they had settled.

Another matter on which he disagreed with Jackson was the tangled and controversial issue of internal improvements—defined as building roads and canals as well as removing obstacles to navigation on rivers—identified in western states with facilitating the exchange of commodities. Although General Jackson had supported a system of national roads as important to the defense of the frontier, President Jackson, with the aid of Congressman Polk, consistently opposed the federal funding of internal improvements, nominally because it was unconstitutional—on the grounds that any such improvements would benefit some sections of the country at the expense of all—but also because his party anticipated that the cost would be met by imposing high tariffs on imported goods.

Henry Clay as early as 1810 had proposed his "American system," in which tariffs would be used to protect American manufactures even while encouraging the use of American raw materials, a plan favored by politicians from the industrial eastern states. The agrarian South was opposed to tariffs as having no advantage to farmers while increasing the cost of manufactured goods, whether from abroad or from New England. This southern opposition came to a head when the tariff of 1828, the "Tariff of Abominations," was followed by Henry Clay's "compromise" tariff bill of 1832, regarded as inadequate by many southerners including Jackson's vice president, John Calhoun of South Carolina. In response, Calhoun put forward the doctrine of nullification, which would allow individual states to ignore laws with which they disagreed. Anathema to the Whigs, the idea of nullification was also opposed by Jackson as unconstitutional, forcing Calhoun's resignation as vice president even as he was elected to the Senate as a champion of states' rights.

The point of all this is that internal improvements were linked inextricably to high tariffs, yet in 1830 David Crockett had supported a bill for building a national road, providing it ran from Washington to Memphis, in his home state, a position verifying Jackson's opinion about sectional particularism. And in 1831, for similar reasons, Crockett sponsored a bill authorizing national support for improvements to navigation on the Ohio and Mississippi Rivers, arguing that waterways that passed through many states would not otherwise be cleared of obstructions because interstate rivalry precluded cooperation. It was the president's newfound opposition to the national funding of internal improvements that inspired Crockett's remark in Congress in 1831 that although "our great man at the head of the nation has changed his course, I will not change mine. . . . I shall insist upon it that I am still a Jackson man, but General Jackson is not" (Shackford: 112).

Crockett's essentially populist views led him to oppose appropriations for the military academy at West Point, which he considered an institution favoring (and creating) elites, a position taken by many in the Tennessee legislature, and which was likewise supported by Congressman Polk. By contrast, Crockett spoke against the president's proposal for the removal of all Native American tribes to reservations located west of the Mississippi, a measure that catered to the expansive spirit along the frontier. Since the colonel had proved to be no Indian lover during the Creek War, his opposition to a bill, which though unjust was favored by his constituents, has puzzled many commentators.

Shackford notes that opposition to the Indian Bill came mostly from the East, where the conflicts with Native Americans were long past. Indeed, in the 1820s novels and poems by eastern authors promoting a sentimental view of an essentially extinct people began to appear, heralded by Cooper's *Last of the Mohicans*. By 1830, Crockett had become increasingly friendly toward the positions of the anti-Jackson party which had begun to cast a hospitable eye in his direction as a Democrat who had become well known for his hostility toward the president. Since the anti-Jacksonians were especially strong in the Northeast, Shackford regards Crockett's position on Indian removal as a first step toward his eventual alliance with the Whig party of Webster and Clay.

In 1830, Crockett opposed Jackson in the matter of political appointments, pointing out that the president had campaigned by promising retrenchment of the burgeoning government bureaucracy. Having won the election, Jackson was conducting business as usual, with the active help of Calhoun's replacement as vice president, Martin Van Buren of New York. The Jackson administration sought to consolidate its power by appointing office holders friendly to its policies, creating by the spoils system what Crockett called "a Set of Jackson worshippers." He maintained that he wore no collar around his neck that identified him as Andrew Jackson's "dog" (Shackford: 118–19).

He had, he declared, in the same letter to a correspondent, been "herled" by Jackson supporters "from their party," in effect throwing him in the direction of the opposition party. The specific charge Crockett made against Jackson was that he had removed the postmaster general appointed by President Monroe and kept by the Adams administration so as to replace him with a Democrat of his own persuasion. Later it was discovered that there was a huge deficit in the Post Office funds, the blame for which was laid on Jackson's man—the "dog" in question—by the president's opponents.

Shackford notes that this refusal to wear a collar with Jackson's name on it also appeared in the anonymous *Life and Adventures of Colonel David Crockett of West Tennessee,* published in 1833 and credited to Matthew St. Clair Clarke, clerk of the House of Representatives from 1822 to 1833 and a friend of the president of the second National Bank, Nicholas Biddle. President Jackson regarded the bank with great hostility as an anti-democratic institution, and any friend of Biddle was no friend of Jackson. The book was the first of several connected with or credited to Crockett, and like the others, it was essentially a proto-Whig document attacking Jackson's record, especially his removal of government deposits from the second National Bank in 1833.

The bank had been created during President Monroe's administration at the behest of financial and manufacturing interests who thought of a centralized institution as an instrument for controlling the currency thereby stabilizing the national economy. But the bank was opposed by agrarian interests who thought it had been created chiefly for the benefit of eastern elites opposed to westerners' desire for easy credit, which was regarded by the moneyed class as promoting inflation, thereby devaluing investments.

During Biddle's leadership national prosperity boomed, but Jackson regarded the bank as an autocratic institution favoring his opponents whose power would be (and was) greatly reduced by his removal of government funds. The president redistributed the money to state banks, supposedly more responsive to local (agrarian) needs, a step that was both a decentralization maneuver and one that eastern Democrats saw as spreading the wealth while sapping the strength of the Whigs. But western farmers were not pleased with the removal and redistribution of the funds, which made the money more available to speculators than to impoverished settlers.

Given that Crockett was the representative of a poor region tenanted by farmers, and that he was ideologically a Populist, his loud and frequent attacks on Jackson's removal of the "deposites," as he spelled it, indicates that he was aware of the negative effect of the measure on his constituents. At the same time, his attitude toward the president and the removal of the deposits was in sympathy with the position of the Whigs. They obviously thought of the colonel as a backwoodsman from Tennessee useful to them as a spokesman for their opposition to the Tennessean now in the executive mansion; a mini-Jackson, Crockett in his hunting outfit of buckskins and fur hat was a version of a ventriloquist's dummy. He may not have worn a collar identifying him as Jackson's dog, but he soon became harnessed to a leash held in the hands of Nicholas Biddle; as Arthur M. Schlesinger Jr. observed more than fifty years ago, the "Davy" Crockett of popular fame was distinctly a Whig creation.

It has been pointed out by Shackford and others that the emergence of the comic Davy Crockett was helped along by the popular success of Major Jack Downing, the creation of Seba Smith, a newspaper editor and Democrat in Portland, Maine. Writing letters with an inimitable Down East flavor from Washington, the fictitious major became a humorous witness to the activities of Jackson's administration, making shrewd observations that became increasingly satiric as the president's hand tightened the reins of government while loosening the distribution of political largesse.

These letters were collected as a book in 1833, their publication hastened by the appearance of a second Jack Downing, the creation of Charles Augustus Davis, whose letters were much more critical of Jackson's administration than were those of Smith's creation. Collected in 1834, the letters of the alternative Jack Downing had first appeared in a New York newspaper and were addressed to its editor, Theodore Dwight. Dwight had been one of the Connecticut Wits, and was a sympathetic chronicler of the Hartford Convention, who even by the 1830s had remained an unreconstructed Federalist for whom Jacksonian democracy was anathema.

Also worthy of mention is another work of literature that assisted in the creation of Davy Crockett, *The Lion of the West,* a prize-winning play first produced in 1831. The comedy was written by the multitalented New Yorker James Kirke Paulding, who had collaborated with his friend Washington Irving, on the satiric periodical *Salmagundi* (1807–08), after which he had written a number of satires and poems. Because he was an author of a series of biographical studies of naval commanders in the War of 1812 and was throughout much of his career steadfastly hostile to Great Britain, Paulding was appointed by President Madison to the Board of Navy Commissioners in 1815. In 1824 he was made navy agent for New York by President Monroe and served President (and fellow New Yorker) Martin Van Buren—Jackson's handpicked successor—as secretary of the navy. In sum, Paulding was a Democrat who made a successful transition from Jeffersonianism to Jacksonianism. He was in addition a northerner sympathetic to the pro-slavery cause, made clear by his *Slavery in the United States* (1836), and was friendly toward the people who kept slaves, as he demonstrated in *Letters from the South* (1817).

It is generally accepted that the protagonist of Paulding's farce, Colonel Nimrod Wildfire, a congressman from Kentucky, was at least in part inspired by stories already in circulation about Colonel Crockett. Though in *Letters from the South* Paulding was uneasy about the backwoodsman type, describing a fight between a wagoneer and a riverboatman in satiric terms, in his play (as revised for production first by an American then a British dramatist) the characterization of the hunter from Kentucky was otherwise. Though uncouth in dress and manners (he wears a fringed leather hunting coat and an animal pelt for a hat) and given to boasting about his fighting abilities—claiming to be a "half horse half alligator" able to "lick his weight in wild cats"—the colonel is a courageous and gallant frontiersman with a heart of gold. As acted by James H. Hackett, who had commissioned the play, Wildfire proved to be a popular figure who held the stage for the next twenty years, and is an obvious source for the almanac version of Davy Crockett.

Perhaps anticipating a libel suit, Paulding saw to it, even before the play was first produced, that newspaper stories appeared denying that Wildfire was modeled after Colonel Crockett, who was after all from Tennessee, not Kentucky, and (unlike Andrew Jackson) was not notorious for fights with others, whether with fists or firearms. But it is also undeniable that there was a connection between the two colonels in the mind of the public, and when Paulding's play was staged in Washington in 1833, the story went, Crockett attended a performance during which Hackett as Wildfire bowed in the congressman's direction. When the "other" colonel responded in kind the audience applauded the gesture.

It was also in 1833 that Clarke's *Life* of Crockett first appeared, in which the author borrowed an episode from Paulding's play (the account of a fight between a backwoodsman and a boatman that had been previously used in the author's book on the South, now put into the colorful language of Wildfire). Clarke included other anecdotes that firmly cemented the colonel to his wild-man stage counterpart, and since much of the *Life* contains biographical material that could only have been supplied by Crockett, Shackford concludes that he must have been a party to its composition, despite his subsequent declaration that he had nothing to do with the book. Subsequent scholars have agreed with Shackford that Clarke's *Life* was part of a calculated plan by the anti-Jacksonians to exploit the image of the "other" Democrat and frontier hero from Tennessee (Shackford: 256–57).

By 1831, despite his continuing efforts on behalf of western Tennesseans on the vacant lands issue, Crockett was beginning to have problems with his constituents over his claim of being an anti-Jackson Jackson man. He published that year a Circular Letter setting forth the reasons for his several positions on retrenchment, internal improvements, and the like, but to no avail. Crockett was defeated in his bid for reelection that year, in part, Shackford believes, because his bitter antipathy toward the Jacksonian Democrats was beginning to diminish his good-natured and playful attitude toward politics.

In 1828, Crockett had acquired land in Weakley County, and having bought adjacent property with a house already on it, in 1831 he once more moved westward with his family. In 1833, he again ran for Congress, this time successfully, though he seems to have felt that his political career was not enhanced by Clarke's *Life,* which was published that same year. Its portrayal of Crockett as a slangy, boastful hunter from the backwoods may have pleased the Whigs but it seems to have been regarded by the colonel as not very helpful to his increasingly ambitious plans for national office. Nor was it very flattering to the western constituency on whose votes he depended.

He therefore declared that he had no connection with the book, and set to work on his autobiographical *Narrative,* apparently with the help of an old (and literate) friend, Thomas Chilton, a member of Congress from Kentucky. The book covered much of the same ground as the *Life,* but gave more stress to Crockett's military career and his heroic ordeals as a hunter and pioneer and had little of the broad humor and anecdotal style of the other book. In it he repeatedly attacked Jackson and Martin Van Buren and gave hints of his availability as a Whig candidate for president, the *Narrative* not being published until 1834, after he had been returned once again to Congress.

During Crockett's absence from Washington, the battle between Jackson and Nicholas Biddle over the future of the National Bank had heated up, with the president attacking the bank as a monopolistic agent of corruption. (Shackford tells us that during his career in Congress, Crockett was one of many legislators granted loans by the bank that were in effect gifts, clear evidence of Biddle's desire to curry favor with the legislature.) At the urging of Henry Clay, Biddle asked Congress to renew the bank's charter, four years before it was to expire. As Biddle and Clay anticipated, Jackson vetoed the bill after it had passed the Senate and House, a show of executive force that they thought would cause Jackson to lose the forthcoming election. They were wrong, and no sooner had Jackson been returned to office than he removed the government funds deposited in the bank.

When he returned to Washington in 1833, Crockett had immediately set to work on behalf of his version of the Tennessee Land Bill, at the same time fulminating in private correspondence against Jackson because of the president's naked display of power in removing the deposits, which had the effect of "deranging" the stability of currency and "destroying" the nation's system of commerce (Shackford: 147). He repeatedly used the phrase "King Andrew," popular with Whigs (who took their name from the anti-Tory party in England), and with them he maintained that the president was a despot indifferent to the will of the people.

With his "authorized" autobiography now in print, Crockett went on a tour of the Northeast in late April and early May of 1834, hoping to increase the sales of his book. The trip was also a test of the political waters in Whig country, first in the expectation of gaining support for his land bill, and second with some vague hope of making a run for the presidency against Jackson's appointed heir, Martin Van Buren. The vice president was variously characterized by Crockett and the Whigs as "Old Kinderhook," "the Magician," and "the little Red Fox."

But the only palpable result of this trip was another book, *An Account of Colonel Crockett's Tour to the North and Down East* (1835), a first-person narrative published in his name but credited by Shackford to William Clark, a fellow congressman and a Whig. Shackford uncovers evidence that Crockett was active in contributing materials to Clark, but though faithful to the facts of the congressman's tour, the book is a thoroughgoing piece of Whig propaganda. Thanks to a well-managed schedule of events during his tour, Colonel Crockett received a tumultuous welcome in Philadelphia, New York, and Boston. The event was comparable to President Jackson's tour of the Northeast the year before; indeed it may have been arranged by the Whigs as a calculated response to the general's trip.

We may not doubt the colorful congressman's widespread

popularity, but that much of the applause was politically inspired we may also accept, and the book that renders an account of the tour is filled with "Crockett's" euphoric praise of
progress in the places he visited, from improvements to navigation (the Union system of canals connecting Philadelphia to
Pittsburgh) to the factory system in the Northeast. He also spoke
of the necessity of protective tariffs to foster local manufactur-
ers, and his description of the Lowell mills, with their miles of
attractive young women tending looms, reads like an advertis-
ing brochure written by Abbot Lawrence himself. He claimed
that in New York he had sat down to dinner with "Major Jack
Downing," and his account of the tour closes with an exchange
of "letters" with the fictitious Yankee opponent of Jackson.
Like the version of the "Major" created by Charles Augustus
Davis, the western colonel, by the end of the account of his
tour, had become a figment of the Whig imagination.

Much of the tour's cost was covered by his hosts, and in
Philadelphia Crockett was given a watch-chain seal engraved
with his famous motto, "Go ahead," sentiments beloved by
Whiggish champions of progress (one of the first locomotives
put in service in Massachusetts was named "Davy Crockett").
In Boston he was given a hunting coat of local manufacture. In
Lowell he received a bolt of fabric spun in the mills from wool
supposedly shipped from Mississippi, thus proving the value of
factories in the Northeast (and tariffs) to farmers in the
South—a major stress of Clay's "American system," the royal
arch supporting the Whig notion of national union.

When Crockett returned to Philadelphia from Washington
on the following 4th of July, he was given (by the "Young
Whigs") a new rifle crafted to his specifications, and in response to a heavy hint by the congressman he was at the same
time presented with "a half a dozen cannisters of his best sports-
man's powder" by none other than the aging Éleuthère Irénée
Du Pont (*Tour*, quoted in Shackford: 168). Independence Day
in Philadelphia, the city where the Declaration of Independence
had been written, was a special occasion, and Crockett shone,
delivering rhetorical fireworks in an address denouncing the return to America of tyranny in the form of Andrew Jackson.

During his grand tour, Crockett had made similar speeches along the way, all printed in the *Tour,* all repeating the same themes, all walking the line dictated by the Whig party, and all apparently written for him to read aloud. The result is probably the most boring book associated with Crockett's authorship, though the *Life of Martin Van Buren,* which appeared over his name later the same year, is a close rival, being a complex and at times incomprehensible recounting of the "Magician's" political career. But these efforts were to no avail if Crockett expected to garner Whig support for his land bill, for it was defeated when the vote was called on February 18, 1835, as was Colonel Crockett in the congressional election later that same year.

His loss to Adam Huntsman—another hero of the War of 1812 whose artificial limb inspired Crockett's unfortunate epithet, "timber-leg"—resulted in his declaration that the people of Tennessee could go to hell and that he was going to Texas. And so he did, his adventures inspiring one more ghostwritten book, a narrative written after his death but trailing inglorious clouds of defeat generated by Colonel Crockett's congressional career. Out of those clouds, however, in part inspired by his martyrdom at the Alamo, sprung the phoenix called Davy Crockett, granting him an immortality he never sought but for which we may be sure he would have been grateful.

IV.

Richard Penn Smith, the author of *Col. Crockett's Exploits and Adventures in Texas,* was a well-connected Philadelphian; born in 1799, he was the grandson of William Smith, first provost of what would become the University of Pennsylvania. A lawyer with a creative bent inherited from his father, Smith had by 1836 written twenty plays and a novel, as well as sketches, short stories, and poetry. His first literary endeavor was a series of newspaper essays published in the early 1820s under the title "The Plagiary," a meaningful coincidence given that his subsequent dramatic works were mostly adaptations of French plays.

As we shall see, Smith's spurious account of Crockett's apotheosis at the Alamo is likewise dependent on other men's work and, having been written at a great rate of speed, is a tour de force of literary amalgamation. Though no great shakes in terms of style, the book managed to convince its readers that it was genuine, in part because Crockett's autobiography is itself stylistically uneven and occasionally boring. Smith's book was instantly popular, selling ten thousand copies in the first year of publication by Carey and Hart, and it received enthusiastic reviews in Great Britain, where it was regarded as a dependable account of the conflict in Texas. Smith's twentieth-century biographer regards the book as superior to the author's plays, which were overwrought and melodramatic, and regrets that he did not repeat his experiment in a realistic, humorous style. For whatever reason, Smith thenceforth abandoned his writing career, but his last book satisfied its immediate purpose: as the publishers had hoped, it emptied their shelves of unsold copies of *Col. Crockett's Tour.*

Ever since the nativist enthusiasm for Davy Crockett in the 1930s, led by V. L. Parrington, Walter Blair, Franklin J. Meine, and Constance Rourke, most studies of popular culture in the United States have focused on the comic almanac adventures of the famed "Kentucky" hunter, which have been credited with creating a mythic Crockett. And yet, with their crude woodcuts, raw humor, and emphasis on violence, the almanac stories bear little resemblance to the historic Crockett, who was of course from Tennessee. James Shackford's biography, published in 1956, was intended to rescue the virtually forgotten original from the mythic version, but over the past fifty years it has continued to be the "Davy" of almanac fame who has monopolized scholarly attention.

Following the lead of Richard Slotkin, perhaps the most influential revisionist historian of the American West in recent times, modern students of popular culture have been drawn to literature that has attracted a large audience. It is a criterion clearly related to the populist tendency of democracy, which ranks the tastes and preferences of the general public higher than those of elites. Moreover, the distinction between the "two" Crocketts has been blurred by Slotkin himself, who confuses the chronology and contents of the "authorized" and ghostwritten Crockett autobiographies. As a result Slotkin gives the *Sketches and Eccentricities* undue emphasis, regarding its "folkloric" collection of "tall tales, trickster pranks, and magical triumphs" as having had the greater influence because it was published *after* Crockett's own narrative of his life (*Fatal Environment:* 166).

Thus, in his discussion of Crockett's death at the Alamo, Slotkin notes that his "publishers and editorial associates immediately increased the number and circulation of the almanacs that bore Crockett's name, and published a sequel to his earlier biographies which purported to be the journal found on his dead body" (171). This conflates two quite distinct genres: whatever their origins, the almanacs were aimed at the masses, where Smith's book, like the earlier accounts of Crockett's life and adventures from which it derives, was intended for a relatively sophisticated readership. Moreover, the almanacs were ephemeral productions, and their great rarity today indicates how few escaped destruction at the end of the year for which they were published. On the other hand, Smith's account of Crockett's Texas adventures continued to be reprinted for nearly a century, often in tandem with Crockett's own *Narrative,* and provided biographers and historians with what they assumed was authentic material.

In 1883 there appeared a compilation of biographies of celebrated western heroes by D. M. Kelsey, the frontispiece of which was a depiction of "Custer's Last Rally on the Little Big Horn." In celebrating "Pioneer Heroes" from de Soto to Generals Miles and Crook, Kelsey rendered an account of Crockett's life that combined the authentic *Narrative* with Smith's *Exploits and Adventures,* and it was shortly afterward that Theodore Roosevelt wrote "Remember the Alamo," with its dependence on Smith's account of Crockett's final days. When in 1923 Hamlin Garland brought together Crockett's autobiography and excerpts from the ghostwritten *Tour,* he also included the main body of Smith's narrative despite a bibliographic note declaring that the book was spurious.

Garland himself seemed to be dubious about its authenticity, calling Smith's an "apocryphal work," but he also noted that it "remains the only account of the great woodsman's death, and it is in character" (10). The bibliographic note takes a somewhat harder but still positive tack, noting that "this pseudo-Crockett . . . is itself interesting," if only because "the existence of such a book that there was current at the time a popular legend and literature of the frontier which made it possible for catch-penny hacks to manufacture a reasonably characteristic, reasonably convincing 'autobiography' of a dead hero while his death was still in the news" (11).

This rationale still seems valid, for Smith's fictional narrative bears witness not only to the contemporary popularity of Colonel Crockett, intensified by his martyrdom at the Alamo, but to the author's skill in producing a convincing story from a patchwork of anecdotes borrowed from earlier books supposedly written by Crockett along with other elements popular at the time. Smith gave verisimilitude to his narrative by incorporating bona fide materials about the mounting friction between the Americans in Texas and the authorities in Mexico, binding the whole with a reasonably accurate description of the landscape through which Crockett had passed. As his biographer notes, Smith used a realistic, often slangy style, and he included a number of humorous and picaresque anecdotes; though the narrative is often sketchy and occasionally flat, anyone familiar with the other books credited to Crockett, including the bona fide autobiography, will recognize the terrain.

In 1933, Franklin Meine published his anthology, *Tall Tales of the Southwest,* and aroused the ire of James Shackford by ignoring the "real" David Crockett. Meine included "only a selection from the entirely spurious *Exploits,* the only Crockett book with which David had *nothing* to do" (viii). This, Shackford continues, "paved the way" for Constance Rourke's "fictional" biography of Crockett in 1934, "which gave 'Davy' the identical tall-tale treatment Mr. Meine had given him." This was what Parrington meant when he referred to Davy Crockett as "a mythical figure that drew to itself the unappropriated picturesque that sprang spontaneously from the crude western life," only Shackford identified the mythmaking process with the 1930s, not the 1830s (II: 173).

Rourke used a number of anecdotes about her hero's travels through Arkansas and Texas as told by Smith, and devoted a chapter to "the brightly colored story [about] the shadowy companions who joined Crockett somewhere along the way," including Thimblerig (supposedly inspired by the famous gambler Jonathan Harrison Green) and the Bee hunter (179). Though aware that Smith had been identified as the author, Rourke felt that "a pattern of evidence may yet be woven to prove that it had a basis in fact. . . . The tale was—and remains—part of the spreading Crockett legend . . . and so must have a place in this narrative." Indeed, Smith's book is still of great relevance to anyone interested in the "mythic" Crockett, not because it may have been written by Crockett but because it is a self-conscious attempt to construct a narrative out of contemporary popular materials.

There is an early reference in Smith's book to Sam Patch, who gained fame and a short-lived immortality by leaping from great heights into rivers and falls. A millworker in Rhode Island, Patch obtained local notice by his dives into the Pawtucket River, but he first caught the attention of a greater public after going to work in a factory in Paterson, New Jersey. Appearing high above the Passaic River where a crowd had gathered to watch as the span of a great bridge was being slowly drawn across the chasm, Patch stole the show by shouting what became his famous slogan, "Some things can be done as well as others!" then jumping into the water far below. He thereby commenced a career of sorts, the high point of which was reached when he leaped into Niagara Falls from a platform on Goat Island before a huge audience.

Patch's series of breathtaking jumps ended with yet another, even greater leap, this time into the Genesee Falls in Rochester: Sam promoted the event with a poster declaring, "HIGHER YET! SAM'S LAST JUMP. SOME THINGS CAN BE DONE AS WELL AS OTHERS. THERE IS NO MISTAKE IN SAM PATCH" (Dorson, *America in Legend*: 94). The words proved prophetic: this was truly his last leap because it killed him. Smith works Patch's slogan into his narrative at several junctures, thereby associating Crockett with another eccentric hero of the day, perhaps with a somber implication.

Like Patch, Crockett had been elevated suddenly from a humble station in life and then had become trapped in his own notoriety; moreover, his heroic stature, like Patch's, was regarded as something of a joke: not even his Whig champions took Crockett seriously. Patch literally rose to a great height and suffered a great fall—his wooden tombstone read "Here lies Sam Patch; such is Fame"—and a similar epitaph could have decorated Crockett's grave, had his body not been burned and buried with the other defenders of the Alamo. As I have already stated, had Crockett abandoned his political career after his second term as a state legislator, his fame would have remained local, but once elected to Congress, he gained a platform from which, like Patch, he took a fatal leap.

The first part of Smith's *Exploits and Adventures* relies heavily on material in Clarke's 1832 *Life,* and takes material as well from letters Crockett had sent to his (and Smith's) publishers, Carey and Hart. The former includes the colonel's account of his campaigning methods and the cunning trick played on a rum-seller, and though the victim is not a swindling Yankee like Job Snelling—a type that was then emerging in contemporary popular literature—several Yankee tricksters do appear in Clarke's book. From Crockett's letters to his publishers Smith took details of the colonel's departure for Texas, and, as Constance Rourke notes, "whole passages were taken over from [Mary Austin] Holley's 'Texas' and from David B. Edwards's 'History of Texas,' among others" (267–68).

Smith soon introduced characters into the narrative that were apparently of his own creation, including both Thimblerig and the unnamed philanthropist-fiddler, a sentimental type perhaps inspired by Laurence Sterne. But the lovelorn Bee hunter was lifted from Cooper's recent *The Prairie,* much as Crockett's feat of marksmanship, first used in Clarke's *Life,* is a parody of a famous episode in *The Pioneers* where Leatherstocking actually does hit the center of a bullseye twice. Crockett's encounter with the young bumpkin rehearsing "a knock-down and drag-out fight" was taken from a sketch in Augustus Baldwin Longstreet's *Georgia Scenes,* published in 1835, indicating the extent to which Smith was up-to-date not only on major authors of his day but on southwestern humor as well.

Most narratives about Crockett's martyrdom in the cause for freedom in Texas ignore the fact that one of the many objections American colonists had to arbitrary Mexican rule was the law against slavery incorporated in the Mexican constitution of 1824, the year that independence from Spain was finally achieved. The founders of the American colony had pinned their hopes for prosperity on raising cotton, from which fortunes were being made along the Mississippi delta, and cotton growing on a large scale depended on slave labor.

Crockett himself owned a few slaves, as did many small farmers in the Southwest, but he seems never to have been an ardent champion of pro-slavery during a time when advocates for abolition were beginning to make themselves heard. Smith, being from Philadelphia, could hardly have been unaware of the controversy. Because of its Quaker heritage the city had early on become a center for anti-slavery activities: both Ben Franklin and Dr. Benjamin Rush were presidents of the first anti-slavery society founded in America (1775), and Pennsylvania had been among the first states to abolish slavery (in 1780).

In his speech given aboard a Mississippi steamboat in chapter six of *Exploits and Adventures,* Crockett maintains that because he is in "a slave-holding state," to avoid being lynched he should declare that "I am neither an abolitionist nor a colonizationist [i.e., a proponent of sending freed slaves to Africa], but simply Colonel Crockett of Tennessee, now bound for Texas." But then he proceeds to raise a toast to "the abolition of slavery," quickly clarifying his sentiments by maintaining that "there are no slaves in the country more servile than the [Democratic] party slaves in Congress." Beyond this rhetorical trick, there is scant mention in Smith's book of the slavery controversy.

Thimblerig's vivid account of Natchez, "where nigger women are knocked down by the auctioneer, and knocked up by the purchaser," and "where the poorest slave has plenty of

yellow boys [mulatto children], but not of Benton's mintage,"
raised the specter of miscegenation, a source of ribald humor in
the South and righteous indignation in the North. The reference is also to Missouri's Senator Thomas Hart Benton's championing of hard currency: the slang term for gold coins was
"yellow boys" ("yaller boys" in *Huckleberry Finn*). Here as
elsewhere in Smith's book Crockett's derisive reference to Benton was inspired by the Missouri Democrat's support of President Jackson's attack on the National Bank.

   Though among Smith's dramas was *The Eighth of January,* a
melodrama celebrating the Battle of New Orleans and produced the year that Jackson became president, we may assume
that the author was a Whig. He may even have been one of
those "Young Whigs" of Philadelphia who gave Crockett his
new rifle, mention of which is made in his *Narrative,* when in
fact that valuable weapon was left at home. Most northern
Whigs remained equivocal on the issue of slavery for fear of of-
fending the southern Democrats to the point of secession, and
Smith is no exception. Still, his Whig bias is chiefly shown by
his frequent echoes of Crockett's attacks on prominent Democrats in his autobiography and in the spurious *Tour.*

   The speech the colonel gives attacking Van Buren is in
the spirit of the biography of "Old Kinderhook" credited to
Crockett, and his discontent with politics in general is echoed
throughout, either directly in his "advice" to political candidates, or indirectly by allusion and figures of speech. Shackford
declares that Smith's book was in no way "related to the political exploitation of Crockett . . . but was instead a publisher's
exploitation of his name and fame in a literary type of sham"
(281). And yet, the heavy Whig bias, though perhaps used by
Smith to make his hoax convincing, most certainly kept the
anti-Jackson spirit very much alive, an unintentional irony as
we shall see.

   As anti-Mexican propaganda, the spurious diary supported
the expansionist cause, and was therefore a different political
use of Crockett—a posthumous commemoration of his martyrdom gauged to arouse hatred of Santa Anna and sympathy for
Texan independence. As Parrington long ago pointed out, the

political exploitation of Davy Crockett came in three stages: "The exploitation of Davy's canebrake waggery, the exploitation of his anti-Jacksonian spleen, and the exploitation of his dramatic death at the Alamo" (II: 173). In 1836 and thereafter, the greatest exponents of territorial expansion in the United States were southern Democrats, who sought to extend the agrarian frontier and thereby enlarge the slavery system. Whigs, by contrast, tended to oppose expansion, less because of the slavery issue than because they feared the lure of free land would reduce the pool of white factory workers. The leaders of the movement to make Texas an independent republic, like Sam Houston and Stephen Austin, were Democrats, and Houston in particular was a friend of Andrew Jackson. At least in private the president approved of the war for Texan independence, counting on eventual annexation by the United States. As a result, Smith's book as a political document is divided against itself, expressing Whiggish hostility toward the Democratic party while championing the Democratic cause of Texan freedom from Mexican rule, meaning among other things the right to keep slaves.

The issue becomes even more complex if one accepts Shackford's argument that the defenders of the Alamo were commanded by anti-Jackson Democrats, Colonels James Bowie and William B. Travis, who had been sent to San Antonio by General Houston with orders not to defend but to destroy the fort. Other accounts maintain that the two colonels were sent to determine whether or not the fort could be held, but whatever the truth, Houston's strategy was the Fabian tactic used by George Washington, which was to retreat until the advancing enemy had extended itself too far, then attack—precisely what happened later at the battle of San Jacinto, resulting in the capture of Santa Anna.

Defying the odds (and perhaps Houston's authority), Colonels Bowie and Travis decided to hold the Alamo against thousands of Mexican troops with a garrison of 185 men, some of whom were incapacitated by illness. Perhaps, as Shackford maintains, in joining the defenders of the Alamo Crockett was expressing his fierce hatred of Jackson—though no one doubts the sincerity of his desire for Texan independence. Moreover, Crockett must have realized that any political future he might have in Texas would be enhanced by his participation in the revolution.

He did not, however, set out from Tennessee with the aim of raising volunteers for the war with Mexico, as Smith (and John Wayne) would have it. Only after arriving in Nacogdoches did Crockett resolve to join the revolution, swearing to support a provisional government—famously adding the word "republican" to the oath. But if in joining Bowie and Travis at the Alamo Crockett was inspired chiefly by his hatred of Jacksonian Democrats, the defeat of the Americans by Santa Anna not only validated but strengthened Sam Houston's strategy. Thus the martyrdom of the Alamo defenders was an unintended blessing for the cause of Texan independence: when Houston's soldiers attacked the Mexican forces at San Jacinto, they were inspired by the cry, "Remember the Alamo!"

Smith includes in his last chapter an account of the manner of Crockett's death, the one of five that puts Santa Anna in the worst light possible, a story that Bill Groneman has traced to a New York newspaper story for July 9, 1846. It was apparently copied, with some revisions, into Smith's book, which actually ends with an account of the merciless butchery of the American soldiers under Colonel Fannin near Goliad. These stories of Santa Anna's cruelty appeared while he was still held prisoner, and may have been a bid for the Mexican general's execution, but once again Houston took the wisest course, setting Santa Anna free in hopes of gaining Texan independence. Moreover, the most popular and long-lived version of Davy Crockett's death was printed in the *Crockett Almanack for 1837* (composed in 1836), which is included here in an appendix, for most celebrants of the myth preferred that their hero had not surrendered but died fighting to the last.

Thus Teddy Roosevelt acknowledges that "some say that when Crockett fell from his wounds, he was taken alive, and was then shot by Santa Anna," but TR clearly favored the story that "old Davy Crockett" was the last man alive at the Alamo, and that he died facing "his foes with his back to the wall,

ringed around by the bodies of the men he had slain" (86, 87).
Constance Rourke likewise, who may have read Hamlin Garland's edited version of Smith's narrative, which left out the final chapter, insists that despite the story told "in later years"
about Crockett's capture and execution, he "was not taken
prisoner," but died "fighting bitterly . . . in the thickest of the
swift and desperate clash" (219–20). On the other hand, perhaps the most effective account is the one in Crockett's fictional
diary, which ends with the words "No time for memorandums
now.—Go ahead!—Liberty and independence for ever!" The
best response to questions for which there are no exact answers
is silence.

Suggestions for Further Reading

Blair, Walter. "Six Davy Crocketts." *Southwest Review*, 25 (1940), 443–62.

———. *Tall Tale America: A Legendary History of Our Humorous Heroes*. New York: Coward-McCann, 1944.

Crockett, David. *A Narrative of the Life of David Crockett of the State of Tennessee*. A Facsimile Edition with Annotations and an Introduction by James A. Shackford and Stanley J. Folmsbee. Knoxville: The University of Tennessee Press, 1953.

Dorson, Richard M. *America in Legend: Folklore from the Colonial Period to the Present*. New York: Pantheon Books, 1973.

———, ed. *Davy Crockett: American Comic Legend*. New York: Rockland Editions, 1939. (See also Dorson's "The Sources of *Davy Crockett: American Comic Legend*." *Midwest Folklore* 8 [1958], 615–24.)

Hauck, Richard Boyd. *Crockett: A Bio-Bibliography*. Westport, Connecticut: Greenwood Press, 1982.

Kilgore, Dan. *How Did Davy Die?* College Station, Texas: Texas A & M Press, 1978.

Lofaro, Michael A. *Davy Crockett's Riproarious Shemales and Sentimental Sisters: Women's Tall Tales from the Crockett Almanacs (1835–1856)*. Mechanicsburg, Pennsylvania: Stackpole Books, 2001.

———, ed. *Davy Crockett: The Man, the Legend, the Legacy, 1786–1986*. Knoxville: The University of Tennessee Press, 1985.

Lofaro, Michael A. and Joe Cummings, eds. *Crockett at Two Hundred: New Perspectives on the Man and the Myth*. Knoxville: The University of Tennessee Press, 1989.

Meine, Franklin J., ed. *The Crockett Almanacs: Nashville Series, 1835–1838*. Chicago: The Caxton Club, 1955.

Paulding, James Kirke. *The Lion of the West: A Farce in Two Acts*. Edited by James N. Tidwell. Palo Alto, California: Stanford University Press, 1954.

Rourke, Constance. *Davy Crockett*. New York: Harcourt, Brace and Company, 1934.

Shackford, James Atkins. *David Crockett: The Man and the Legend*. Edited by John B. Shackford. Chapel Hill: The University of North Carolina Press, 1956.

TEXTS CITED IN
THE INTRODUCTION AND NOTES

Davis, Richard Harding. *The West from a Car Window*. New York: Harper & Brothers, 1892.

Garland, Hamlin, Introduction. *The Autobiography of David Crockett*. New York: Charles Scribner's Sons, 1923.

Groneman, Bill. *Eyewitness to the Alamo*. Revised edition. Plano: Woodware Publishing: Republic of Texas Press, 2001.

Kelsey, D. M. *Our Pioneer Heroes and their Daring Deeds . . . Explorers, Renowned Frontier Fighters, and Celebrated Early Settlers of America, from the Earliest Times to the Present. Profusely Illustrated*. Philadelphia: G. O. Pelton, 1883.

McCullough, B. W. *The Life and Writings of Richard Penn Smith, with a Reprint of His Play, "The Deformed."* Philadelphia: University of Pennsylvania Press, 1917.

Morris, Edmund. *The Rise of Theodore Roosevelt*. New York: Coward, McCann & Geoghegan, 1975.

Nofi, Albert A. *The Alamo and the Texas War for Independence: September 30, 1835–April 21, 1836*. Conshohocken, Pennsylvania: Combined Books, 1992.

Parrington, Vernon Louis. *Main Currents in American Thought: An Interpretation of American Literature from the Beginnings to 1920*. 3 volumes. New York: Harcourt, Brace and Company, 1927, 1930.

Remini, Robert V. *The Life of Andrew Jackson*. New York: Harper & Row, 1994.

Roosevelt, Theodore, and Henry Cabot Lodge. *Hero Tales from American History. The Works of Theodore Roosevelt*, National Edition, Vol. X. New York: Charles Scribner's Sons, 1926.

Schlesinger. Arthur M. Jr. *The Age of Jackson.* Boston: Little, Brown & Company, 1945.

Slotkin, Richard. *The Fatal Environment: The Myth of the Frontier in the Age of Industrialization, 1800–1890.* New York: Atheneum, 1985.

———. *Gunfighter Nation: The Myth of the Frontier in Twentieth-Century America.* New York: Atheneum, 1992.

Note on the Text

This edition of Co*l. Crockett's Exploits and Adventures in Texas* has been set from the original edition of 1836, published by Carey and Hart of Philadelphia under the name "T.K. and P.G. Collins," a fictitious firm. All peculiarities of grammar and spelling have been preserved as intrinsic to the pretext of Crockett's authorship. We have added to Richard Penn Smith's title the words "On to the Alamo," in order to provide a clue to the contents, which would have been obvious to readers in 1836 but less so to a modern-day audience.

Col. Crockett's
Exploits and Adventures
in Texas

COL. CROCKETT'S

EXPLOITS AND ADVENTURES

IN TEXAS:

WHEREIN IS CONTAINED

A FULL ACCOUNT OF HIS JOURNEY FROM TENNESSEE TO THE RED
RIVER AND NATCHITOCHES, AND THENCE ACROSS
TEXAS TO SAN ANTONIO;

INCLUDING

HIS MANY HAIR-BREADTH ESCAPES;

TOGETHER WITH

A TOPOGRAPHICAL, HISTORICAL, AND POLITICAL
VIEW OF TEXAS.

Say, what can politicians do,
  When things run riot, plague, and vex us ?
But shoulder *flook*, and start anew,
  Cut stick, and GO AHEAD in TEXAS !!!
                                THE AUTHOR.

WRITTEN BY HIMSELF.
[RICHARD PENN SMITH]

THE NARRATIVE BROUGHT DOWN FROM THE DEATH OF
COL. CROCKETT TO THE BATTLE OF SAN JACINTO,
BY AN EYE-WITNESS.

PHILADELPHIA:
T. K. AND P. G. COLLINS.[1]
1836.

DAVID CROCKETT.

PREFACE.

Colonel Crockett, at the time of leaving Tennessee for Texas, made a promise to his friends that he would keep notes of whatever might occur to him of moment, with the ulterior view of laying his adventures before the public. He was encouraged in this undertaking by the favourable manner in which his previous publications had been received: and if he had been spared throughout the Texian struggle, it cannot be doubted that he would have produced a work replete with interest, and such as would have been universally read. His plain and unpolished style may occasionally offend the taste of those who are sticklers for classic refinement; while others will value it for that frankness and sincerity which is the best voucher for the truth of the facts he relates. The manuscript has not been altered since it came into the possession of the editor; though it is but proper to state that it had previously undergone a slight verbal revision; and the occasional interlineations were recognised to be in the handwriting of the Bee hunter,[2] so frequently mentioned in the progress of the narrative. These corrections were doubtless made at the author's own request, and received his approbation.

This worthy and talented young man was well known in New Orleans. His parents were wealthy, he had received a liberal education, was the pride and soul of the circle in which he moved, but his destiny was suddenly overshadowed by an act in which he had no agency, but his proud father in a moment of anger turned his face upon him, and the romantic youth, with a wounded spirit, commenced the roving life which he had pursued with success for four or five years. His father recently

found out the great injustice that had been done his proud spirited son, recalled him, and a reconciliation took place; but the
young man had become enamoured of Texas, and a young
woman at Nacogdoches, and had already selected a plantation
in Austin's colony,[3] on which he intended to have settled in the
course of the coming year. The following letter will explain the
manner in which the manuscript was preserved, and how it
came into my possession:—

San Jacinto, May 3, 1836.

My dear friend,—

I write this from the town of Lynchburg, on the San Jacinto, to
inform you that I am laid up in ordinary at this place, having
been wounded in the right knee by a musket ball, in the glorious
battle of the 20th ultimo. Having some friends residing here, I
was anxious to get among them, for an invalid has not much
chance of receiving proper attention from the army surgeons in
the present state of affairs. I send you a literary curiosity, which I
doubt not you will agree with me should be laid before the public. It is the journal of Colonel Crockett, from the time of his leaving Tennessee up to the day preceding his untimely death at the
Alamo. The manner of its preservation was somewhat singular.
The Colonel was among the six who were found alive in the fort
after the general massacre had ceased. General Castrillon,[4] as you
have already learned, was favourably impressed with his manly
and courageous deportment, and interceded for his life, but in
vain. After the fort had been ransacked, these papers were found
in the Colonel's baggage, by the servant of Castrillon, who immediately carried them to his master. After the battle of San Jacinto, they were found in the baggage of Castrillon, and as I was
by at the time, and recognised the manuscript, I secured it, and
saved it from being cast away as worthless, or torn up as cartridge paper. By way of beguiling the tedious hours of my illness,
I have added a chapter, and brought down a history of the events
to the present time. Most of the facts I have recorded, I gathered
from Castrillon's servant, and other Mexican prisoners. The manuscript is at your service to do with as you please, but I should ad-

vise its publication, and should it be deemed necessary, you are at liberty to publish this letter also, by way of explanation.

With sincere esteem, your friend,

Charles T. Beale.

To Alex. J. Dumas Esq., New Orleans.[5]

The deep interest that has been taken, for several years past, in the sayings and doings of Colonel Crockett, has induced me to lay this last of his literary labours before the public, not doubting that it will be read with as much avidity as his former publications, though in consequence of the death of the author before he had revised the sheets for the press, it will necessarily be ushered into the world with many imperfections on its head, for which indulgence is craved by the public's obedient servant,

Alex. J. Dumas.

New Orleans, June, 1836

Adventures in Texas.

CHAPTER I.

It is a true saying that no one knows the luck of a lousy calf, for though in a country where, according to the Declaration of Independence, the people are all born free and equal, those who have a propensity to go ahead[1] may aim at the highest honours, and they may ultimately reach them too, though they start at the lowest rowel of the ladder,—still it is a huckelberry above by persimmon to cipher out how it is with six months' schooling only, I, David Crockett, find myself the most popular bookmaker of the day; and such is the demand for my works that I cannot write them half fast enough, no how I can fix it. This problem would bother even my friend Major Jack Downing's[2] rule of three, to bring out square after all his practice on the Post Office accounts and the public lands[3] to boot.

I have been told that there was one Shakspeare more than two hundred years ago, who was brought up a hostler, but finding it a dull business, took to writing plays, and made as great a stir in his time as I do at present; which will go to show, that one ounce of the genuine horse sense is worth a pound of your book learning any day, and if a man is only determined to go ahead, the more kicks he receives in his breech the faster he will get on his journey.

Finding it necessary to write another book, that the whole world may be made acquainted with my movements, and to save myself the trouble of answering all the questions that are poked at me, as if my own private business was the business of the nation, I set about the work, and offer the people another proof of my capacity to write my own messages and state papers, should I be pitched upon to run against the Little Flying

Dutchman,[4] a thing not unlikely from present appearances; but
somehow I feel rather dubious that my learning may not make
against me, as "the greatest and the best"[5] has set the example
of writing his long rigmaroles by proxy, which I rather reckon
is the easiest plan.

I begin this book on the 8th day of July, 1835, at Home,
Weakley county, Tennessee. I have just returned from a two
weeks' electioneering canvass, and I have spoken every day to
large concourses of people with my competitor. I have him
badly plagued, for he does not know as much about "the Government,"[6] the deposites, and the Little Flying Dutchman,
whose life I wrote, as I can tell the people; and at times he is as
much bothered as a fly in a tar pot to get out of the mess. A
candidate is often stumped in making stump-speeches. His
name is Adam Huntsman;[7] he lost a leg in an Indian fight, they
say, during the last war, and the Government run him on the
score of his military services. I tell him in my speech that I have
great hopes of writing one more book, and that shall be the
second fall of Adam, for he is on the Eve of an almighty thrash-
ing. He relishes the joke about as much as a doctor does his
own physic. I handle the administration without gloves, and I
do believe I will double my competitor, if I have a fair shake,
and he does not work like a mole in the dark. Jacksonism is dying here faster than it ever sprung up, and I predict that "the
Government" will be the most unpopular man, in one more
year, that ever had any pretensions to the high place he now
fills. Four weeks from to-morrow will end the dispute in our
elections, and if old Adam is not beaten out of his hunting shirt
my name isn't Crockett.

While on the subject of election matters, I will just relate a
little anecdote, about myself, which will show the people to the
east, how we manage these things on the frontiers. It was when
I first run for Congress; I was then in favour of the Hero,[8] for
he had chalked out his course so sleek in his letter to the Tennessee legislature, that, like Sam Patch,[9] says I, "there can be no
mistake in him," and so I went ahead. No one dreamt about
the monster and the deposites at that time, and so, as I afterward found, many, like myself, were taken in by these fair

promises, which were worth about as much as a flash in the pan when you have a fair shot at a fat bear.

But I am losing sight of my story.—Well, I started off to the Cross Roads, dressed in my hunting shirt, and my rifle on my shoulder. Many of our constituents had assembled there to get a taste of the quality of the candidates at orating. Job Snelling,[10] a gander-shanked Yankee, who had been caught somewhere about Plymouth Bay, and been shipped to the west with a cargo of cod fish and rum, erected a large shantee, and set up shop for the occasion. A large posse of the voters had assembled before I arrived, and my opponent had already made considerable headway with his speechifying and his treating, when they spied me about a rifle shot from the camp, sauntering along as if I was not a party in the business. "There comes Crockett," cried one. "Let us hear the colonel," cried another, and so I mounted the stump that had been cut down for the occasion, and began to bushwhack in the most approved style.

I had not been up long before there was such an uproar in the crowd that I could not hear my own voice, and some of my constituents let me know, that they could not listen to me on such a dry subject as the welfare of the nation, until they had something to drink, and that I must treat 'em. Accordingly I jumped down from the rostrum, and led the way to the shantee, followed by my constituents, shouting, "Huzza for Crockett," and "Crockett for ever!"

When we entered the shantee, Job was busy dealing out his rum in a style that showed he was making a good day's work of it, and I called for a quart of the best, but the crooked critur returned no other answer than by pointing at a board over the bar, on which he had chalked in large letters, "*Pay to-day and trust to-morrow.*" Now that idea brought me all up standing; it was a sort of cornering in which there was no back out, for ready money in the west, in those times, was the shyest thing in all natur, and it was most particularly shy with me on that occasion.

The voters, seeing my predicament, fell off to the other side, and I was left deserted and alone, as the Government will be, when he no longer has any offices to bestow. I saw, plain as day,

that the tide of popular opinion was against me, and that, unless I got some rum speedily, I should lose my election as sure
as there are snakes in Virginny,—and it must be done soon, or
even burnt brandy wouldn't save me. So I walked away from
the shantee, but in another guess sort from the way I entered it,
for on this occasion I had no train after me, and not a voice
shouted "Huzza for Crockett." Popularity sometimes depends
on a very small matter indeed; in this particular it was worth a
quart of New England rum, and no more.

Well, knowing that a crisis was at hand, I struck into the
woods with my rifle on my shoulder, my best friend in time of
need, and as good fortune would have it, I had not been out
more than a quarter of an hour before I treed a fat coon, and in
the pulling of a trigger he lay dead at the root of the tree. I soon
whipped his hairy jacket off his back, and again bent my way
towards the shantee, and walked up to the bar, but not alone,
for this time I had half a dozen of my constituents at my heels.
I threw down the coon skin upon the counter, and called for a
quart, and Job, though busy in dealing out rum, forgot to point
at his chalked rules and regulations, for he knew that a coon
was as good a legal tender for a quart, in the west, as a New
York shilling, any day in the year.

My constituents now flocked about me, and cried "Huzza
for Crockett," "Crockett for ever," and finding that the tide
had taken a turn, I told them several yarns, to get them in a
good humour, and having soon despatched the value of the
coon, I went out and mounted the stump, without opposition,
and a clear majority of the voters followed me to hear what
I had to offer for the good of the nation. Before I was half
through, one of my constituents moved that they would hear
the balance of my speech, after they had washed down the first
part with some more of Job Snelling's extract of cornstalk and
molasses, and the question being put, it was carried unanimously. It wasn't considered necessary to call the yeas and
nays, so we adjourned to the shantee, and on the way I began
to reckon that the fate of the nation pretty much depended
upon my shooting another coon.

While standing at the bar, feeling sort of bashful while Job's rules and regulations stared me in the face, I cast down my eyes, and discovered one end of the coon skin sticking between the logs that supported the bar. Job had slung it there in the hurry of business. I gave it a sort of quick jerk, and it followed my hand as natural as if I had been the rightful owner. I slapped it on the counter, and Job, little dreaming that he was barking up the wrong tree, shoved along another bottle, which my constituents quickly disposed of with great good humour, for some of them saw the trick, and then we withdrew to the rostrum to discuss the affairs of the nation.

I don't know how it was, but the voters soon became dry again, and nothing would do, but we must adjourn to the shantee, and as luck would have it, the coon skin was still sticking between the logs, as if Job had flung it there on purpose to tempt me. I was not slow in raising it to the counter, the rum followed of course, and I wish I may be shot, if I didn't, before the day was over, get ten quarts for the same identical skin, and from a fellow too, who in those parts was considered as sharp as a steel trap, and as bright as a pewter button.[11]

This joke secured me my election, for it soon circulated like smoke among my constituents, and they allowed, with one accord, that the man who could get the whip hand of Job Snelling in fair trade, could outwit Old Nick himself, and was the real grit for them in Congress. Job was by no means popular; he boasted of always being wide awake, and that any one who could take him in was free to do so, for he came from a stock that sleeping or waking had always one eye open, and the other not more than half closed. The whole family were geniuses. His father was the inventor of wooden nutmegs, by which Job said he might have made a fortune, if he had only taken out a patent and kept the business in his own hands; his mother Patience manufactured the first white oak pumpkin seeds of the mammoth kind, and turned a pretty penny the first season; and his aunt Prudence was the first to discover that corn husks, steeped in tobacco water, would make as handsome Spanish wrappers as ever came from Havanna, and that oak leaves would answer all the purposes of filling, for no one would discover the difference except the man who smoked them, and then it would be too late to make a stir about it. Job himself bragged of having made some useful discoveries; the most profitable of which was the art of converting mahogany sawdust into cayenne pepper, which he said was a profitable and safe business; for the people have been so long accustomed to having dust thrown in their eyes, that there wasn't much danger of being found out.

The way I got to the blind side of the Yankee merchant was pretty generally known before the election day, and the result was, that my opponent might as well have whistled jigs to a milestone as attempt to beat up for votes in that district. I beat him out and out, quite back into the old year, and there was scarce enough left of him, after the canvass was over, to make a small grease spot. He disappeared without even leaving as much as a mark behind; and such will be the fate of Adam Huntsman, if there is a fair fight and no gouging.

After the election was over, I sent Snelling the price of the rum, but took good care to keep the fact from the knowledge of my constituents. Job refused the money, and sent me word, that it did him good to be taken in occasionally, as it served to brighten his ideas; but I afterwards learnt that when he found out the trick that had been played upon him, he put all the rum I had ordered in his bill against my opponent, who, being elated with the speeches he had made on the affairs of the nation, could not descend to examine into the particulars of the bill of a vender of rum in the small way.

CHAPTER II.

August 11, 1835. I am now at home in Weakley county. My canvass is over, and the result is known. Contrary to all expectation, I am beaten two hundred and thirty votes, from the best information I can get; and in this instance, I may say, bad is the best. My mantle has fallen upon the shoulders of Adam, and I hope he may wear it with becoming dignity, and never lose sight of the welfare of the nation, for the purpose of elevating a few designing politicians to the head of the heap. The rotten policy pursued by "the Government" cannot last long; it will either work its own downfall, or the downfall of the republic, soon, unless the people tear the seal from their eyes, and behold their danger time enough to avert the ruin.

I wish to inform the people of these United States what I had to contend against, trusting that the exposé I shall make will be a caution to the people not to repose too much power in the hands of a single man, though he should be "the greatest and the best."—I had, as I have already said, Mr. Adam Huntsman for my competitor, aided by the popularity of both Andrew Jackson and governor Carroll[1] and the whole strength of the Union Bank at Jackson. I have been told by good men, that some of the managers of the bank on the days of the election were heard [to] say, that they would give twenty-five dollars a vote for votes enough to elect Mr. Huntsman. This is a pretty good price for a vote, and in ordinary times a round dozen might be got for the money.

I have always believed, since Jackson removed the deposites, that his whole object was to place the treasury where he could use it to influence elections; and I do believe he is determined to sacrifice every dollar of the treasury to make the Little Flying

Dutchman his successor. If this is not my creed I wish I may be shot. For fourteen years since I have been a candidate I never saw such means used to defeat any candidate, as were put in practice against me on this occasion. There was a disciplined band of judges and officers to hold the elections at almost every poll. Of late years they begin to find out that there's an advantage in this, even in the west. Some officers held the election, and at the same time had nearly all they were worth bet on the election. Such judges I should take it are like the handle of a jug, all on one side; and I am told it doesn't require much schooling to make the tally list correspond to a notch with the ballot box, provided they who make up the returns have enough loose tickets in their breeches pockets. I have no doubt that I was completely rascalled out of my election, and I do regret that duty to myself and to my country compels me to expose such villany.

Well might Governor Poindexter[2] exclaim—"Ah! My country, what degradation thou hast fallen into!" Andrew Jackson was, during my election canvass, franking the extra Globe[3] with a prospectus in it to every post office in this district, and upon one occasion he had my mileage and pay as a member drawn up and sent to this district, to one of his minions, to have it published just a few days before the election. This is what I call small potatoes and few of a hill. He stated that I had charged mileage for one thousand miles and that it was but seven hundred and fifty miles, and held out the idea that I had taken pay for the same mileage that Mr. Fitzgerald[4] had taken, when it was well known that he charged thirteen hundred miles from here to Washington, and he and myself both live in the same county. It is somewhat remarkable how this fact should have escaped the keen eye of "the Government."

The General's pet, Mr. Grundy,[5] charged for one thousand miles from Nashville to Washington, and it was sanctioned by the legislature, I suppose because he would huzza! for Jackson; and because I think proper to refrain from huzzaing until he goes out of office, when I shall give a screamer, that will be heard from the Mississippi to the Atlantic, or my name's not Crockett—for this reason he came out openly to electioneer against me. I now say, that the oldest man living never heard of the President of a great nation to come down to open election-eering for his successor. It is treating the nation as if it was the property of a single individual, and he had the right to be-queath it to whom he pleased—the same as a patch of land for which he had the patent. It is plain to be seen that the poor su-perannuated old man is surrounded by a set of horse leeches, who will stick to him while there is a drop of blood to be got, and their maws are so capacious that they will never get full enough to drop off. The Land office, the Post office, and the Treasury itself, may all be drained, and we shall still find them craving for more. They use him to promote their own private interest, and for all his sharp sight, he remains as blind as a dead lion to the jackals who are tearing him to pieces. In fact, I do believe he is a perfect tool in their hands, ready to be used to answer any purpose to promote either their interest or grat-ify their ambition.

I come within two hundred and thirty votes of being elected, notwithstanding I had to contend against "the greatest and the best," with the whole power of the Treasury against me. The Little Flying Dutchman will no doubt calculate upon having a true game cock in Mr. Huntsman, but if he doesn't show them the White feather[6] before the first session is over, I agree never to be set down for a prophet, that's all. I am gratified that I have spoken the truth to the people of my district regardless of consequences. I would not be compelled to bow down to the idol for a seat in Congress during life. I have never known what it was to sacrifice my own judgment to gratify any party, and I have no doubt of the time being close at hand when I will be rewarded for letting my tongue speak what my heart thinks. I have suffered myself to be politically sacrificed to save my country from ruin and disgrace, and if I am never again elected, I will have the gratification to know that I have done my duty.—Thus much I say in relation to the manner in which my downfall was effected, and in laying it before the public, "I take the responsibility." I may add in the words of the man in the play, "Crockett's occupation's gone."—[7]

Two weeks and more have elapsed since I wrote the forego-

ing account of my defeat, and I confess the thorn still rankles,
not so much on my own account as the nation's, for I had set
my heart on following up the travelling deposites until they
should be fairly gathered to their proper nest, like young chickens, for I am aware of the vermin that are on the constant look-
out to pounce upon them, like a cock at a blackberry, which
they would have done long since, if it had not been for a few
such men as Webster, Clay, and myself.[8] It is my parting advice,
that this matter be attended to without delay, for before long
the little chickens will take wing, and even the powerful wand
of the magician of Kinderhook will be unable to point out the
course they have flown.

As my country no longer requires my services, I have made
up my mind to go to Texas. My life has been one of danger, toil,
and privation, but these difficulties I had to encounter at a time
when I considered it nothing more than right good sport to sur-
mount them; but now I start anew upon my own hook, and
God only grant that it may be strong enough to support the
weight that may be hung upon it. I have a new row to hoe, a
long and a rough one, but come what will I'll go ahead.

A few days ago I went to a meeting of my constituents. My
appetite for politics was at one time just about as sharp set as a
saw mill, but late events has given me something of a surfeit,—
more than I could well digest; still habit they say is second
natur, and so I went, and gave them a piece of my mind touching "the Government" and the succession, by way of a codicil
to what I have often said before.

I told them to keep a sharp look-out for the deposites, for it
requires an eye as insinuating as a dissecting knife to see what
safety there is in placing one million of the public funds in some
little country shaving shop with no more than one hundred
thousand dollars capital. This bank, we will just suppose, without being too particular, is in the neighbourhood of some of the
public lands, where speculators, who have every thing to gain
and nothing to lose, swarm like crows about carrion. They buy
the United States' land upon a large scale, get discounts from the
aforesaid shaving shop, which are made upon a large scale also,
upon the United States' funds; they pay the whole purchase

money with these discounts, and get a clear title to the land, so that when the shaving shop comes to make a Flemish account[9] of her transactions, "the Government" will discover that he has not only lost the original deposite, but a large body of the public lands to boot. So much for taking the responsibility.

I told them that they were hurrying along a broad M'Adamized road[10] to make the Little Flying Dutchman the successor, but they would no sooner accomplish that end, than they would be obliged to buckle to, and drag the Juggernaut through many narrow and winding and out-of-the-way paths, and hub deep in the mire. That they reminded me of the Hibernian, who bet a glass of grog with a hod carrier, that he could not carry him in his hod up a ladder to the third story of a new building. He seated himself in the hod, and the other mounted the ladder with his load upon his shoulder. He ascended to the second story pretty steadily, but as he approached the third his strength failed him, he began to totter, and Pat was so delighted at the prospect of winning his bet, that he clapped his hands and shouted, "By the powers the grog's mine," and he made such a stir in the hod, that I wish I may be shot if he didn't win it, but he broke his neck in the fall. And so I told my constituents that they might possibly gain the victory, but in doing so, they would ruin their country.

I told them moreover of my services, pretty straight up and down, for a man may be allowed to speak on such subjects when others are about to forget them; and I also told them of the manner in which I had been knocked down and dragged out, and that I did not consider it a fair fight any how they could fix it. I put the ingredients in the cup pretty strong I tell you, and I concluded my speech by telling them that I was down with politics for the present, and that they might all go to hell, and I would go to Texas.

When I returned home I felt a sort of cast down at the change that had taken place in my fortunes, and sorrow, it is said, will make even an oyster feel poetical. I never tried my hand at that sort of writing, but on this particular occasion such was my state of feeling, that I began to fancy myself inspired; so I took pen in hand, and as usual I went ahead. When I had got fairly through, my poetry looked as zigzag as a worm fence; the lines wouldn't tally, no how; so I showed them to Peleg Longfellow,[11] who has a first-rate reputation with us for that sort of writing, having some years ago made a carrier's address[12] for the Nashville Banner, and Peleg lopped off some lines, and stretched out others; but I wish I may be shot if I don't rather think he has made it worse than it was when I placed it in his hands. It being my first, and no doubt last piece of poetry, I will print it in this place, as it will serve to express my feelings on leaving my home, my neighbours, and friends and country, for a strange land, as fully as I could in plain prose.

> Farewell to the mountains whose mazes to me
> Were more beautiful far than Eden could be;
> No fruit was forbidden, but Nature had spread
> Her bountiful board, and her children were fed.
> The hills were our garners—our herds wildly grew,
> And Nature was shepherd and husbandman too.
> I felt like a monarch, yet thought like a man,
> As I thank'd the Great Giver, and worshipp'd his plan.
>
> The home I forsake where my offspring arose:
> The graves I forsake where my children repose.
> The home I redeem'd from the savage and wild;
> The home I have loved as a father his child;
> The corn that I planted, the fields that I clear'd,
> The flocks that I raised, and the cabin I rear'd;
> The wife of my bosom—Farewell to ye all!
> In the land of the stranger I rise—or I fall.
>
> Farewell to my country!—I fought for thee well.
> When the savage rush'd forth like the demons from hell.
> In peace or in war I have stood by thy side—
> My country, for thee I have lived—would have died!
> But I am cast off—my career now is run,
> And I wander abroad like the prodigal son—
> Where the wild savage roves, and the broad prairies spread,
> The fallen—despised—will again go ahead!

CHAPTER III.

In my last chapter I made mention of my determination to cut and quit the States until such time as honest and independent men should again work their way to the head of the heap; and as I should probably have some idle time on hand before that state of affairs shall be brought about, I promised to give the Texians a helping hand, on the high road to freedom.[1]—Well, I was always fond of having my spoon in a mess of that kind, for if there is any thing in this world particularly worth living for, it is freedom; any thing that would render death to a brave man particularly pleasant, it is freedom.

I am now on my journey, and have already tortled[2] along as far as Little Rock on the Arkansas, about one hundred and twenty-five miles from the mouth. I had promised to write another book, expecting, when I made that promise, to write about politics, and use up "the Government," his successor, the removal of the deposites, and so on, matters and things that come as natural to me as bear hunting; but being rascalled out of my election, I am taken all aback, and I must now strike into a new path altogether. Still I will redeem my promise, and make a book, and it shall be about my adventures in Texas, hoping that my friends, Messrs. Webster and Clay and Biddle,[3] will keep a sharp look-out upon "the Government" during my absence.—I am told that every author of distinction writes a book of travels now-a-days.

My thermometer stood somewhat below the freezing point as I left my wife and children; still there was some thawing about the eyelids, a thing that had not taken place since I first ran away from my father's house when a thoughtless vagabond boy. I dressed myself in a clean hunting shirt, put on a new fox skin cap with the tail hanging behind, took hold of my rifle Betsey,[4] which all the world knows was presented to me by the patriotic citizens of Philadelphia, as a compliment for my unflinching opposition to the tyrannic measures of "the Government," and thus equipped I started off, with a heavy heart, for Mill's Point, to take steamboat down the Mississippi, and go ahead in a new world.

While walking along, and thinking whether it was altogether the right grit to leave my poor country at a time she most needed my services, I came to a clearing,[5] and I was slowly rising a slope, when I was startled by loud, profane, and boisterous voices, (as loud and profane as have been heard in the White House of late years,) which seemed to proceed from a thick covert of undergrowth, about two hundred yards in advance of me, and about one hundred to the right of my road.

"You kin, kin you?"

"Yes, I kin, and am able to do it! Boo—oo—oo!—O! wake snakes, and walk your chalks! Brimstone and —— fire! Don't hold me, Nick Stoval! The fight's made up, and let's go at it. —— my soul if I don't jump down his throat and gallop every chitterling out of him, before you can say 'quit!'"

"Now, Nick, don't hold him! Jist let the wild cat come, and I'll tame him. Ned'll see me a fair fight—won't you, Ned?"

"O! yes, I'll see you a fair fight; blast my old shoes if I don't."

"That's sufficient, as Tom Haynes said, when he saw the elephant. Now let him come."

Thus they went on, with countless oaths interspersed, which I dare not even hint at, and with much that I could not distinctly hear.

In mercy's name! thought I, what a band of ruffians is at work here. I quickened my gait, and had come nearly opposite to the thick grove whence the noise proceeded, when my eye caught indistinctly, through the foliage of the dwarf oaks and hickories that intervened, glimpses of a man or men, who seemed to be in a violent struggle; and I could occasionally catch those deep drawn emphatic oaths, which men in conflict utter, when they deal blows. I hurried to the spot, but before I reached it, I saw the combatants come to the ground, and after a short struggle, I saw the uppermost one (for I could not see the other) make a heavy plunge with both his thumbs, and at the same instant I heard a cry in the accent of keenest torture, "Enough! My eye is out!"

I stood completely horror-struck for a moment. The accomplices in the brutal deed had all fled at my approach, at least I supposed so, for they were not to be seen.

"Now blast your corn-shucking soul," said the victor, a lad about eighteen, as he rose from the ground, "come cutt'n your shines 'bout me agin, next time I come to the Court House, will you!—Get your owl-eye in agin if you can."

At this moment he saw me for the first time. He looked as though he couldn't help it, and was for making himself particularly scarce, when I called to him, "Come back, you brute, and assist me in relieving the poor critur you have ruined for ever."

Upon this rough salutation, he sort of collected himself, and with a taunting curl of the nose he replied, "You needn't kick before you're spurr'd. There an't nobody there, nor han't been nother. I was jist seein' how I could a' fout." So saying he bounded to his plough, which stood in the corner of the fence about fifty yards from the battle ground.

Now would any man in his senses believe that a rational being could make such a darned fool of himself? but I wish I may be shot, if his report was not as true as the last Post office report, every word, and a little more satisfactory. All that I had heard and seen was nothing more nor less than what is called a rehearsal of a knock-down and drag-out fight, in which the young man had played all the parts for his own amusement, and by way of keeping his hand in. I went to the ground from which he had risen, and there was the prints of his two thumbs, plunged up to the balls in the mellow earth, about the distance of a man's eyes apart, and the ground around was broken up, as if two stags had been engaged upon it.

As I resumed my journey I laughed outright at this adventure, for it reminded me of Andrew Jackson's attack upon the United States Bank. He had magnified it into a monster, and then begun to rip and tear and swear and gouge, until he thought he had the monster on its back; and when the fight was over, and he got up to look about for his enemy, he could find none for the soul of him, for his enemy was altogether in his heated imagination. These fighting characters are never at peace, unless they have something to quarrel with, and rather than have no fight at all they will trample on their own shadows.

The day I arrived at Little Rock, I no sooner quit the steamer than I streaked it straight ahead for the principal tavern, which is nothing to boast of, nohow, unless a man happens to be like the member of Congress from the south, who was converted to Jacksonism, and then made a speech as long as the longitude about his political honesty. Some men it seems, take a pride in saying a great deal about nothing—like windmills, their tongues must be going whether they have any grist to grind or not. This is all very well in Congress, where every member is expected to make a speech to let his constituents know that some things can be done as well as others;[6] but I set it down as being rather an imposition upon good nature to be compelled to listen, without receiving the consideration of eight dollars per day, besides mileage, as we do in Congress. Many members will do nothing else for their pay but listen, day in and day out, and I wish I may be shot, if they do not earn every penny of it, provided they don't sleep, and Benton[7] or little Isaac Hill[8] will spin their yarns but once in a week. No man who has not tried it can imagine what dreadful hard work it is to listen. Splitting gum logs in the dog days is child's play to it. I've tried both, and give the preference to the gum logs.

Well, as I said, I made straight for the tavern, and as I drew nigh, I saw a considerable crowd assembled before the door. So, thought I, they have heard that Colonel Crockett intended to pay a visit to their settlement, and they have already got together to receive him in due form. I confess I felt a little elated at the idea, and commenced ransacking the lumber room of my brain, to find some one of my speeches that I might furbish up for the occasion; and then I shouldered my Betsey, straightened myself, and walked up to the door, charged to the muzzle, and ready to let fly.

But strange as it may seem, no one took any more notice of me, than if I had been Martin Van Buren, or Dick Johnson,[9] the celebrated wool grower. This took me somewhat aback, and I inquired what was the meaning of the gathering; and I learnt that a travelling showman had just arrived, and was about to exhibit for the first time the wonderful feats of Harlequin, and Punch and Judy, to the impatient natives. It was drawing towards nightfall, and expectation was on tiptoe; the children were clinging to their mother's aprons, with their chubby faces dimpled with delight, and asking "What is it like? when will it begin?" and similar questions, while the women, as all good wives are in duty bound to do, appealed to their husbands for information; but the call for information was not responded to in this instance, as is sometimes the case in Congress;—their husbands understood the matter about as well as "the Government" did the Post office accounts.

The showman at length made his appearance, with a countenance as wo-begone as that of "the Government" when he found his batch of dirty nominations rejected by the Senate, and mentioned the impossibility that any performance should take place that evening, as the lame fiddler had overcharged his head, and having but one leg at best, it did not require much to destroy his equilibrium. And as all the world knows, a puppet show without a fiddle is like roast pork and no apple sauce. This piece of intelligence was received with a general murmur of dissatisfaction; and such was the indignation of his majesty, the sovereign people, at being thwarted in his rational amusements, that, according to the established custom in such cases made and provided, there were some symptoms of a disposition to kick up a row, break the show, and finish the amusements of the day by putting Lynch's law in practice upon the poor showman. There is nothing like upholding the dignity of the people, and so Lieut. Randolph[10] thought, when with his cowardly and sacrilegious hand he dared to profane the anointed nose of "the Government," and bring the whole nation into contempt. If I had been present, may disgrace follow my career in Texas, if I wouldn't have become a whole hog Jackson man upon the spot, for the time being, for the nose of "the Government" should be held more sacred than any other member, that it may be kept in good order to smell out all the corruption that is going forward—not a very pleasant office, and by no means a sinecure.

The indignant people, as I have already said, were about to exercise their reserved rights upon the unlucky showman, and Punch and Judy too, when, as good fortune would have it, an old gentleman drove up to the tavern door in a sulky, with a box of books and pamphlets of his own composition—(for he was an author like myself)—thus being able to vouch for the moral tendency of every page he disposed of. Very few booksellers can do the same, I take it. His linen and flannels, which he had washed in the brooks by the wayside, were hanging over the back of the crazy vehicle to dry, while his own snuffy countenance had long bid defiance to sun, wind, and water to bleach it.

His jaded beast stopped instinctively upon seeing a crowd, while the old man remained seated for some moments before he could recall his thoughts from the world of imagination, where they were gleaning for the benefit of mankind. He looked, it must be confessed, more like a lunatic than a moral lecturer; but being conscious of his own rectitude, he could not conceive how his outward Adam could make him ridiculous in the eyes of another; but a fair outside is every thing to the world. The tulip flower is highly prized, although indebted for its beauty to the corruption engendered at the root: and so it is with man.

We occasionally meet with one possessing sufficient philosophy to look upon life as a pilgrimage, and not as a mere round of pleasure: who, treating this world as a place of probation, is ready to encounter suffering, and not expecting the sunshine of prosperity, escapes being overclouded by disappointment. Such is the character of the old preacher, whose ridiculous appearance in the eyes of the thoughtless and ignorant is only exceeded by the respect and veneration of those who are capable of estimating his real worth. I learnt that he was educated for the church, but not being able to obtain a living, he looked upon the whole earth as his altar, and all mankind as his flock.

He was penniless, and therefore had no predilection for this or that section of the globe, for wherever he might be, his journey of probation still continued, and in every spot he found that human nature was the same. His life was literally that of a pilgrim. He was an isolated being, though his heart overflowed with the milk of human kindness; for being indiscriminate in his affection, very few valued it. He who commences the world with a general love for mankind, and suffers his feelings to dictate in his reason, runs a great hazard of reaping a plentiful harvest of ingratitude, and of closing a tedious existence in misanthropy. But it was not so with the aged preacher.

Being unable to earn his bread as an itinerant lecturer,—for in those cases it is mostly poor preach and worse pay—he turned author, and wrote histories which contained but little information, and sermons which, like many others, had nothing to boast of, beyond being strictly orthodox. He succeeded in obtaining a sulky, and a horse to drag it, by a plea of mercy, which deprived the hounds of their food, and with these he travelled over the western states, to dispose of the product of his brain; and when poverty was deprived of the benefit of his labour, in the benevolence of his heart he would deliver a moral lecture, which had the usual weight of homilies on this subject. A lecture is the cheapest thing that a man can bestow in charity, and many of our universal philanthropists have made the discovery.

The landlord now made his appearance, and gave a hearty welcome to the reverend traveller, and shaking him by the hand, added, that he never came more opportunely in all his life.

"Opportunely!" exclaimed the philosopher.

"Yes," rejoined the other; "you have a heart and head that labour for the benefit of us poor mortals."

"O! true, an excellent market for my pamphlets," replied the other, at the same time beginning to open the trunk that lay before him.

"You misunderstand me," added the landlord.

"A poor showman, with a sick wife and five children, has arrived from New Orleans——"

"I will sell my pamphlets to relieve their wants, and endeavour to teach them resignation."

"He exhibits to-night in my large room: you know the room, sir—I let him have it gratis."

"You are an honest fellow. I will witness his show, and add my mite to his assistance."

"But," replied the innkeeper, "the lame fiddler is fond of the bottle, and is now snoring in the hayloft."

"Degrading vice!" exclaimed the old man, and taking "God's Revenge against Drunkenness" from the trunk, and standing erect in the sulky, commenced reading to his astonished audience. The innkeeper interrupted him by observing that the homily would not fill the empty purse of the poor showman, and unless a fiddler could be obtained, he must depend on charity, or go supperless to bed. And moreover, the people, irritated at their disappointment, had threatened to tear the show to pieces.

"But what's to be done?" demanded the parson.

"Your reverence shakes an excellent bow," added the innkeeper, in an insinuating tone.

"I!" exclaimed the parson; "I fiddle for a puppet show!"

"Not for the puppet show, but for the sick wife and five hungry children."

A tear started into the eyes of the old man, as he added in an undertone, "If I could be concealed from the audience——"

"Nothing easier," cried the other; "we will place you behind the scenes, and no one will ever dream that you fiddled at a puppet show."

The matter being thus settled, they entered the house, and shortly afterward the sound of a fiddle squeaking like a giggling girl, tickled into ecstacies, restored mirth and good humour to the disappointed assemblage, who rushed in, helter-skelter, to enjoy the exhibition.

All being seated, and silence restored, they waited in breathless expectation for the rising of the curtain. At length Harlequin made his appearance, and performed astonishing feats of activity on the slack rope; turning somersets backward and forward, first on this side, and then on that, with as much ease as if he had been a politician all his life,—the parson sawing vigorously on his fiddle all the time. Punch followed, and set the audience in a roar with his antic tricks and jests; but when Judy entered with her broomstick, the burst of applause was as great as ever I heard bestowed upon one of Benton's slang-whang[11] speeches in Congress, and I rather think quite as well merited.

As the plot thickened, the music of the parson became more animated; but unluckily in the warmth of his zeal to do justice to his station, his elbow touched the side scene, which fell to the floor, and exposed him, working away in all the ecstacies of little Isaac Hill, while reading one of his long orations about things in general to empty benches. No ways disconcerted by the accident, the parson seized upon it as a fine opportunity of conveying a lesson to those around him, at the same time that he might benefit a fellow mortal. He immediately mounted the chair upon which he was seated, and addressed the audience to the following effect:—

"Many of you have come here for amusement, and others no doubt to assist the poor man, who is thus struggling to obtain a subsistence for his sick wife and children.—Lo! the moral of a puppet show!—But is this all; has he not rendered unto you your money's worth? This is not charity. If you are charitably inclined, here is an object fully deserving of it." He preached upon this text for full half an hour, and concluded with taking his hat to collect assistance from his hearers for the friendless showman and his family.

The next morning, when his sulky was brought to the door, the showman and his wife came out to thank their benefactor. The old man placed his trunk of pamphlets before him, and proceeded on his pilgrimage, the little children following him through the village with bursts of gratitude.

CHAPTER IV.

The public mind having been quieted by the exhibition of the puppet show, and allowed to return to its usual channel, it was not long before the good people of Little Rock began to inquire what distinguished stranger had come among them; and learning that it was neither more nor less than the identical Colonel Crockett, the champion of the fugitive deposites, than straight they went ahead at getting up another tempest in a teapot; and I wish I may be shot, if I wasn't looked upon as almost as great a sight as Punch and Judy.

Nothing would answer but I must accept of an invitation to a public dinner. Now as public dinners have become so common, that it is enough to take away the appetite of any man, who has a proper sense of his own importance, to sit down and play his part in the humbug business, I had made up my mind to write a letter declining the honour, expressing my regret, and winding up with a flourish of trumpets about the patriotism of the citizens of Little Rock, and all that sort of thing, when the landlord came in, and says he, "Colonel, just oblige me by stepping into the back yard a moment."

I followed the landlord in silence, twisting and turning over in my brain, all the while, what I should say in my letter to the patriotic citizens of Little Rock, who were bent on eating a dinner for the good of their country; when he conducted me to a shed in the yard, where I beheld, hanging up, a fine fat cub bear, several haunches of venison, a wild turkey as big as a young ostrich, and small game too tedious to mention. "Well, Colonel, what do you think of my larder?" says he. "Fine!" says I; "let us liquor." We walked back to the bar, I took a horn,[1] and without loss of time I wrote to the committee, that I accepted of the invitation to a public dinner with pleasure,— that I would always be found ready to serve my country either by eating or fasting; and that the honour the patriotic citizens of Little Rock had conferred upon me rendered it the proudest moment of my eventful life. The chairman of the committee was standing by while I wrote the letter, which I handed to him; and so this important business was soon settled.

As there was considerable time to be killed, or got rid of in some way, before the dinner could be cooked, it was proposed that we should go beyond the village, and shoot at a mark, for they had heard that I was a first-rate shot, and they wanted to see for themselves whether fame had not blown her trumpet a little too strong in my favour; for since she had represented "the Government" as being a first-rate statesman, and Colonel Benton as a first-rate orator, they could not receive such reports without proper allowance, as Congress thought of the Post of-fice report.

Well, I shouldered my Betsey, and she is just about as beauti-ful a piece as ever came out of Philadelphia, and I went out to the shooting ground, followed by all the leading men in Little Rock, and that was a clear majority of the town, for it is re-markable that there are always more leading men in small vil-lages than there are followers.

I was in prime order. My eye was as keen as a lizard, and my nerves were as steady and unshaken as the political course of Henry Clay; so at it we went, the distance one hundred yards. The principal marksmen, and such as had never been beat, led the way, and there was some pretty fair shooting, I tell you. At length it came to my turn. I squared myself, raised my beauti-ful Betsey to my shoulder, took deliberate aim, and smack I sent the bullet right into the centre of the bull's eye. "There's no mistake in Betsey," said I, in a sort of careless way, as they were all looking at the target, sort of amazed, and not at all over pleased.

"That's a chance shot, Colonel," said one who had the repu-tation of being the best marksmen in those parts.

"Not as much chance as there was," said I, "when Dick

Johnson took his darkie[2] for better for worse. I can do it five times out of six any day in the week." This I said in as confident a tone as "the Government" did when he protested that he forgave Colonel Benton[3] for shooting him, and he was now the best friend he had in the world. I knew it was not altogether as correct as it might be, but when a man sets about going the big figure, halfway measures won't answer no how; and "the greatest and the best" had set me the example, that swaggering will answer a good purpose at times.

They now proposed that we should have a second trial; but knowing that I had nothing to gain, and every thing to lose, I was for backing out and fighting shy; but there was no let-off, for the cock of the village, though whipped, determined not to stay whipped; so to it again we went. They were now put upon their mettle, and they fired much better than the first time; and it was what might be called pretty sharp shooting. When it came to my turn,[4] I squared myself, and turning to the prime shot, I gave him a knowing nod, by way of showing my confidence; and says I, "Look-out for the bull's eye, stranger." I blazed away, and I wish I may be shot if I didn't miss the target. They examined it all over, and could find neither hair nor hide of my bullet, and pronounced it a dead miss; when says I, "Stand aside and let me look, and I war'nt you I get on the right trail of the critter." They stood aside, and I examined the bull's eye pretty particular, and at length cried out, "Here it is; there is no snakes if it ha'n't followed the very track of the other." They said it was utterly impossible, but I insisted on their searching the hole, and I agreed to be stuck up as a mark myself, if they did not find two bullets there. They searched for my satisfaction, and sure enough it all came out just as I had told them; for I had picked up a bullet that had been fired, and stuck it deep into the hole, without any one perceiving it. They were all perfectly satisfied, that fame had not made too great a flourish of trumpets when speaking of me as a marksman; and they all said they had enough of shooting for that day, and they moved, that we adjourn to the tavern and liquor.

We had scarcely taken drinks round before the landlord announced that dinner was ready, and I was escorted into the dining room by the committee, to the tune of "See the conquering hero comes," played upon a drum, which had been beaten until it got a fit of the sullens, and refused to send forth any sound; and it was accompanied by the weasing of a fife that was sadly troubled with a spell of the asthma. I was escorted into the dining room, I say, somewhat after the same fashion that "the Government" was escorted into the different cities when he made his northern tour; the only difference was, that I had no sycophants about me, but true hearted hospitable friends, for it was pretty well known that I had, for the present, abandoned all intention of running for the Presidency against the Little Flying Dutchman.

The dinner was first-rate. The bear meat, the venison, and wild turkey would have tempted a man who had given over the business of eating altogether; and every thing was cooked to the notch precisely. The enterprising landlord did himself immortal honour on this momentous occasion; and the committee, thinking that he merited public thanks for his patriotic services, handed his name to posterity to look at in the lasting columns of the Little Rock Gazette; and when our children's children behold it, they will think of the pure patriots who sat down in good fellowship to feast on the bear meat and venison; and the enthusiasm the occasion is calculated to awaken will induce them to bless the patriot who, in a cause so glorious, spared no pains in cooking the dinner, and serving it in a becoming manner—And this is fame![5]

The fragments of the meats being cleared off, we went through the customary evolution of drinking thirteen regular toasts, after every one of which our drum with the loose skin grumbled like an old horse with an empty stomach; and our asthmatic fife squeaked like a stuck pig, a spirit-stirring tune, which we put off christening until we should come to prepare our proceedings for posterity. The fife appeared to have but one tune in it; possibly it mought have had more, but the poor fifer, with all his puffing and blowing, his too-too-tooing, and shaking his head and elbow, could not, for the body and soul of him, get more than one out of it. If the fife had had an extra tune to its name, sartin it wouldn't have been quite so hide bound on such an occasion, but have let us have it, good, bad, or indifferent. We warn't particular by no means.

Having gone through with the regular toasts, the president of the day drank, "Our distinguished guest, Col. Crockett," which called forth a prodigious clattering all around the table, and I soon saw that nothing would do, but I must get up and make them a speech. I had no sooner elongated my outward Adam, than they at it again, with renewed vigour, which made me sort of feel that I was still somebody, though no longer a member of Congress.

In my speech I went over the whole history of the present administration; took a long shot at the flying deposites, and gave an outline, a sort of charcoal sketch, of the political life of "the Government's" heir presumptive.[6] I also let them know how I had been rascalled out of my election, because I refused to bow down to the idol; and as I saw a number of young politicians around the table, I told them, that I would lay down a few rules for their guidance, which, if properly attended to, could not fail to lead them on the highway to distinction and public honour. I told them, that I was an old hand at the business, and as I was about to retire for a time, I would give them a little instruction gratis, for I was up to all the tricks of the trade, though I had practised but few.

"Attend all public meetings," says I, "and get some friend to move that you take the chair; if you fail in this attempt, make a push to be appointed secretary; the proceedings of course will be published, and your name is introduced to the public. But should you fail in both undertakings, get two or three acquaintances, over a bottle of whisky, to pass some resolutions, no matter on what subject; publish them even if you pay the printer—it will answer the purpose of breaking the ice, which is the main point in these matters. Intrigue until you are elected an officer of the militia; this is the second step toward promotion, and can be accomplished with ease, as I know an instance of an election being advertised, and no one attending, the innkeeper at whose house it was to be held, having a military turn, elected himself colonel of his regiment." Says I, "You may not accomplish your ends with as little difficulty, but do not be discouraged—Rome wasn't built in a day.

"If your ambition or circumstances compel you to serve your country, and earn three dollars a day, by becoming a member of the legislature, you must first publicly avow that the constitution of the state is a shackle upon free and liberal legislation; and is, therefore, of as little use in the present enlightened age, as an old almanac of the year in which the instrument was framed. There is policy in this measure, for by making the constitution a mere dead letter, your headlong proceedings will be attributed to a bold and unshackled mind; whereas, it might otherwise be thought they arose from sheer mulish ignorance. 'The Government' has set the example in his attack upon the constitution of the United States, and who should fear to follow where 'the Government' leads?

"When the day of election approaches, visit your constituents far and wide. Treat liberally, and drink freely, in order to rise in their estimation, though you fall in your own. True, you may be called a drunken dog by some of the clean shirt and silk stocking gentry, but the real rough necks will style you a jovial fellow,—their votes are certain, and frequently count double. Do all you can to appear to advantage in the eyes of the women. That's easily done—you have but to kiss and slabber their children, wipe their noses, and pat them on the head; this cannot fail to please their mothers, and you may rely on your business being done in that quarter.

"Promise all that is asked," said I, "and more if you can think of any thing. Offer to build a bridge or a church, to divide a country, create a batch of new offices, make a turnpike, or any thing they like. Promises cost nothing, therefore deny nobody who has a vote or sufficient influence to obtain one.

"Get up on all occasions, and sometimes on no occasion at all, and make long-winded speeches, though composed of nothing else than wind—talk of your devotion to your country, your modesty and disinterestedness, or on any such fanciful subject. Rail against taxes of all kinds, office holders, and bad harvest weather; and wind up with a flourish about the heroes who fought and bled for our liberties in the times that tried men's souls.[7] To be sure you run the risk of being considered a bladder of wind, or an empty barrel; but never mind that, you will find enough of the same fraternity to keep you in countenance.

"If any charity be going forward, be at the top of it, provided it is to be advertised publicly; if not, it isn't worth your while. None but a fool would place his candle under a bushel on such an occasion.

"These few directions," said I, "if properly attended to, will do your business; and when once elected, why a fig for the dirty children, the promises, the bridges, the churches, the taxes, the offices, and the subscriptions, for it is absolutely necessary to forget all these before you can become a thorough-going politician, and a patriot of the first water."

My speech was received with three times three, and all that; and we continued speechifying and drinking until nightfall, when it was put to vote, that we would have the puppet show over again, which was carried *nem.con.*[8] The showman set his wires to work, just as "the Government" does the machinery in his big puppet show; and we spent a delightful and rational evening. We raised a subscription for the poor showman; and I went to bed, pleased and gratified with the hospitality and kindness of the citizens of Little Rock. There are some first-rate men there, of the real half horse half alligator breed,[9] with a sprinkling of the steamboat, and such as grow nowhere on the face of the universal earth, but just about the back bone of North America.

CHAPTER V.

The day after our public dinner I determined to leave my hospitable friends at Little Rock, and cross Arkansas to Fulton on the Red River, a distance of about one hundred and twenty miles. They wanted me to stay longer; and the gentleman who had the reputation of being the best marksman in those parts was most particularly anxious that we should have another trial of skill; but says I to myself, "Crockett, you've had just about glory enough for one day, so take my advice, and leave well enough alone." I declined shooting, for there was nothing at all to be gained by it, and I might possibly lose some little of the reputation I had acquired. I have always found that it is a very important thing for a man who is fairly going ahead, to know exactly how far to go, and when to stop. Had "the Government" stopped before he meddled with the constitution, the deposites, and "taking the responsibility," he would have retired from office with almost as much credit as he entered upon it, which is as much as any public man can reasonably expect. But the General is a whole team, and when fairly started, will be going ahead; and one might as well attempt to twist a streak of lightning into a true lover's knot as to stop him.

Finding that I was bent on going, for I became impatient to get into Texas, my kind friends at Little Rock procured me a good horse to carry me across to Red River. There are no bounds to the good feeling of the pioneers of the west; they consider nothing a trouble that will confer a favour upon a stranger that they chance to take a fancy to: true, we are something like chestnut burs on the outside, rather prickly if touched roughly, but there's good fruit within.

My horse was brought to the door of the tavern, around which many of the villagers were assembled. The drum and fife were playing what was intended for a lively tune, but the skin of the drum still hung as loose as the hide of a fat man far gone in a consumption; and the fife had not yet recovered from the asthma. The music sounded something like a fellow singing, "Away with melancholy," on the way to the gallows. I took my leave of the landlord, shook hands with the showman, who had done more than an average business, kissed his wife, who had recovered, and bidding farewell to all my kind-hearted friends, I mounted my horse, and left the village, accompanied by four or five gentlemen. The drum and fife now appeared to exert themselves, and made more noise than usual, while the crowd sent forth three cheers to encourage me on my way.

I tried to raise some recruits for Texas among my companions, but they said they had their own affairs to attend to, which would keep them at home for the present, but no doubt they would come over and see us as soon as the disturbances should be settled. They looked upon Texas as being part of the United States, though the Mexicans did claim it; and they had no doubt the time was not very distant when it would be received into the glorious Union.

My companions did not intend seeing me farther on my way than the Washita river, near fifty miles. Conversation was pretty brisk, for we talked about the affairs of the nation and Texas; subjects that are by no means to be exhausted, if one may judge by the long speeches made in Congress, where they talk year in and year out; and it would seem that as much still remains to be said as ever. As we drew nigh to the Washita, the silence was broken alone by our own talk and the clattering of our horses' hoofs; and we imagined ourselves pretty much the only travellers, when we were suddenly somewhat startled by the sound of music. We checked our horses, and listened, and the music continued. "What can all that mean?" says I. "Blast my old shoes if I know, Colonel," says one of the party. We listened again, and we now heard, "Hail, Columbia, happy land!" played in first-rate style. "That's fine," says I. "Fine as silk, Colonel, and leetle finer," says the other; "but hark, the tune's changed." We took another spell of listening, and now the musician struck up, in a brisk and lively manner, "Over the water to Charley." "That's mighty mysterious," says one; "Can't cipher it out no-how," says another; "A notch beyant my measure," says a third. "Then let us go ahead," says I, and off we dashed at a pretty rapid gait, I tell you—by no means slow.

As we approached the river we saw to the right of the road a new clearing on a hill, where several men were at work, and they running down the hill like wild Indians, or rather like the office holders in pursuit of the deposites. There appeared to be no time to be lost, so they ran, and we cut ahead for the crossing. The music continued all this time stronger and stronger, and the very notes appeared to speak distinctly, "Over the water to Charley."

When we reached the crossing we were struck all of a heap, at beholding a man seated in a sulky in the middle of the river, and playing for life on a fiddle. The horse was up to his middle in the water; and it seemed as if the flimsy vehicle was ready to be swept away by the current. Still the fiddler fiddled on composedly, as if his life had been insured, and he was nothing more than a passenger. We thought he was mad, and shouted to him. He heard us, and stopped his music. "You have missed the crossing," shouted one of the men from the clearing. "I know I have," returned the fiddler. "If you go ten feet farther you will be drowned." "I know I shall," returned the fiddler. "Turn back," said the man. "I can't," said the other. "Then how the devil will you get out?" "I'm sure I don't know: come you and help me."

The men from the clearing, who understood the river, took our horses and rode up to the sulky, and after some difficulty, succeeded in bringing the traveller safe to shore, when we recognised the worthy parson who had fiddled for us at the puppet show at Little Rock. They told him that he had had a narrow escape, and he replied, that he had found that out an hour ago. He said he had been fiddling to the fishes for a full hour, and had exhausted all the tunes that he could play without notes. We then asked him what could have induced him to think of fiddling at a time of such peril; and he replied, that he had remarked in his progress through life, that there was nothing in univarsal natur so well calculated to draw people together as the sound of a fiddle; and he knew, that he might bawl until he was hoarse for assistance, and no one would stir a peg; but they would no sooner hear the scraping of his catgut, than they would quit all other business, and come to the spot in flocks. We laughed heartily at the knowledge the parson showed of human natur.—And he was right.

Having fixed up the old gentleman's sulky right and tight, and after rubbing down his poor jaded animal, the company insisted on having a dance before we separated. We all had our flasks of whisky; we took a drink all around, and though the parson said he had had about enough fiddling for one day, he struck up with great good humour; at it we went, and danced straight fours for an hour and better. We all enjoyed ourselves very much, but came to the conclusion, that dancing wasn't altogether the thing without a few petticoats to give it variety.

The dance being over, our new friends pointed out the right fording, and assisted the parson across the river. We took another drink all round, and after shaking each other cordially by the hand, we separated, wishing each other all the good fortune that the rugged lot that has been assigned us will afford. My friends retraced the road to Little Rock, and I pursued my journey; and as I thought of their disinterested kindness to an entire stranger, I felt that the world is not quite as heartless and selfish as some grumblers would have us think.

The Arkansas is a pretty fine territory, being about five hundred and fifty miles in length from east to west, with a mean width of near two hundred, extending over an area of about one hundred thousand square miles. The face of the country from its great extent is very much diversified. It is pretty well watered, being intersected by the Arkansas river and branches of the Red, Washita, and White rivers. The Maserne mountains, which rise in Missouri, traverse Arkansas and extend into Texas. That part of the territory to the south-east of the Masernes is for the most part low, and in many places liable to be overflooded annually. To the north-west of the mountains the country presents generally an open expanse of prairie without wood, except near the borders of the streams. The seasons of the year partake of those extremes of heat and cold, which might be expected in so great an extent, and in a country which affords so much difference of level. The summers are as remarkable as is the winters for extremes of temperature. The soil exhibits every variety, from the most productive to the most sterile. The forest trees are numerous and large; such as oak, hickory, sycamore, cotton-wood, locust, and pine. The cultivated fruit trees are the apple, pear, peach, plum, nectarine, cherry, and quince; and the various kinds of grain, such as wheat, rye, oats, barley, and Indian corn, succeed amazing well. Cotton, Indian corn, flour, peltry, salted provisions, and lumber, are the staples of this territory. Arkansas was among the most ancient settlements of the French in Louisiana. That nation had a hunting and trading post on the Arkansas river as early as the beginning of the eighteenth century. Arkansas, I rather reckon, will be admitted as a state into the Union during the next session of Congress; and if the citizens of Little Rock are a fair sample of her children, she cannot fail to go ahead.

I kept in company with the parson until we arrived at Greenville, and I do say, he was just about as pleasant an old gentleman to travel with, as any man who wasn't too darned particular could ask for. We talked about politics, religion, and natur, farming and bear hunting, and the many blessings that an all bountiful Providence[1] has bestowed upon our happy country. He continued to talk upon this subject, travelling over the whole ground as it were, until his imagination glowed, and his soul became full to overflowing; and he checked his horse, and I stopped mine also, and a stream of eloquence burst forth from his aged lips, such as I have seldom listened to: it came from the overflowing fountain of a pure and grateful heart. We were alone in the wilderness, but as he proceeded it seemed to me as if the tall trees bent their tops to listen; that the mountain stream laughed out joyfully as it bounded on like some living thing; that the fading flowers of autumn smiled, and sent forth fresher fragrance, as if conscious that they would revive in spring; and even the sterile rocks seemed to be endued with some mysterious influence. We were alone in the wilderness, but all things told me that God was there. That thought renewed my strength and courage. I had left my country, felt somewhat like an outcast, believed that I had been neglected and lost sight of: but I was now conscious that there was still one watchful Eye over me; no matter whether I dwelt in the populous cities, or threaded the pathless forest alone; no matter whether I stood in the high places among men, or made my solitary lair in the untrodden wild, that Eye was still upon me. My very soul leaped joyfully at the thought; I never felt so grateful in all my life; I never loved my God so sincerely in all my life. I felt that I still had a friend.

When the old man finished I found that my eyes were wet with tears. I approached and pressed his hand, and thanked him, and says I, "Now let us take a drink." I set him the example, and he followed it, and in a style too that satisfied me, that if he had ever belonged to the Temperance society,[2] he had either renounced membership or obtained a dispensation. Having liquored, we proceeded on our journey, keeping a sharp look-out for mill seats and plantations as we rode along.

I left the worthy old man at Greenville, and sorry enough I was to part with him, for he talked a great deal, and he seemed to know a little about every thing. He knew all about the history of the country; was well acquainted with all the leading men; knew where all the good lands lay in most of the western states, as well as the cutest clerk[3] in the Land office; and had traced most of the rivers to their sources. He was very cheerful and happy, though to all appearances very poor. I thought that he would make a first-rate agent for taking up lands, and mentioned it to him; he smiled, and pointing above, said, "My wealth lies not in this world."

I mounted my horse, and pushed forward on my road to Fulton. When I reached Washington, a village a few miles from the Red river, I rode up to the Black Bear tavern, when the following conversation[4] took place between me and the landlord, which is a pretty fair sample of the curiosity of some folks:—

"Good morning, mister—I don't exactly recollect your name now," said the landlord as I alighted.

"It's of no consequence," said I.

"I'm pretty sure I've seen ye somewhere."

"Very likely you may, I've been there frequently."

"I was sure 'twas so; but strange I should forget your name," says he.

"It is indeed somewhat strange that you should forget what you never knew," says I.

"It is unaccountable strange. It's what I'm not often in the habit of, I assure you. I have, for the most part, a remarkably detentive memory. In the power of people that pass along this way, I've scarce ever made, as the doctors say, a *slapsus slinkum*[5] of this kind afore."

"Eh heh!" I shouted, while the critter continued.

"Travelling to the western country, I presume, mister?"

"Presume any thing you please, sir," says I, "but don't trouble me with your presumptions."

"O Lord, no, sir—I won't do that—I've no ideer of that—not the least ideer in the world," says he; "I suppose you've been to the westward afore now?"

"Well, suppose I have?"

"Why, on that supposition, I was going to say you must be pretty well—that is to say, you must know something about the place."

"Eh heh!" I ejaculated, looking sort of mazed full in his face. The tarnel critter still went ahead.

"I take it you're a married man, mister?"

"Take it as you will, that is no affair of mine," says I.

"Well, after all, a married life is the most happiest way of living; don't you think so, mister?"

"Very possible," says I.

"I conclude you have a family of children, sir?"

"I don't know what reason you have to conclude so."

"O, no reason in the world, mister, not the least," says he; "but I thought I might just take the liberty to make the presumption, you know, that's all, sir. I take it, mister, you're a man about my age?"

"Eh heh!"

"How old do you call yourself, if I may be so bold?"

"You're bold enough, the devil knows," says I; and as I spoke rather sharp, the varment seemed rather staggered, but he soon recovered himself, and came up to the chalk again.

"No offence, I hope—I—I—I—wouldn't be thought uncivil by any means; I always calculate to treat everybody with civility."

"You have a very strange way of showing it."

"True, as you say, I ginnerally take my own way in these ere matters.—Do you practise law, mister, or farming, or mechanicals?"

"Perhaps so," says I.

"Ah, I judge so; I was pretty certain it must be the case. Well, it's as good business as any there is followed now-a-days."

"Eh heh!" I shouted, and my lower jaw fell in amazement at his perseverance.

"I take it you've money at interest, mister?" continued the varment, without allowing himself time to take breath.

"Would it be of any particular interest to you to find out?" says I.

"O, not at all, not the least in the world, sir. I'm not at all inquisitive about other people's matters; I mind's my own business—that's my way."

"And a very odd way you have of doing it too."

"I've been thinking what persuasion you're of—whether you're a Unitarian or Baptist, or whether you belong to the Methodisses."

"Well, what's the conclusion?"

"Why, I have concluded that I'm pretty near right in my conjectures. Well, after all, I'm inclined to think they're the nearest right of any persuasion—though some folks think differently."

"Eh heh!" I shouted again.

"As to pollyticks, I take it, you—that is to say. I suppose you——"

"Very likely."

"Ah! I could have sworn it was so from the moment I saw you. I have a nack at finding out a man's sentiments. I dare say, mister, you're a justice in your own country?"

"And if I may return the compliment, I should say you're a just ass everywhere." By this time I began to get weary of his impertinence, and led my horse to the trough to water, but the darned critter followed me up.

"Why, yes," said he, "I'm in the commission of the peace, to be sure—and an officer in the militia—though between you and I, I wouldn't wish to boast of it."

My horse having finished drinking, I put one foot in the stirrup, and was preparing to mount—"Any more inquiries to make?" said I.

"Why, no, nothing to speak on," said he. "When do you return, mister?"

"About the time I come back," said I; and leaping into the saddle galloped off. The pestiferous varment bawled after me, at the top of his voice,—

"Well, I shall look for ye then. I hope you won't fail to call."

Now, who in all natur do you reckon the crittur was, who afforded so fine a sample of the impertinent curiosity that some people have to pry into other people's affairs? I knew him well enough at first sight, though he seemed to have forgotten me. It was no other than Job Snelling, the manufacturer of cayenne pepper out of mahogany sawdust, and upon whom I played the trick with the coon skin. I pursued my journey to Fulton, and laughed heartily to think what a swither I had left poor Job in, at not gratifying his curiosity; for I knew he was one of those fellows who would peep down your throat just to ascertain what you had eaten for dinner.

When I arrived at Fulton, I inquired for a gentleman to whom my friends at Little Rock had given me a letter of introduction. I was received in the most hospitable manner; and as the steamboat did not start for Natchitoches until the next day, I spent the afternoon in seeing all that was to be seen. I left my horse with the gentleman, who promised to have him safely returned to the owner; and I took the steamboat, and started on my way down the Red river, right well pleased with my reception at Fulton.

CHAPTER VI.

There was a considerable number of passengers on board the boat, and our assortment was somewhat like the Yankee merchant's cargo of notions, pretty particularly miscellaneous, I tell you. I moved through the crowd from stem to stern, to see if I could discover any face that was not altogether strange to me; but after a general survey, I concluded that I had never seen one of them before. There were merchants and emigrants and gamblers, but none who seemed to have embarked in the particular business that for the time being occupied my mind—I could find none who were going to Texas. All seemed to have their hands full enough of their own affairs, without meddling with the cause of freedom. The greater share of glory will be mine, thought I, so go ahead, Crockett.

I saw a small cluster of passengers at one end of the boat, and hearing an occasional burst of laughter, thinks I, there's some sport started in that quarter, and having nothing better to do, I'll go in for my share of it. Accordingly I drew nigh to the cluster, and seated on a chest was a tall lank sea sarpent looking blackleg,[1] who had crawled over from Natchez under the hill, and was amusing the passengers with his skill at thimblerig;[2] at the same time he was picking up their shillings just about as expeditiously as a hungry gobbler would a pint of corn. He was doing what might be called an average business in a small way, and lost no time in gathering up the fragments.

I watched the whole process for some time, and found that he had adopted the example set by the old tempter himself, to get the weathergage of us poor weak mortals. He made it a point to let his victims win always the first stake, that they

might be tempted to go ahead; and then, when they least sus-
pected it, he would come down upon them like a hurricane in a
cornfield, sweeping all before it.

I stood looking on, seeing him pick up the chicken feed from
the green horns, and thought if men are such darned fools as to
be cheated out of their hard earnings by a fellow who had just
brains enough to pass a pea from one thimble to another, with
such slight of hand, that you could not tell under which he had
deposited it; it is not astonishing that the magician of Kinderhook should play thimblerig upon the big figure, and attempt
to cheat the whole nation. I thought that "the Government"
was playing the same game with the deposites, and with such
address too, that before long it will be a hard matter to find
them under any of the thimbles where it is supposed they have
been originally placed.

The thimble conjurer saw me looking on, and eyeing me as if
he thought I would be a good subject, said carelessly, "Come,
stranger, won't you take a chance?" the whole time passing the
pea from one thimble to the other, by way of throwing out a
bait for the gudgeons to bite at. "I never gamble, stranger,"
says I, "principled against it; think it a slippery way of getting
through the world at best." "Them are my sentiments to a
notch," says he; "but this is not gambling by no means. A little
innocent pastime, nothing more. Better take a hack by way of
trying your luck at guessing." All this time he continued working with his thimbles; first putting the pea under one, which
was plain to be seen, and then uncovering it, would show that
the pea was there; he would then put it under the second thimble, and do the same, and then under the third; all of which he
did to show how easy it would be to guess where the pea was
deposited, if one would only keep a sharp look-out.

"Come, stranger," says he to me again, "you had better take
a chance. Stake a trifle, I don't care how small, just for the fun
of the thing."

"I am principled against betting money," says I, "but I don't
mind going in for drinks for the present company, for I'm as
dry as one of little Isaac Hill's regular set speeches."

"I admire your principles," says he, "and to show that I play with these here thimbles just for the sake of pastime, I will take that bet, though I'm a whole hog[3] temperance man. Just say when, stranger."

He continued all the time slipping the pea from one thimble to another; my eye was as keen as a lizard's, and when he stopped, I cried out, "Now; the pea is under the middle thimble." He was going to raise it to show that it wasn't there, when I interfered, and said, "Stop, if you please," and raised it myself, and sure enough the pea was there; but it mought have been otherwise if he had had the uncovering of it.

"Sure enough you've won the bet," says he. "You've a sharp eye, but I don't care if I give you another chance. Let us go fifty cents this bout; I'm sure you'll win."

"Then you're a darned fool to bet, stranger," says I; "and since that is the case, it would be little better than picking your pocket to bet with you; so I'll let it alone."

"I don't mind running the risk," said he.

"But I do," says I; "and since I always let well enough alone, and I have had just about glory enough for one day, let us all go to the bar and liquor."

This called forth a loud laugh at the thimble conjurer's expense; and he tried hard to induce me to take just one chance more, but he mought just as well have sung psalms to a dead horse, for my mind was made up; and I told him, that I looked upon gambling as about the dirtiest way that a man could adopt to get through this dirty world; and that I would never bet any thing beyond a quart of whisky upon a rifle shot, which I considered a legal bet, and gentlemanly and rational amusement. "But all this cackling," says I, "makes me very thirsty, so let us adjourn to the bar and liquor."

He gathered up his thimbles, and the whole company followed us to the bar, laughing heartily at the conjurer; for, as he had won some of their money, they were sort of delighted to see him beaten with his own cudgel. He tried to laugh too, but his laugh wasn't at all pleasant, and rather forced. The barkeeper placed a big-bellied bottle before us; and after mixing our liquor, I was called on for a toast, by one of the company, a chap just about as rough hewn as if he had been cut out of a gum log with a broad axe, and sent into the market without even being smoothed off with a jack plane,—one of them chaps who, in their journey through life, are always ready for a fight or a frolic, and don't care the toss of a copper which.

"Well, gentlemen," says I, "being called upon for a toast, and being in a slave-holding state, in order to avoid giving offence, and running the risk of being Lynched,[4] it may be necessary to promise that I am neither an abolitionist nor a colonizationist, but simply Colonel Crockett, of Tennessee, now bound for Texas." When they heard my name they gave three cheers for Colonel Crockett; and silence being restored, I continued, "Now, gentlemen, I will offer you a toast, hoping, after what I have stated, that it will give offence to no one present; but should I be mistaken, I must imitate the 'old Roman,' and take the responsibility. I offer, gentlemen, The abolition of slavery: Let the work first begin in the two houses of Congress. There are no slaves in the country more servile than the party slaves in Congress. The wink or the nod of their masters is all sufficient for the accomplishment of the most dirty work."

They drank the toast in a style that satisfied me, that the Little Magician might as well go to a pigsty for wool, as to beat round in that part for voters; they were all either for Judge White[5] or Old Tippecanoe.[6] The thimble conjurer having asked the barkeeper how much was to pay, was told there were sixteen smallers, which amounted to one dollar. He was about to lay down the blunt,[7] but not in Benton's metallic currency, which I find has already become as shy as honesty with an office holder, but he planked down one of Biddle's notes, when I interfered, and told him that the barkeeper had made a mistake.

"How so?" demanded the barkeeper.

"How much do you charge," says I, "when you retail your liquor?"

"A fip a glass."

"Well, then," says I, "as Thimblerig here, who belongs to the temperance society, took it in wholesale, I reckon you can afford to let him have it at half price?"

Now, as they had all noticed that the conjurer went what is

called the heavy wet, they laughed outright, and we heard no more about temperance from that quarter. When we returned to the deck the blackleg set to work with his thimbles again, and bantered me to bet; but I told him that it was against my principle, and as I had already reaped glory enough for one day, I would just let well enough alone for the present. If the "old Roman" had done the same in relation to the deposites and "the monster," we should have escaped more difficulties than all the cunning of the Little Flying Dutchman, and Dick Johnson to boot, will be able to repair. I shouldn't be astonished if the new Vice President's head should get wool gathering, before they have half unravelled the knotted and twisted thread of perplexities that the old General has spun,—in which case his charming spouse will no doubt be delighted, for then they will be all in the family way. What a handsome display they will make in the White House. No doubt the first act of Congress will be to repeal the duties on Cologne and Lavender waters, for they will be in great demand about the Palace, particularly in the dog days.

One of the passengers, hearing that I was on board of the boat, came up to me, and began to talk about the affairs of the nation, and said a good deal in favour of "the Magician," and wished to hear what I had to say against him. He talked loud,[8] which is the way with all politicians educated in the Jackson school; and by his slang-whanging, drew a considerable crowd around us. Now, this was the very thing I wanted, as I knew I should not soon have another opportunity of making a political speech; he no sooner asked to hear what I had to say against his candidate, than I let him have it, strong and hot as he could take, I tell you.

"What have I to say against Martin Van Buren? He is an artful, cunning, intriguing, selfish, speculating lawyer, who, by holding lucrative offices for more than half his life, has contrived to amass a princely fortune, and is now seeking the presidency, principally for sordid GAIN, and to gratify the most selfish ambition. His fame is unknown to the history of our country, except as a most adroit political manager and successful office hunter. He never took up arms in defence of his country, in her days of darkness and peril. He never contributed a dollar of his surplus wealth to assist her in her hours of greatest want and weakness. OFFICE and MONEY have been the gods of his idolatry; and at their shrines has the ardent worship of his heart been devoted, from the earliest days of his manhood to the present moment. He can lay no claim to pre-eminent services as a statesman; nor has he ever given any evidences of superior talent, except as a political electioneerer and intriguer. As a politician he is 'all things to all men.' He is for internal improvement, and against it; for the tariff, and against it; for the bank monopoly, and against it; for abolition of slavery, and against it; and for any thing else, and against any thing else; just as he can best promote his popularity and subserve his own private interest. He is so totally destitute of moral courage, that he never dares to give an opinion upon any important question until he first finds out whether it will be popular, or not. He is celebrated as the 'Little Non Committal Magician,' because he enlists on no side of any question until he discovers which is the strongest party; and then always moves in so cautious, sly, and secret a manner, that he can change sides at any time, as easily as a juggler or a magician can play off his arts of legerdemain.

"Who is Martin Van Buren? He is the candidate of the office holders and office expectants, who nominated him for the presidency, at a convention assembled in the city of Baltimore, in May last. The first account we have of his political life is while he was a member of the Senate of New York, at the time when Mr. Clinton[9] was nominated as the federal candidate for the presidency, in opposition to Mr. Madison. The support he then gave Mr. Clinton afforded abundant evidence of that spirit of opposition to the institutions of his country, which was prominently developed in the conduct of those with whom he was united. Shortly after the success of Mr. Madison, and during the prosecution of the war, Rufus King, of New York, (for whom Mr. Van Buren voted,) was elected to the Senate of the United States, avowedly opposed to the administration. Upon his entrance into that body, instead of devoting his energies to maintain the war, he commenced a tirade of abuse against the administration for having attempted relief to the oppressed seamen of our gallant navy, who had been compelled by British violence to arm themselves against their country, their firesides, and their friends. Thus Martin Van Buren countenanced, by his vote in the Senate of New York, an opposition to that war, which, a second time, convinced Great Britain that Americans could not be awed into bondage and subjection.

"Subsequent to this time Mr. Van Buren became himself a member of the United States Senate, and, while there, *opposed* every proposition to improve the west or to add to her numerical strength.

"He voted *against* the continuance of the national road through Ohio, Indiana, Illinois, and *against* appropriations for its preservation.

"He voted *against* the graduation of the price of the public lands.

"He voted *against* ceding the refuse lands to the states in which they lie.

"He voted *against* making donations of the lands to actual settlers.

"He again voted *against* ceding the refuse lands, not worth twenty-five cents per acre, to the new states for purposes of education and internal improvement.

"He voted *against* the bill providing 'settlement and preemption rights' to those who had assisted in opening and improving the western country, and thus deprived many an honest poor man of a home.

"He voted *against* donations of land to Ohio, to prosecute the Miami Canal; and, although a member of the Senate, he was not present when the vote was taken upon the engrossment of the bill giving land to Indiana for her Wabash and Erie Canal, and was known to have opposed it in all its stages.

"He voted *in favour* of erecting toll gates on the national road; thus demanding a tribute from the west for the right to pass upon her own highways, constructed out of her own money—a thing never heard of before.

"After his term of service had expired in the Senate, he was elected Governor of New York, by a plurality of votes. He was afterward sent to England as minister plenipotentiary, and upon his return was elected Vice President of the United States, which office he now holds, and from which the office holders are seeking to transfer him to the presidency."

My speech was received which great applause, and the politician, finding that I was better acquainted with his candidate than he was himself, for I wrote his life,[10] shut his fly trap, and turned on his heel without saying a word. He found that he had barked up the wrong tree. I afterward learnt that he was a mail contractor in those parts, and that he also had large dealings in the Land office, and therefore thought it necessary to chime in with his penny whistle, in the universal chorus. There's a large band of the same description, but I'm thinking Uncle Sam will some day find out that he has paid too much for the piper.

CHAPTER VII.

After my speech, and setting my face against gambling, poor Thimblerig was obliged to break off conjuring for want of customers, and call it half a day. He came and entered into conversation with me, and I found him a good-natured intelligent fellow, with a keen eye for the main chance. He belonged to that numerous class, that it is perfectly safe to trust as far as a tailor can sling a bull by the tail—but no farther. He told me that he had been brought up a gentleman; that is to say, he was not instructed in any useful pursuit by which he could obtain a livelihood, so that when he found he had to depend upon himself for the necessaries of life, he began to suspect, that dame nature would have conferred a particular favour if she had consigned him to the care of any one else. She had made a very injudicious choice when she selected him to sustain the dignity of a gentleman.

The first bright idea that occurred to him as a speedy means of bettering his fortune, would be to marry an heiress. Accordingly he looked about himself pretty sharp, and after glancing from one fair object to another, finally his hawk's eye rested upon the young and pretty daughter of a wealthy planter. Thimblerig run his brazen face with his tailor for a new suit, for he abounded more in that metallic currency than he did in either Benton's mint drops or in Biddle's notes; and having the gentility of his outward Adam thus endorsed by his tailor—an important endorsement, by-the-way, as times go—he managed to obtain an introduction to the planter's daughter.

Our worthy had the principle of going ahead strongly developed. He was possessed of considerable address, and had brass enough in his face to make a wash-kettle; and having once got access to the planter's house, it was no easy matter to dislodge him. In this he resembled those politicians who commence life as office holders; they will hang on tooth and nail, and even when death shakes them off, you'll find a commission of some kind crumpled up in their clenched fingers. Little Van appears to belong to this class—there's no beating his snout from the public crib. He'll feed there while there's a grain of corn left, and even then, from long habit, he'll set to work and gnaw at the manger.

Thimblerig got the blind side of the planter, and every thing to outward appearances went on swimmingly. Our worthy boasted to his cronies that the business was settled, and that in a few weeks he should occupy the elevated station in society that nature had designed him to adorn. He swelled like the frog in the fable,[1] or rather like Johnson's wife,[2] of Kentucky, when the idea occurred to her of figuring away at Washington. But there's many a slip 'twixt the cup and the lip, says the proverb, and suddenly Thimblerig discontinued his visits at the planter's house. His friends inquired of him the meaning of this abrupt termination of his devotions.

"I have been treated with disrespect," replied the worthy, indignantly.

"Disrespect! in what way?"

"My visits, it seems, are not altogether agreeable."

"But how have you ascertained that?"

"I received a hint to that effect; and I can take a hint as soon as another."

"A hint!—and have you allowed a hint to drive you from the pursuit? For shame. Go back again."

"No, no, never! a hint is sufficient for a man of my gentlemanly feelings. I asked the old man for his daughter."

"Well, what followed? what did he say?"

"Didn't say a word."

"Silence gives consent all the world over."

"So I thought. I then told him to fix the day."

"Well, what then?"

"Why, then he kicked me down stairs, and ordered his slaves

to pump upon me.[3] That's hint enough for me, that my visits are not properly appreciated; and blast my old shoes if I condescend to renew the acquaintance, or notice them in any way until they send for me."

As Thimblerig's new coat became rather too seedy to play the part of a gentleman much longer in real life, he determined to sustain that character upon the stage, and accordingly joined a company of players. He began, according to custom, at the top of the ladder, and was regularly hissed and pelted through every gradation until he found himself at the lowest rowel. "This," said he, "was a dreadful check to proud ambition;" but he consoled himself with the idea of peace and quiet in his present obscure walk; and though he had no prospect of being elated by the applause of admiring multitudes, he no longer trod the scene of mimic glory in constant dread of becoming a target for rotten eggs and oranges.—"And there was much in that," said Thimblerig. But this calm could not continue for ever.

The manager, who, like all managers who pay salaries regularly, was as absolute behind the scenes as the "old Roman" is in the White House, had fixed upon getting up an eastern spectacle, called the Cataract of the Ganges. He intended to introduce a fine procession, in which an elephant was to be the principal feature. Here a difficulty occurred. What was to be done for an elephant? Alligators were plenty in those parts, but an elephant was not to be had for love or money. But an alligator would not answer the purpose, so he determined to make a pasteboard elephant as large as life, and twice as natural. The next difficulty was to find members of the company of suitable dimensions to perform the several members of the pasteboard star. The manager cast his eye upon the long gaunt figure of the unfortunate Thimblerig, and cast him for the hinder legs, the rump, and part of the back of the elephant. The poor player expostulated, and the manager replied, that he would appear as a star on the occasion, and would no doubt receive more applause than he had during his whole career. "But I shall not be seen," said the player. "All the better," replied the manager, "as in that case you will have nothing to apprehend from eggs and oranges."

Thimblerig, finding that mild expostulation availed nothing, swore that he would not study the part, and accordingly threw it up in dignified disgust. He said that it was an outrage upon the feelings of the proud representative of Shakspeare's heroes, to be compelled to play pantomime in the hinder parts of the noblest animal that ever trod the stage. If it had been the fore quarters of the elephant, it might possibly have been made a speaking part; at any rate he might have snorted through the trunk, if nothing more; but from the position he was to occupy, damned the word could he utter, or even roar with propriety. He therefore positively refused to act, as he considered it an insult to his reputation to tread the stage in such a character; and he looked upon the whole affair as a profanation of the legitimate drama. The result was, our worthy was discharged from the company, and compelled to commence hoeing another row.

He drifted to New Orleans, and hired himself as marker to a gambling table. Here he remained but a few months, for his ideas of arithmetic differed widely from those of his employer, and accordingly they had some difficulty in balancing the cash account; for when his employer, in adding up the receipts, made it nought and carry two, Thimblerig insisted that it should be nought and carry one; and in order to prove that he was correct, he carried himself off, and left nothing behind him.

He now commenced professional blackleg on his own hook, and took up his quarters in Natchez under the hill.[4] Here he remained, doing business in a small way, until Judge Lynch commenced his practice in that quarter, and made the place too hot for his comfort. He shifted his habitation, but not having sufficient capital to go the big figure, he practised the game of thimblerig until he acquired considerable skill, and then commenced passing up and down the river in the steamboats; and managed, by close attention to business, to pick up a decent livelihood in the small way, from such as had more pence in their pockets than sense in their noddles.

I found Thimblerig to be a pleasant talkative fellow. He communicated the foregoing facts with as much indifference as if there had been nothing disgraceful in his career; and at times he would chuckle with an air of triumph at the adroitness he had displayed in some of the knavish tricks he had practised. He looked upon this world as one vast stage, crowded with empiries and jugglers; and that he who could practise his deceptions with the greatest skill was entitled to the greatest applause.

I asked him to give me an account of Natchez and his adventures there, and I would put it in the book I intended to write, when he gave me the following, which betrays that his feelings were still somewhat irritated at being obliged to give them leg bail[5] when Judge Lynch made his appearance. I give it in his own words,

"Natchez is a land of fevers, alligators, niggers, and cotton bales: where the sun shines with force sufficient to melt the diamond, and the word ice is expunged from the dictionary, for its definition cannot be comprehended by the natives: where to refuse grog before breakfast would degrade you below the brute creation; and where a good dinner is looked upon as an angel's visit, and voted a miracle: where the evergreen and majestic magnolia tree, with its superb flower, unknown to the northern climes, and its fragrance unsurpassed, calls forth the admiration of every beholder; and the dark moss hangs in festoons from the forest trees like the drapery of a funeral pall: where bears, the size of young jackasses, are fondled in lieu of pet dogs; and knives, the length of a barber's pole, usurp the place of toothpicks: where the filth of the town is carried off by buzzards, and the inhabitants are carried off by fevers: where nigger women are knocked down by the auctioneer, and knocked up by the purchaser: where the poorest slave has plenty of yellow boys,[6] but not of Benton's mintage; and indeed the shades of colour are so varied and mixed, that a nigger is frequently seen black and blue at the same time. And such is Natchez.

"The town is divided into two parts, as distinct in character as they are in appearance. Natchez on the hill, situated upon a high bluff overlooking the Mississippi, is a pretty little town with streets regularly laid out, and ornamented with divers handsome public buildings. Natchez under the hill,—where, O! where, shall I find words suitable to describe the peculiarities of that unholy spot? 'Tis, in fact, the jumping off place. Satan looks on it with glee, and chuckles as he beholds the orgies of his votaries. The buildings are for the most part brothels, taverns, or gambling houses, and frequently the whole three may be found under the same roof. Obscene songs are sung at the top of the voice in all quarters. I have repeatedly seen the strumpets tear a man's clothes from his back, and leave his body beautified with all the colours of the rainbow.

"One of the most popular tricks is called the 'Spanish burial.' When a greenhorn makes his appearance among them, one who is in the plot announces the death of a resident, and that all strangers must subscribe to the custom of the place upon such an occasion. They forthwith arrange a procession; each person, as he passes the departed, kneels down and pretends to kiss the treacherous corpse. When the unsophisticated attempts this ceremony the dead man clinches him, and the mourners beat the fellow so entrapped until he consents to treat all hands; but should he be penniless, his life will be endangered by the severity of the castigation. And such is Natchez under the hill.

"An odd affair occurred while I was last there," continued Thimblerig. "A steamboat stopped at the landing, and one of the hands went ashore under the hill to purchase provisions, and the adroit citizens of that delectable retreat contrived to rob him of all his money. The captain of the boat, a determined fellow, went ashore in the hope of persuading them to refund,—but that cock wouldn't fight. Without farther ceremony, assisted by his crew and passengers, some three or four hundred in number, he made fast an immense cable to the frame tenement where the theft had been perpetrated, and allowed fifteen minutes for the money to be forthcoming; vowing, if it was not produced within that time, to put steam to his boat, and drag the house into the river. The money was instantly produced.

"I witnessed a sight during my stay there," continued the thimble conjurer, "that almost froze my blood with horror, and will serve as a specimen of the customs of the far south. A planter, of the name of Foster, connected with the best families of the state, unprovoked, in cold blood, murdered his young and beautiful wife, a few months after marriage. He beat her deliberately to death in a walk adjoining his dwelling, carried the body to the hut of one of his slaves, washed the dirt from her person, and, assisted by his negroes, buried her upon his plantation. Suspicion was awakened, the body disinterred, and the villain's guilt established. He fled, was overtaken, and secured in prison. His trial was, by some device of the law, delayed until the third term of the court. At length it came on, and so clear and indisputable was the evidence, that not a doubt was entertained of the result; when, by an oversight on the part of the sheriff, who neglected swearing into office his deputy who summoned the jurors, the trial was abruptly discontinued, and all proceedings against Foster were suspended, or rather ended.

"There exists, throughout the extreme south, bodies of men who style themselves Lynchers.[7] When an individual escapes punishment by some technicality of the law, or perpetrates an offence not recognised in courts of justice, they seize him, and inflict such chastisement as they conceive adequate to the offence. They usually act at night, and disguise their persons. This society at Natchez embraces all the lawyers, physicians, and principal merchants of the place. Foster, whom all good men loathed as a monster unfit to live, was called into court, and formally dismissed. But the Lynchers were at hand. The moment he stept from the court-house he was knocked down, his arms bound behind him, his eyes bandaged, and in this condition was marched to the rear of the town, where a deep ravine afforded a fit place for his punishment. His clothes were torn from his back, his head partially scalped, they next bound him to a tree; each Lyncher was supplied with a cowskin, and they took turns at the flogging until the flesh hung in ribands from his body. A quantity of heated tar was then poured over his head, and made to cover every part of his person; they finally showered a sack of feathers on him, and in this horrid guise, with no other apparel than a miserable pair of breeches, with a drummer at his heels, he was paraded through the principal streets at midday. No disguise was assumed by the Lynchers;

the very lawyers employed upon his trial took part in his punishment.

"Owing to long confinement his gait had become cramped, and his movements were very faltering. By the time the procession reached the most public part of the town, Foster fell down from exhaustion, and was allowed to lie there for a time, without exciting the sympathies of any one,—an object of universal detestation. The blood oozing from his stripes had become mixed with the feathers and tar, and rendered his aspect still more horrible and loathsome. Finding him unable to proceed further, a common dray was brought, and with his back to the horse's tail, the drummer standing over him playing the rogue's march, he was reconducted to prison, the only place at which he would be received.

"A guard was placed outside of the jail to give notice to the body of Lynchers when Foster might attempt to escape, for they had determined on branding him on the forehead and cutting his ears off. At two o'clock in the morning of the second subsequent day, two horsemen with a led horse stopped at the prison, and Foster was with difficulty placed astride. The Lynchers wished to secure him; he put spurs to his beast, and passed them. As he rode by they fired at him; a ball struck his hat, which was thrown to the ground, and he escaped; but if ever found within the limits of the state, will be shot down as if a price was set on his head.

"Sights of this kind," continued Thimblerig, "are by no means unfrequent. I once saw a gambler, a sort of friend of mine, by-the-way, detected cheating at faro, at a time when the bets were running pretty high. They flogged him almost to death, added the tar and feathers, and placed him aboard a dug-out, a sort of canoe, at twelve at night; and with no other instruments of navigation than a bottle of whisky and a paddle, set him adrift in the Mississippi. He has never been heard of since, and the presumption is, that he either died of his wounds or was run down in the night by a steamer. And this is what we call Lynching in Natchez."

Thimblerig had also been at Vicksburg in his time, and

entertained as little liking for that place as he did for Natchez. He had luckily made his escape a short time before the recent clearing-out of the slight-of-hand gentry; and he reckoned some time would elapse before he would pay them another visit. He said they must become more civilized first. All the time he was talking to me he was seated on a chest, and playing mechanically with his pea and thimbles, as if he was afraid that he would lose the slight unless he kept his hand in constant practice. Nothing of any consequence occurred in our passage down the river, and I arrived at Natchitoches in perfect health, and in good spirits.

CHAPTER VIII.

Natchitoches is a post town and seat of justice for the parish of Natchitoches, Louisiana, and is situated on the right bank of the Red river. The houses are chiefly contained in one street, running parallel to the river; and the population I should reckon at about eight hundred. The soil in this parish is generally sterile, and covered with pine timber, except near the margin of Red river, where the greatest part of the inhabitants are settled on the alluvial banks. Some other, though comparatively small, tracts of productive soil skirt the streams. An extensive body of low ground, subject to annual submersion, extends along the Red river, which, it is said, will produce forty bushels of frogs to the acre, and alligators enough to fence it.

I stayed two days at Natchitoches, during which time I procured a horse to carry me across Texas to the seat of war. Thimblerig remained with me, and I found his conversation very amusing; for he is possessed of humour and observation, and has seen something of the world. Between whiles he would amuse himself with his thimbles, to which he appeared greatly attached, and occasionally he would pick up a few shillings from the tavern loungers. He no longer asked me to play with him, for he felt somewhat ashamed to do so, and he knew it would be no go.

I took him to task in a friendly manner and tried to shame him out of his evil practices. I told him that it was a burlesque on human natur, that an able bodied man, possessed of his full share of good sense, should voluntarily debase himself, and be indebted for subsistence to such pitiful artifice.

"But what's to be done, Colonel?" says he. "I'm in the

slough of despond, up to the very chin. A miry and slippery path to travel."

"Then hold your head up," says I, "before the slough reaches your lips."

"But what's the use?" says he; "it's utterly impossible for me to wade through; and even if I could, I should be in such a dirty plight, that it would defy all the waters in the Mississippi to wash me clean again. "No," he added, in a desponding tone, "I should be like a live eel in a frying pan, Colonel, sort of out of my element, if I attempted to live like an honest man at this time o' day."

"That I deny. It is never too late to become honest," said I. "But even admit what you say to be true—that you cannot live like an honest man, you have at least the next best thing in your power, and no one can say nay to it."

"And what is that?"

"Die like a brave one. And I know not whether, in the eyes of the world, a brilliant death is not preferred to an obscure life of rectitude. Most men are remembered as they died, and not as they lived. We gaze with admiration upon the glories of the setting sun, yet scarcely bestow a passing glance upon its noonday splendour."

"You are right; but how is this to be done?"

"Accompany me to Texas. Cut aloof from your degrading habits and associates here, and in fighting for their freedom, regain your own."

He started from the table, and hastily gathering up the thimbles with which he had been playing all the time I was talking to him, he thrust them into his pocket, and after striding two or three times across the room, suddenly stopped, his leaden eye kindled, and grasping me by the hand violently, he exclaimed with an oath, "By —— I'll be a man again. Live honestly, or die bravely. I go with you to Texas."

I said what I could to confirm him in his resolution, and finding that the idea had taken fast hold of his mind, I asked him to liquor, which he did not decline, notwithstanding the temperance habits that he boasted of; we then took a walk on the banks of the river.

The evening preceding my departure from Natchitoches, a gentleman, with a good horse and a light wagon, drove up to the tavern where I lodged. He was accompanied by a lady who carried an infant in her arms. As they alighted I recognised the gentleman to be the politician at whom I had discharged my last political speech, on board the boat coming down the Red river. We had let him out in our passage down, as he said he had some business to transact some distance above Natchitoches. He entered the tavern, and seemed to be rather shy of me, so I let him go, as I had no idea of firing two shots at such small game.

The gentleman had a private room, and called for supper; but the lady, who used every precaution to keep the child concealed from the view of any one, refused to eat supper, saying she was unwell. However, the gentleman made a hearty meal, and excused the woman, saying "My wife is subject to a pain in the stomach, which has deprived her of her food." Soon after supper the gentleman desired a bed to be prepared, which being done, they immediately retired to rest.

About an hour before daybreak, next morning, the repose of the whole inn was disturbed by the screams of the child. This continued for some time, and at length the landlady got up to see what it was ailed the noisy bantling. She entered the chamber without a light, and discovered the gentleman seated in the bed alone, rocking the infant in his arms, and endeavouring to quiet it by saying, "Hush, my dear—mamma will soon return again." However the child still squalled on, and the long absence of the mother rendered it necessary that something should be done to quiet it.

The landlady proposed taking up the child, to see what was the reason of its incessant cries. She approached the bed, and requested the man to give her the infant, and tell her whether it was a son or a daughter; but this question redoubled his consternation, for he was entirely ignorant which sex the child belonged to; however, with some difficulty, he made the discovery, and informed the landlady it was a son.

She immediately called for a light, which was no sooner brought than the landlady began to unfold the wrapper from the child, and exclaim, "O, what a fine big son you have got!" But on a more minute examination they found, to their great astonishment, and to the mortification and vexation of the supposed father, that the child was a mulatto.

The wretched man, having no excuse to offer, immediately divulged the whole matter without reserve. He stated, that he had fell in with her on the road to Natchitoches the day before, and had offered her a seat in his vehicle. Soon perceiving that she possessed an uncommon degree of assurance, induced him to propose that they should pass as man and wife, to which she readily assented. No doubt she had left her own home in order to rid herself of the stigma which she had brought on herself by her lewd conduct; and at midnight she had eloped from the bed, leaving the infant to the paternal care of her pretended husband.

Immediate search was made for the mother of the child, but in vain. And, as the song says, "Single misfortunes ne'er come alone," to his great consternation and grief, she had taken his horse, and left the poor politician destitute of every thing except a fine *yellow boy*, but of a widely different description from those which Benton put in circulation.[1]

By this time all the lodgers in the tavern had got up and dressed themselves, from curiosity to know the occasion of the disturbance. I descended to the street in front of the inn. The stars were faintly glimmering in the heavens, and the first beams of the morning sun were struggling through the dim clouds that skirted the eastern horizon. I thought myself alone in the street, when the hush of morning was suddenly broken by a clear, joyful, and musical voice, which sang, as near as I could catch it, the following scrap of a song:

> "O, *what is the time of the merry round year*
> *That is fittest and sweetest for love!*
> *Ere sucks the bee, ere buds the tree;*
> *And primroses by two, by three,*
> *Faintly shine in the path of the lonely deer,*
> *Like the few stars of twilight above.*"

I turned towards the spot whence the sounds proceeded, and discovered a tall figure[2] leaning against the sign post. His eyes were fixed on the streaks of light in the east; his mind was absorbed, and he was clearly unconscious of any one being near him. He continued his song in so full and clear a tone, that the street re-echoed—

> *"When the blackbird and thrush, at early dawn,*
> *Prelude from leafy spray—*
> *Amid dewy scents and blandishments,*
> *Like a choir attuning their instruments,*
> *Ere the curtain of nature aside be drawn*
> *For the concert the livelong day."*

I now drew nigh enough to see him distinctly. He was a young man, not more than twenty-two. His figure was light and graceful, at the same time that it indicated strength and activity. He was dressed in a hunting shirt, which was made with uncommon neatness, and ornamented tastily with fringe. He held a highly finished rifle in his right hand, and a hunting pouch, covered with Indian ornaments, was slung across his shoulders. His clean shirt collar was open, secured only by a black riband around his neck. His boots were polished, without a soil upon them; and on his head was a neat fur cap, tossed on in a manner which said, "I don't care a d——n," just as plainly as any cap could speak it. I thought it must be some popinjay of a lark, until I took a look at his countenance. It was handsome, bright, and manly. There was no mistake in that face. From the eyes down to his breast he was sunburnt as dark as mahogany, while the upper part of his high forehead was as white and polished as marble. Thick clusters of black hair curled from under his cap. I passed on, unperceived, and he continued his song:—

> *"In the green spring-tide, all tender and bright,*
> *When the sun sheds a kindlier gleam*
> *O'er velvet bank, that sweet flowers prank,*

That have fresh dews and sunbeams drank—
Softest, and most chaste, as enchanted light
In the visions of maiden's dream."

The poor politician, whose misfortunes had roused up the inmates of the tavern at such an unusual hour, now returned from the stable, where he had been in search of his horse and his woman; but they were both among the missing. He held a whip in his hand, and about a dozen men followed him, some from curiosity to see the result of the adventure, and others from better feelings. As he drew nigh to the front of the tavern, chafing with mortification at both his shame and his loss, his rage increasing to a flame as his windy exclamations became louder and louder, he chanced to espy the fantastic personage I have just described, still leaning against the sign post, carelessly humming his song, but in a lower tone, as he perceived he was not alone.

The irritated politician no sooner saw the stranger against the sign post, whose self satisfied air was in striking contrast with the excited feelings of the other, than he paused for a moment, appeared to recognise him; then coming up in a blustering manner, and assuming a threatening attitude, he exclaimed fiercely—

"You're an infernal scoundrel—do you hear? an infernal scoundrel, sir!"

"I do, but it's news to me," replied the other, quietly.

"News, you scoundrel! do you call it news?"

"Entirely so."

"You needn't think to carry it off so quietly. I say, you're an infernal scoundrel, and I'll prove it."

"I beg you will not; I shouldn't like to be proved a scoundrel," replied the other, smiling with most provoking indifference.

"No, I dare say you wouldn't. But answer me directly—did you, or did you not say, in presence of certain ladies of my acquaintance, that I was a mere——"

"Calf?—O, no, sir; the truth is not to be spoken at all times."

"The truth! Do you presume to call me a calf, sir?"

"O, no, sir; I call you——nothing," replied the stranger, just as cool and as pleasant as a morning in spring.

"It's well you do; for if you had presumed to call me——"

"A man, I should have been grossly mistaken."

"Do you mean to say, I am not a man, sir?"

"That depends on circumstances."

"What circumstances?" demanded the other, fiercely.

"If I should be called as an evidence in a court of justice, I should be bound to speak the truth."

"And you would say, I was not a man, hey?—Do you see this cowskin?"

"Yes; and I have seen it with surprise ever since you came up," replied the stranger, calmly, at the same time handing me his rifle, to take care of.

"With surprise!" exclaimed the politician who saw that his antagonist had voluntarily disarmed himself;—"Why, did you suppose I was such a coward, that I dare not use the article when I thought it was demanded?"

"Shall I tell you what I thought?"

"Do—if you dare."

"I thought to myself, what use has a calf for a cowskin?" He turned to me, and said, "I had forgot, Colonel—shall I trouble you to take care of this also?" Saying which he drew a long hunting knife from his belt, and placed it in my hand. He then resumed his careless attitude against the sign post.

"You distinctly call me a calf, then?"

"If you insist upon it, you may."

"You hear, gentlemen," said he, speaking to the bystanders— "Do you hear the insult?—What shall I do with the scoundrel?"

"Dress him, dress him!" exclaimed twenty voices, with shouts and laughter.

"That I'll do at once." Then turning to the stranger, he cried out fiercely, "Come one step this way, you rascal, and I'll flog you within an inch of your life."

"I've no occasion."

"You're a coward."

"Not on your word."

"I'll prove it by flogging you out of your skin."

"I doubt it."

"I am a liar then—am I?"

"Just as you please."

"Do you hear that, gentlemen?"

"Ay, we hear," was the unanimous response. "You can't avoid dressing him now."

"O, heavens! grant me patience! I shall fly out of my skin."

"It will be so much the better for your pocket; calf skins are in good demand."

"I shall burst."

"Not here in the street, I beg of you. It would be disgusting."

"Gentlemen, can I any longer avoid flogging him?"

"Not if you are able," was the reply. "Go at him."

Thus provoked, thus stirred up, and enraged, the fierce politician went like lightning at his provoking antagonist. But before he could strike a blow he found himself disarmed of his cowskin, and lying on his back under the spout of a neighbouring pump, whither the young man had carried him to cool his rage; and before he could recover from his astonishment at such unexpected handling, he was as wet as a thrice drowned rat, from the cataracts of water which his laughing antagonist had liberally pumped upon him. His courage, by this time, had fairly oozed out; and he declared, as he arose and went dripping away from the pump, that he would never again trust to quiet appearances; and that the devil himself might, the next time, undertake to cowskin such a cucumber blooded[3] scoundrel for him. The bystanders laughed heartily. The politician now went in pursuit of his horse and his woman, taking his yellow boy with him; and the landlady declared that he richly deserved what he had got, even if he had been guilty of no other offence than the dirty imposition he had practised on her.

The stranger now came to me, and calling me by name, asked for his rifle and knife, which I returned to him. I expressed some astonishment at being known to him, and he said that he had heard of my being in the village, and had sought me out for the purpose of accompanying me to Texas. He told me that he was a bee hunter; that he had travelled pretty much over that country in the way of his business, and that I would find him of considerable use in navigating through the ocean of prairies.

He told me that honey trees are abundant in Texas,[4] and that honey of an excellent quality, and in any quantity, may be obtained from them. There are persons who have a peculiar tact in coursing the bee, and thus discovering their deposites of the luscious food. This employment is not a mere pastime, but is profitable. The wax alone, thus obtained, is a valuable article of commerce in Mexico, and commands a high price. It is much used in churches, where some of the candles made use of are as long as a man's arm. It often happens that the hunters throw away the honey, and save only the wax.

"It is a curious fact," said the bee hunter, "in the natural history of the bee, that it is never found in a wild country, but always precedes civilization, forming a kind of advance guard between the white man and the savage. The Indians, at least, are perfectly convinced of this fact, for it is a common remark among them, when they observe these insects—'there come the white men.'"

Thimblerig came up, and the bee hunter spoke to him, calling him by name, for he had met with him in New Orleans. I told him that the conjurer had determined to accompany me also, at which he seemed well pleased, and encouraged the poor fellow to adhere to that resolution; for he would be a man among men in Texas, and no one would be very particular in inquiring about his fortunes in the states. If once there, he might boldly stand up and feed out of the same rack with the best.

I asked him what was his cause of quarrel with the politician, and he told me that he had met him a few weeks before down at Baton Rouge, where the fellow was going the big figure; and that he had exposed him to some ladies, which completely cut his comb, and he took wing; that this was the first time they had met since, and being determined to have his revenge, he had attacked him without first calculating consequences.

With the assistance of our new friend, who was a generous, pleasant fellow, we procured a horse and rifle for Thimblerig; and we started for Nacogdoches, which is about one hundred and twenty miles west of Natchitoches, under the guidance of the bee hunter.

CHAPTER IX.

Our route, which lay along what is called the old Spanish road, I found to be much better defined on the map, than upon the face of the country. We had, in many instances, no other guide to the path than the blazes on the trees. The bee hunter was a cheerful communicative companion, and by his pleasant conversation rendered our journey any thing but fatiguing. He knew all about the country; had undergone a variety of adventure, and described what he had witnessed with such freshness, and so graphically, that if I could only remember one-half he told me about the droves of wild horses, buffalo, various birds, beautiful scenery of the wide spreading and fertile prairies, and his adventures with the roving tribes of Indians, I should fill my book, I am sure, much more agreeably than I shall be able to do on my own hook. When he'd get tired of talking, he'd commence singing, and his list of songs seemed to be as long as a rainy Sunday. He had a fine clear voice, and though I have heard the Woods sing[1] at the Park Theatre, in New York, I must give the Bee hunter the preference over all I have ever heard, except my friend Jim Crow,[2] who, it must be allowed, is a real steamboat at the business, and goes a leetle ahead of any thing that will come after him.

He gave me, among other matters, the following account of a rencounter between one of the early settlers and the Indians:—

"Andrew Tumlinson,"[3] said he, "belonged to a family which the colonists of De Witt will long remember as one of their chief stays in the dangers of settling those wilds, trod only by the children of the forest. This indefatigable champion of revenge for his father's death, who had fallen some years before by Indian treachery, had vowed never to rest until he had received satisfaction. In order the better to accomplish his end, he was one of the foremost, if possible, in every skirmish with the Indians; and that he might be enabled to do so without restraint, he placed his wife under the care of his brother-in-law, shouldered his rifle, and headed a ranging party, who were resolved to secure peace to those who followed them, though purchased by their own death.

"He had been frequently victorious, in the most desperate fights, where the odds were greatly against him, and at last fell a victim to his own imprudence. A Caddo[4] had been seized as a spy, and threatened with death, in order to compel him to deliver up his knife. The fellow never moved a muscle, or even winked, as he beheld the rifles pointed at him. He had been found lurking in the yard attached to the house of a solitary and unprotected family, and he knew that the whites were exasperated at his tribe for injuries that they had committed. When discovered he was accompanied by his little son.

"Tumlinson spoke to him in Spanish, to learn what had brought him there at such a time, but instead of giving any satisfaction, he sprung to his feet, from the log where he was seated, at the same time seizing his rifle which was lying beside him. The owner of the house, with whom the Indian had been on a friendly footing, expostulated with him, and got him to surrender the gun, telling him that the whites only wished to be satisfied of his friendly intentions, and had no desire to injure one who might be useful in conciliating his red brethren.

"He appeared to acquiesce, and wrapping his blanket more closely around his body, moved on in silence ahead of the whites. Tumlinson approached him, and though the rest of the party privately cautioned him not to go too nigh, as they believed the Indian had a knife under his blanket, he disregarded the warning, trusting for safety to his rifle and dexterity.

"He continued to interrogate the captive until he awakened his suspicions that his life was not safe. The Indian returned no answer but a short caustic laugh at the end of every question. Tumlinson at length beheld his countenance become more savage, which was followed by a sudden movement of the right hand beneath his blanket. He fired, and the next instant the Caddo's knife was in his heart, for the savage sprung with the quickness of the wild cat upon his prey. The rifle ball had passed through the Indian's body, yet his victim appeared to be no more in his grasp than a sparrow in the talons of an eagle, for he was a man of gigantic frame, and he knew that not only his own life, but that of his little son, would be taken on the spot. He called to the boy to fly, while he continued to plunge his knife into the bosom of his prostrate victim. The rest of the party levelled their rifles, and the victor shouted, with an air of triumph,—'Do your worst. I have sacrificed another pale face to the spirits of my fathers.' They fired, and he fell dead across the body of the unfortunate Tumlinson. The poor boy fell also. He had sprung forward some distance, when his father was shot, and was running in a zig-zag manner, taught them in their youth, to avoid the balls of their enemies, by rendering it difficult for the best marksman to draw a sight upon them."

In order to afford me some idea of the state of society in the more thickly settled parts of Texas, the Bee hunter told me that he had set down to the breakfast table, one morning at an inn, at San Felipe, and among the small party around the board were eleven who had fled from the states charged with having committed murder. So accustomed are the inhabitants to the appearance of fugitives from justice that they are particularly careful to make inquiries of the characters of new-comers, and generally obtain early and circumstantial information concerning strangers. "Indeed," said he, "it is very common to hear the inquiry made, 'What did he do that made him leave home?'[5] or, 'What have you come to Texas for?' intimating almost an assurance of one's being a criminal. Notwithstanding this state of things, however, the good of the public, and of each individual, is so evidently dependent on the public morals, that all appear ready to discountenance and punish crime. Even men who have been expatriated by fear of justice, are here among the last who would be disposed to shield a culprit guilty of a crime against life or property." Thimblerig was delighted at this favourable account of the state of society, and said that it would be the very place for him to flourish in; he liked their liberal way of thinking, for it did not at all tally with his ideas of natural law, that a man who happened to give offence to the straight laced rules of action established by a set of people contracted in their notions, should be hunted out of all society, even though willing to conform to their regulations. He was lawyer enough, he said, to know that every offence should be tried on the spot where it was committed; and if he had stolen the pennies from his grandmother's eyes in Louisiana, the people in Texas would have nothing to do with that affair, nohow they could fix it. The dejected conjurer pricked up his ears, and from that moment was as gay and cheerful as a blue bird in spring.

As we approached Nacogdoches, the first object that struck our view was a flag flying at the top of a high liberty pole. Drums were beating, and fifes playing, giving an indication, not to be misunderstood, of the spirit that had been awakened in a comparative desert. The people of the town no sooner saw us than many came out to meet us. The Bee hunter, who was known to them, introduced me; and it seems that they had already received the news of my intended visit, and its object, and I met with a cordial and friendly reception.

Nacogdoches is the capital of the department of that name, and is situated about sixty miles west of the river Sabine, in a romantic dell, surrounded by woody bluffs of considerable eminence, within whose inner borders, in a semicircle embracing the town, flow the two forks of the Nana, a branch of the Naches. It is a flourishing town, containing about one thousand actual citizens, although it generally presents twice that number on account of its extensive inland trade, one-half of which is supported by the friendly Indians. The healthiness of this town yields to none in the province, except Bexar, and to none whatsoever south of the same latitude, between the Sabine and the Mississippi. There was a fort established here, by the French, as far back as the year 1717, in order to overawe the wandering tribes of red men, between their borders and the colonists of Great Britain. The soil around it is of an easy nature and well adapted to cultivation.

I passed the day at Nacogdoches in getting information from the principal patriots as to the grievances imposed upon them

by the Mexican government; and I passed the time very pleasantly, but I rather reckon not quite as much so as my friend the
Bee hunter. In the evening, as I had missed him for several
hours while I was attending to the affairs of the patriots, I inquired for my companion, and was directed, by the landlord,
to an apartment appropriated to his family, and accordingly I
pushed ahead. Before I reached the door, I heard the joyous and
musical voice of the young rover singing as usual.

> "I'd like to have a little farm,
> And leave such scenes as these,
> Where I could live, without a care,
> Completely at my ease.
> I'd like to have a pleasant house
> Upon my little farm,
> Airy and cool in summer time
> In winter close and warm."

"And is there nothing else you'd like to have to make you
happy, Edward?" demanded a gentle voice, which sounded
even more musical in my ear than that of the Bee hunter.

"Yes, in good faith there is, my gentle Kate; and I'll tell you
what it is," he exclaimed, and resumed his song:—

> "I'd like to have a little wife—
> I reckon I know who;
> I'd like to have a little son—
> A little daughter too;
> And when they'd climb upon my knee,
> I'd like a little toy
> To give my pretty little girl,
> Another for my boy."

"O, fie, for shame of you to talk so, Edward!" exclaimed the
same gentle voice.

"Well, my pretty Kate, if you'll only listen, now, I'll tell you
what I wouldn't like."

"Let me hear that, by all means."

> *"I should not like my wife to shake*
> *A broomstick at my head—*
> *For then I might begin to think*
> *She did not love her Ned;*
> *But I should always like to see*
> *Her gentle as a dove;*
> *I should not like to have her scold—*
> *But be all joy and love."*

"And there is not much danger, Edward, of her ever being otherwise."

"Bless your sweet lips, that I am certain of," exclaimed the Bee hunter, and I heard something that sounded marvellously like a kiss. But he resumed his song:—

> *"If I had these I would not ask*
> *For any thing beside;*
> *I'd be content thus smoothly through*
> *The tedious world to glide.*
> *My little wife and I would then*
> *No earthly troubles see—*
> *Surrounded by our little ones,*
> *How happy we would be."*

I have always endeavoured to act up to the golden rule of doing as I would be done by, and as I never liked to be interrupted on such occasions, I returned to the bar-room, where I found Thimblerig seated on a table practising with his thimbles, his large white Vicksburg hat[6] stuck in a most independent and impudent manner on the side of his head. About half a dozen men were looking on with amazement at his skill, but he got no bets. When he caught my eye his countenance became sort of confused, and he hastily thrust the thimbles into his pocket, saying, as he jumped from the table, "Just amusing myself a little, Colonel, to kill time, and show the natives that some things can be done as well as others—Let us take an ideer." So we walked up the to bar, took a nip, and let the matter drop.

My horse had become lame, and I found I would not be able

to proceed with him, so I concluded to sell him and get another. A gentleman offered to give me a mustang in exchange, and I gladly accepted of his kindness. The mustangs are the wild horses, that are to be seen in droves of thousands pasturing on the prairies. They are taken by means of a lazo,[7] a long rope with a noose, which is thrown around their neck, and they are dragged to the ground with violence, and then secured. These horses, which are considerably smaller than those in the states, are very cheap, and are in such numbers, that in times of scarcity of game the settlers and the Indians have made use of them as food. Thousands have been destroyed for this purpose.

I saw nothing of the Bee hunter until bed-time, and then I said nothing to him about what I had overheard. The next morning, as we were preparing for an early start, I went into the private apartment where my companion was, but he did not appear quite as cheerful as usual. Shortly afterward a young woman, about eighteen, entered the room. She was as healthy and blooming as the wild flowers of the prairie. My companion introduced me, she courtesied modestly, and turning to the Bee hunter, said, "Edward, I have made you a new deer skin sack since you were last here. Will you take it with you? Your old one is so soiled."

"No, no, dear Kate, I shall not have leisure to gather wax this time."

"I have not yet shown you the fine large gourd that I have slung for you. It will hold near a gallon of water." She went to a closet, and producing it, suspended it around his shoulders.

"My own kind Kate!" he exclaimed, and looked as if he would devour her with his eyes.

"Have I forgotten any thing?—Ah! yes, your books." She ran to the closet, and brought out two small volumes.

"One is sufficient this time, Kate—my Bible. I will leave the poet with you." She placed it in his hunting bag, saying,

"You will find here some biscuit and deer sinews, in case you should get bewildered in the prairies. You know you lost your way the last time, and were nearly famished."

"Kind and considerate Kate."

I began to find out that I was a sort of fifth wheel to a wagon, so I went to the front of the tavern to see about starting. There was a considerable crowd there, and I made them a short address on the occasion. I told them, among other things, that "I will die with my Betsey in my arms. No, I will not die—I'll grin down[8] the walls of the Alamo, and the Americans will lick up the Mexicans like fine salt."

I mounted my little mustang, and my legs nearly reached the ground. The thimble conjurer was also ready; at length the Bee hunter made his appearance, followed by his sweetheart, whose eyes looked as though she had been weeping. He took a cordial leave of all his friends, for he appeared to be a general favourite; he then approached Kate, kissed her, and leaped upon his horse. He tried to conceal his emotion by singing, carelessly,

> *"Saddled and bridled, and booted rode he,*
> *A plume in his helmet, a sword at his knee."*

The tremulous and plaintive voice of Kate took up the next two lines of the song, which sounded like a prophecy:

> *"But toom cam' the saddle, all bluidy to see,*
> *And hame cam' the steed, but hame never cam' he."*

We started off rapidly, and left Nacogdoches amid the cheering of true patriots and kind friends.

CHAPTER X.

An hour or two elapsed before the Bee hunter recovered his usual spirits, after parting from his kind little Kate of Nacogdoches. The conjurer rallied him good humouredly, and had become quite a different man from what he was on the west side of the Sabine. He sat erect in his saddle, stuck his large white Vicksburger conceitedly on his bushy head, carried his rifle with as much ease and grace as if he had been used to the weapon, and altogether he assumed an air of impudence and independence which showed that he had now a soul above thimbles. The Bee hunter at length recovered his spirits, and commenced talking very pleasantly, for the matters he related were for the most part new to me.

My companions, by way of beguiling the tediousness of our journey, repeatedly played tricks upon each other, which were taken in good part. One of them I will relate. We had observed that the Bee hunter always disappeared on stopping at a house, running in to talk with the inhabitants and ingratiate himself with the women, leaving us to take care of the horses. On reaching our stopping place at night he left us as usual, and while we were rubbing down our mustangs, and hobbling them, a negro boy came out of the house with orders from our companion within to see to his horse. Thimblerig, who possessed a good share of roguish ingenuity, after some inquiries about the gentleman in the house, how he looked and what he was doing, told the boy, in rather a low voice, that he had better not come nearer to him than was necessary, for it was possible he might hurt him, though still he didn't think he would. The boy asked why he need be afraid of him. He replied, he did

not certainly know that there was any reason—he hoped there
was none—but the man had been bitten by a mad dog, and it
was rather uncertain whether he was not growing mad himself.
Still, he would not alarm the boy, but cautioned him not to be
afraid, for there might be no danger, though there was something rather strange in the conduct of his poor friend. This was
enough for the boy; he was almost afraid to touch the horse of
such a man; and when, a moment afterward, our companion
came out of the house, he slunk away behind the horse, and
though he was in a great hurry to get him unsaddled, kept his
eyes fixed steadily on the owner, closely watching his motions.

"Take off that bridle," exclaimed the impatient Bee hunter,
in a stern voice: and the black boy sprung off, and darted away
as fast as his feet could carry him, much to the vexation and
surprise of our companion, who ran after him a little distance,
but could in no way account for his singular and provoking
conduct. When we entered the house things appeared a great
deal more strange; for the negro had rushed hastily into the
midst of the family, and in his terrified state communicated the
alarming tale, that the gentleman had been bitten by a mad
dog. He, unconscious all the time of the trick that was playing
off, endeavoured, as usual, to render himself as agreeable as
possible, especially to the females with whom he had already
formed a partial acquaintance. We could see that they looked
on him with apprehension, and retreated whenever he approached them. One of them took an opportunity to inquire of
Thimblerig the truth of the charge; and his answer confirmed
their fears, and redoubled their caution; though, after confess-
ing with apparent candour, that his friend had been bitten, he
stated that there was no certainty of evil consequences, and it
was a thing which of course could not be mentioned to the
sufferer.

As bed time approached the mistress of the house expressed
her fears, lest trouble should arise in the night; for the house,
according to custom, contained but two rooms, and was not
built for security. She therefore urged us to sleep between him
and the door, and by no means to let him pass us. It so happened, however, that he chose to sleep next the door, and it was

with great difficulty that we could keep their fears within bounds. The ill-disguised alarm of the whole family was not less a source of merriment to him who had been the cause, than of surprise and wonder to the subject of it. Whatever member of the household he approached promptly withdrew, and as for the negro, whenever he was spoken to by him, he would jump and roll his eyes. In the morning, when we were about to depart, we commissioned our belied companion to pay our bill; but as he approached the hostess she fled from him, and shut the door in his face. "I want to pay our bill," said he. "O! if you will only leave the house," cried she, in terror, "you are welcome to your lodging."

The jest, however, did not end here. The Bee hunter found out the trick that had been played upon him, and determined to retaliate. As we were about mounting, the conjurer's big white Vicksburger was unaccountably missing, and nowhere to be found. He was not altogether pleased with the liberty that had been taken with him, and after searching some time in vain, he tied a handkerchief around his head, sprung upon his horse, and rode off with more gravity than usual. We had rode about two miles, the Bee hunter bantering the other with a story of his hat lying in pawn at the house we had left, and urged upon him to return and redeem it; but finding Thimblerig out of humour, and resolved not to return, he began to repent of his jest, and offered to go back and bring it, on condition that the past should be forgotten, and there should be no more retaliation. The other consented to the terms, so lighting a cigar with his sun glass, he set off at a rapid rate on his return. He had not been gone long before I presented Thimblerig with his hat, for I had seen the Bee hunter conceal it, and had secretly brought it along with me. It was some time before our absent friend overtook us, having frightened all the family away by his sudden return, and searched the whole house without success. When he perceived the object of his ride upon the head of the conjurer, and recollected the promise by which he had bound himself not to have any more jesting, he could only exclaim, "Well, it's hard, but it's fair." We all laughed heartily, and good humour was once again restored.

Cane brakes are common in some parts of Texas. Our way led us through one of considerable extent. The frequent passage of men and horses had kept open a narrow path not wide enough for two mustangs to pass with convenience. The reeds, the same as are used in the northern states as fishing rods, had grown to the height of about twenty feet, and were so slender, that having no support directly over the path, they drooped a little inward, and intermingled their tops, forming a complete covering overhead. We rode about a quarter of a mile along this singular arched avenue with the view of the sky completely shut out. The Bee hunter told me that the largest brake is that which lines the banks of Caney Creek, and is seventy miles in length, with scarcely a tree to be seen the whole distance. The reeds are eaten by cattle and horses in the winter when the prairies yield little or no other food.

When we came out of the brake we saw three black wolves jogging like dogs ahead of us, but at too great a distance to reach them with a rifle. Wild turkeys and deer repeatedly crossed our path, and we saw several droves of wild horses pasturing in the prairies. These sights awakened the ruling passion[1] strong within me, and I longed to have a hunt upon a large scale; for though I had killed many bears and deers in my time, I had never brought down a buffalo in all my life, and so I told my friends; but they tried to dissuade me from it, by telling me that I would certainly lose my way, and perhaps perish; for though it appeared as a cultivated garden to the eye, it was still a wilderness. I said little more on the subject until we crossed the Trinidad river, but every mile we travelled I found the temptation grow stronger and stronger.

The night after we crossed the river we fortunately found shelter in the house of a poor woman, who had little but the barest necessaries to offer us. While we were securing our horses for the night we beheld two men approaching the house on foot. They were both armed with rifles and hunting knives, and though I have been accustomed to the sight of men who have not stepped far over the line of civilization, I must say these were just about the roughest samples I had seen anywhere. One was a man of about fifty years old, tall and rawboned. He was dressed in a sailor's round jacket,[2] with a tarpaulin on his head. His whiskers nearly covered his face; his hair was coal black and long, and there was a deep scar across his forehead, and another on the back of his right hand. His companion, who was considerably younger, was bareheaded, and clad in a deer skin dress made after our fashion. Though he was not much darker than the old man, I perceived that he was an Indian. They spoke friendly to the Bee hunter, for they both knew him, and said they were on their way to join the Texian forces, at that time near the San Antonio river. Though they had started without horses, they reckoned they would come across a couple before they went much farther. The right of ownership to horse flesh is not much regarded in Texas, for those that have been taken from the wild droves are soon after turned out to graze on the prairies, the owner having first branded them with his mark, and hobbled them by tying their fore feet together, which will enable another to capture them just as readily as himself.

The old woman set about preparing our supper, and apologized for the homely fare, which consisted of bacon and fried onions, when the Indian went to a bag and produced a number of eggs of wild fowls, and a brace of fat rabbits, which were speedily dressed, and we made as good a meal as a hungry man need wish to set down to. The old man spoke very little; but the Indian, who had lived much among the whites, was talkative, and manifested much impatience to arrive at the army. The first opportunity that occurred I inquired of the Bee hunter who our new friends were, and he told me that the old man had been for many years a pirate with the famous Lafitte,[3] and that the Indian was a hunter belonging to a settler[4] near Galveston Bay. I had seen enough of land rats at Washington, but this was the first time that I was ever in company with a water rat to my knowledge; however, baiting that black spot on his escutcheon, he was a well behaved and inoffensive man. Vice does not appear so shocking when we are familiar with the perpetrator of it.

Thimblerig was for taking airs upon himself after learning who our companions were, and protested to me, that he would not sit down at the same table with a man who had outraged the laws in such a manner; for it was due to society that honest men should discountenance such unprincipled characters, and much more to the same effect; when the old man speedily dissipated the gambler's indignant feelings by calmly saying, "Stranger, you had better take a seat at the table, I think," at the same time drawing a long hunting knife from his belt, and laying it on the table. "I think you had better take some supper with us," he added, in a mild tone, but fixing his eye sternly upon Thimblerig. The conjurer first eyed the knife, and then the fierce whiskers of the pirate, and, unlike some politicians, he wasn't long in making up his mind what course to pursue, but he determined to vote as the pirate voted, and said, "I second that motion, stranger," at the same time seating himself on the bench beside me. The old man then commenced cutting up the meat, for which purpose he had drawn his hunting knife, though the gambler had thought it was for a different purpose; and being relieved from his fears, every thing passed off quite sociable.

Early the following morning we compensated the old woman for the trouble she had been at, and we mounted our horses and pursued our journey, our new friends following on foot, but promising to arrive at the Alamo as soon as we should. About noon we stopped to refresh our horses beneath a cluster of trees that stood in the open prairie, and I again spoke of my longing for a buffalo hunt. We were all seated on the grass, and they strived had to dissuade me from the folly of allowing a ruling passion to lead me into such imminent danger and difficulty as I must necessarily encounter. All this time, while they were running down my weakness, as they called it, Thimblerig was amusing himself with his eternal thimbles and pea upon the crown of his big white hat. I could not refrain from laughing outright to see with what gravity and apparent interest he slipped the pea from one thimble to another while in the midst of a desert. Man is a queer animal, and Colonel Dick Johnson is disposed to make him even queerer than Dame Nature originally intended.

The Bee hunter told me, that if I was determined to leave them, he had in his bag a paper of ground coffee, and biscuit,

which little Kate of Nacogdoches had desired him to carry for
my use, which he handed to me, and proposed drinking her
health, saying that she was one of the kindest and purest of
God's creatures. We drank her health, and wished him all hap-
piness when she should be his own, which time he looked forward to with impatience. He still continued to dissuade me
from leaving them, and all the time he was talking his eyes were
wandering above, when suddenly he stopped, sprang to his
feet, looked around for a moment, then leaped on his mustang,
and without saying a word, started off like mad, and scoured
along the prairie. We watched him, gradually diminishing in
size, until he seemed no larger than a rat, and finally disappeared in the distance. I was amazed, and thought to be sure
the man was crazy; and Thimblerig, who continued his game,
responded that he was unquestionably out of his head.

Shortly after the Bee hunter had disappeared we heard a
noise something like the rumbling of distant thunder. The sky
was clear, there were no signs of a storm, and we concluded it
could not proceed from that cause. On turning to the west we
saw an immense cloud of dust in the distance, but could perceive no object distinctly, and still the roaring continued. "What
can all this mean?" said I. "Burn my old shoes if I know," said
the conjurer, gathering up his thimbles, and at the same time
cocking his large Vicksburger fiercely on his head. We continued looking in the direction whence the sound proceeded, the
cloud of dust became thicker and thicker, and the roaring more
distinct—much louder than was ever heard in the White House
at Washington.

We at first imagined that it was a tornado, but whatever it
was, it was coming directly toward the spot where we stood.
Our mustangs had ceased to graze, and cocked up their ears in
evident alarm. We ran and caught them, took off the hobbles,
and rode into the grove of trees; still the noise grew louder and
louder. We had scarcely got under the shelter of the grove before the object approached near enough for us to ascertain
what it was. It was a herd of buffalo, at least four or five hundred in number, dashing along as swift as the wind, and roaring as if so many devils had broke loose. They passed near the

grove, and, if we had not taken shelter there, we should have been in great danger of being trampled to death. My poor little mustang shook worse than a politician about to be turned out of office, as the drove came sweeping by. At their head, apart from the rest, was a black bull, who appeared to be their leader; he came roaring along, his tail straight an end, and at times tossing up the earth with his horns. I never felt such a desire to have a crack at any thing in all my life. He drew nigh the place where I was standing; I raised my beautiful Betsey to my shoulder, took deliberate aim, blazed away, and he roared, and suddenly stopped. Those that were near him did so likewise, and the concussion occasioned by the impetus of those in the rear was such, that it was a miracle that some of them did not break their legs or necks. The black bull stood for a few moments pawing the ground after he was shot, then darted off around the cluster of trees, and made for the uplands of the prairies. The whole herd followed, sweeping by like a tornado, and I do say, I never witnessed a more beautiful sight to the eye of a hunter in all my life. Bear hunting is no more to be compared to it than Colonel Benton is to Henry Clay. I watched them for a few moments, then clapped spurs to my mustang and followed in their wake, leaving Thimblerig behind me.

I followed on the trail of the herd for at least two hours, by which time the moving mass appeared like a small cloud in the distant horizon. Still, I followed, my whole mind absorbed by the excitement of the chase, until the object was entirely lost in the distance. I now paused to allow my mustang to breathe, who did not altogether fancy the rapidity of my movements, and to consider which course I would have to take to regain the path I had abandoned. I might have retraced my steps by following the trail of the buffalos, but it has always been my principle to go ahead, and so I turned to the west and pushed forward.

I had not rode more than an hour before I found that I was as completely bewildered as "the Government" was when he entered upon an examination of the Post office accounts.[5] I looked around, and there was, as far as the eye could reach, spread before me a country apparently in the highest state of cultivation. Extended fields, beautiful and productive, groves of trees cleared from the underwood, and whose margins were as regular as if the art and taste of man had been employed upon them. But there was no other evidence that the sound of the axe, or the voice of man, had ever here disturbed the solitude of nature. My eyes would have cheated my senses into the belief that I was in an earthly paradise, but my fears told me that I was in a wilderness.

I pushed along, following the sun, for I had no compass to guide me, and there was no other path than that which my mustang made. Indeed, if I had found a beaten track, I should have been almost afraid to have followed it; for my friend the Bee hunter had told me, that once, when he had been lost in the prairies, he had accidentally struck into his own path, and had travelled around and around for a whole day before he discovered his error. This I thought was a poor way of going ahead; so I determined to make for the first large stream, and follow its course.

I had travelled several hours without seeing the trace of a human being, and even game was almost as scarce as Benton's mint drops,[6] except just about election time, and I began to wish that I had followed the advice of my companions. I was a good deal bothered to account for the abrupt manner in which the Bee hunter had absconded; and I felt concerned for the poor thimble conjurer, who was left alone, and altogether unaccustomed to the difficulties that he would have to encounter. While my mind was occupied with these unpleasant reflections, I was suddenly startled by another novelty quite as great as that I have just described.

I had just emerged from a beautiful grove of trees, and was entering upon an extended prairie, which looked like the luxuriant meadows of a thrifty farmer; and as if nothing should be wanting to complete the delusion, but a short distance before me, there was a drove of about one hundred beautiful horses quietly pasturing. It required some effort to convince my mind that man had no agency in this. But when I looked around, and fully realized it all, I thought of him who had preached to me in the wilds of the Arkansas, and involuntarily exclaimed, "God, what hast thou not done for man, and yet how little he does for thee! Not even repays thee with gratitude!"

I entered upon the prairie. The mustangs no sooner espied me than they raised their heads, whinnied, and began coursing around me in an extended circle, which gradually became smaller and smaller, until they closely surrounded me. My little rascally mustang enjoyed the sport, and felt disposed to renew his acquaintance with his wild companions; first turning his head to one, then to another, playfully biting the neck of this one, rubbing noses with that one, and kicking up his heels at a third. I began to feel rather uncomfortable, and plied the spur pretty briskly to get out of the mess, but he was as obstinate as the "old Roman" himself, who will be neither led nor driven. I kicked, and he kicked, but fortunately he became tired first, and he made one start, intending to escape from the annoyance if possible. As I had an annoyance to escape from likewise, I beat the devil's tattoo on his ribs, that he might have some music to dance to, and we went ahead right merrily, the whole drove following in our wake, head up, and tail and mane streaming. My little critter, who was both blood and bottom, seemed delighted at being at the head of the heap; and having once got fairly started, I wish I may be shot if I did not find it impossible to stop him. He kept along, tossing his head proudly, and occasionally neighing, as much as to say, "Come on, my hearties, you see I ha'n't forgot our old amusement yet." And they did come on with a vengeance, clatter, clatter, clatter, as if so many fiends had broke loose. The prairie lay extended before me as far as the eye could reach, and I began to think that there would be no end to the race.

My little animal was full of fire and mettle, and as it was the first bit of genuine sport that he had had for some time, he appeared determined to make the most of it. He kept the lead for full half an hour, frequently neighing as if in triumph and derision. I thought of John Gilpin's celebrated ride,[7] but that was child's play to this. The proverb says, "The race is not always to the swift, nor the battle to the strong,"[8] and so it proved in the present instance. My mustang was obliged to carry weight, while his competitors were as free as nature had made them. A beautiful bay, who had trod close upon my heels the whole way, now came side by side with my mustang, and we had it hip and thigh for about ten minutes, in such style as would have delighted the heart of a true lover of the turf. I now felt an interest in the race myself, and for the credit of my bit of blood, determined to win if it was at all in the nature of things. I plied the lash and spur, and the little critter took it quite kindly, and tossed his head, and neighed, as much as to say, "Colonel, I know what you're after—Go ahead!"—and he cut dirt in beautiful style, I tell you.

This could not last for ever. At length my competitor darted ahead, somewhat the same way that Adam Huntsman served me last election, except that there was no gouging; and my little fellow was compelled to clatter after his tail, like a needy politician after an office holder when he wants his influence, and which my mustang found it quite as difficult to reach. He hung on like grim death for some time longer, but at last his ambition began to flag; and having lost ground, others seemed to think that he was not the mighty critter he was cracked up to be, no how, and they tried to outstrip him also. A second shot ahead, and kicked up his heels in derision as he passed us; then a third, a fourth, and so on, and even the scrubbiest little rascal in the whole drove was disposed to have a fling at their broken down leader. A true picture of politicians and their truckling followers, thought I. We now followed among the last of the drove until we came to the banks of the Navasola river. The foremost leaped from the margin into the rushing stream, the others, politician like, followed him, though he would lead them to destruction; but my wearied animal fell on the banks, completely exhausted with fatigue. It was a beautiful sight to see them stemming the torrent, ascend the opposite bank, and scour over the plain, having been refreshed by the water. I relieved my wearied animal from the saddle, and employed what means were in my power to restore him.

CHAPTER XI.

After toiling for more than an hour to get my mustang upon his feet again, I gave it up as a bad job, as little Van did when he attempted to raise himself to the moon by the waistband of his breeches. Night was fast closing in, and as I began to think that I had had just about sport enough for one day, I might as well look around for a place of shelter for the night, and take a fresh start in the morning, by which time I was in hopes my horse would be recruited. Near the margin of the river a large tree had been blown down, and I thought of making my lair in its top, and approached it for that purpose. While beating among the branches I heard a low growl, as much as to say, "Stranger, the apartments are already taken." Looking about to see what sort of a bed-fellow I was likely to have, I discovered, not more than five or six paces from me, an enormous Mexican cougar eyeing me as an epicure surveys the table before he selects his dish, for I have no doubt the cougar looked upon me as the subject of a future supper. Rays of light darted from his large eyes, he showed his teeth like a negro in hysterics, and he was crouching on his haunches, ready for a spring; all of which convinced me that unless I was pretty quick upon the trigger, posterity would know little of the termination of my eventful career, and it would be far less glorious and useful than I intend to make it.

One glance satisfied me that there was no time to be lost, as Pat thought when falling from a church steeple, and exclaimed, "This would be mighty pleasant, now, if it would only last,"— but there was no retreat, either for me or the cougar, so I levelled my Betsey, and blazed away. The report was followed by a furious growl, (which is sometimes the case in Congress,) and the next moment, when I expected to find the tarnal critter struggling with death, I beheld him shaking his head as if nothing more than a bee had stung him. The ball had struck him on the forehead, and glanced off, doing no other injury than stunning him for an instant, and tearing off the skin, which tended to infuriate him the more. The cougar wasn't long in making up his mind what to do, nor was I neither; but he would have it all his own way, and vetoed my motion to back out. I had not retreated three steps before he sprang at me like a steamboat; I stepped aside, and as he lit upon the ground I struck him violently with the barrel of my rifle, but he didn't mind that, but wheeled round and made at me again. The gun was now of no use, so I threw it away, and drew my hunting knife, for I knew we should come to close quarters before the fight would be over. This time he succeeded in fastening on my left arm, and was just beginning to amuse himself by tearing the flesh off with his fangs, when I ripped my knife into his side, and he let go his hold much to my satisfaction.

He wheeled about and came at me with increased fury, occasioned by the smarting of his wounds. I now tried to blind him, knowing that if I succeeded he would become an easy prey; so as he approached me I watched my opportunity, and aimed a blow at his eyes with my knife, but unfortunately it struck him on the nose, and he paid no other attention to it than by a shake of the head and a low growl. He pressed me close, and as I was stepping backward my foot tripped in a vine, and I fell to the ground. He was down upon me like a nighthawk upon a June bug. He seized hold of the outer part of my right thigh, which afforded him considerable amusement; the hinder part of his body was toward my face; I grasped his tail with my left hand, and tickled his ribs with my hunting knife, which I held in my right. Still, the critter wouldn't let go his hold; and as I found that he would lacerate my leg dreadfully unless he was speedily shaken off, I tried to hurl him down the bank into the river, for our scuffle had already brought us to the edge of the bank. I stuck my knife into his side, and summoned all my strength to throw him over. He resisted, was desperate heavy;

but at last I got him so far down the declivity that he lost his balance, and he rolled over and over until he landed on the margin of the river; but in his fall he dragged me along with him. Fortunately I fell uppermost, and his neck presented a fair mark for my hunting knife. Without allowing myself time even to draw breath, I aimed one desperate blow at his neck, and the knife entered his gullet up to the handle, and reached his heart. He struggled for a few moments, and died. I have had many fights with bears, but that was mere child's play; this was the first fight ever I had with a cougar, and I hope it may be the last.

I now returned to the tree top to see if any one else would dispute my lodging; but now I could take peaceable and quiet possession. I parted some of the branches, and cut away others to make a bed in the opening; I then gathered a quantity of moss, which hung in festoons from the trees, which I spread on the litter, and over this I spread my horse blanket; and I had as comfortable a bed as a weary man need ask for. I now took another look at my mustang, and from all appearances he would not live until morning. I ate some of the cakes that little Kate of Nacogdoches had made for me, and then carried my saddle into my tree top, and threw myself down upon my bed, with no very pleasant reflections at the prospect before me.

I was weary, and soon fell asleep, and did not awake until daybreak the next day. I felt somewhat stiff and sore from the wounds I had received in the conflict with the cougar; but I considered myself as having made a lucky escape. I looked over the bank, and as I saw the carcass of the cougar lying there, I thought that it was an even chance that we had not exchanged conditions; and I felt grateful that the fight had ended as it did. I now went to look after my mustang, fully expecting to find him as dead as the cougar; but what was my astonishment to find that he had disappeared without leaving trace of hair or hide of him. I first supposed that some beasts of prey had consumed the poor critter; but then they wouldn't have eaten his bones; and he had vanished as effectually as the deposites, without leaving any mark of the course they had taken. This bothered me amazing; I couldn't figure it out by any rule that I had ever heard of, so I concluded to think no more about it.

I felt a craving for something to eat, and looking around for some game, I saw a flock of geese on the shore of the river. I shot a fine fat gander, and soon stripped him of his feathers; and gathering some light wood, I kindled a fire, run a long stick through my goose, for a spit, and put it down to roast, supported by two sticks with prongs. I had a desire for some coffee; and having a tin cup with me, I poured the paper of ground coffee that I had received from the Bee hunter into it, and made a strong cup, which was very refreshing. Off of my goose and biscuit I made a hearty meal, and was preparing to depart, without clearing up the breakfast things, or knowing which direction to pursue, when I was somewhat taken aback by another of the wild scenes of the west. I heard a sound like the trampling of many horses, and I thought to be sure the mustangs or buffalos were coming upon me again; but on raising my head I beheld in the distance about fifty mounted Cumanches,[1] with their spears glittering in the morning sun, dashing toward the spot where I stood at full speed. As the column advanced it divided, according to their usual practice, into two semicircles, and in an instant I was surrounded. Quicker than thought I sprang to my rifle, but as my hand grasped it, I felt that resistance against so many would be of as little use as pumping for thunder in dry weather.

The chief was for making love to my beautiful Betsey, but I clung fast to her, and assuming an air of composure, I demanded whether their nation was at war with the Americans. "No," was the reply. "Do you like the Americans?" "Yes, they are our friends." "Where do you get your spear heads, your rifles, your blankets, and your knives from?" "Get them from our friends, the Americans." "Well, do you think if you were passing through their nation, as I am passing through yours, they would attempt to rob you of your property?" "No, they would feed me, and protect me; and the Cumanche will do the same by his white brother."

I now asked him what it was had directed him to the spot where I was, and he told me, that they had seen the smoke from a great distance, and had come to see the cause of it. He inquired what had brought me there alone; and I told him that I had come to hunt, and that my mustang had become exhausted, and though I thought he was about to die, that he had escaped from me; at which the chief gave a low chuckling laugh, and said it was all a trick of the mustang, which is the most wily and cunning of all animals. But he said that as I was a brave hunter he would furnish me with another; he gave orders, and a fine young horse was immediately brought forward.

When the party approached there were three old squaws at their head, who made a noise with their mouths, and served as trumpeters. I now told the chief that, as I now had a horse, I would go for my saddle, which was in the place where I had slept. As I approached the spot I discovered one of the squaws devouring the remains of my roasted goose, but my saddle and bridle were nowhere to be found. Almost in despair of seeing them again, I observed, in a thicket at a little distance, one of the trumpeters kicking and belabouring her horse to make him move off, while the sagacious beast would not move a step from the troop. I followed her, and, thanks to her restive mustang, secured my property, which the chief made her restore to me. Some of the warriors had by this time discovered the body of the cougar, and had already commenced skinning it; and seeing how many stabs were about it, I related to the chief the desperate struggle I had had; he said, "Brave hunter, brave man," and wished me to be adopted into his tribe, but I respectfully declined the honour. He then offered to see me on my way; and I asked him to accompany me to the Colorado river, if he was going in that direction, which he agreed to do. I put my saddle on my fresh horse, mounted, and we darted off, at a rate not much slower than I had rode the day previous with the wild herd, the old squaws at the head of the troop braying like young jackasses the whole way.

About three hours after starting we saw a drove of mustangs quietly pasturing in the prairie at a distance. One of the Indians immediately got his lasso ready, which was a long rope made of hide plaited like whip cord, with an iron ring at one end, through which the rope was passed so as to form a noose; and thus prepared, he darted ahead of the troop to make a capture. They allowed him to approach pretty nigh, he all the time flourishing his lasso; but before he got within reaching distance, they started off at a brisk canter, made two or three wide circuits around him, as if they would spy-out what he was after, then abruptly changed their course, and disappeared. One mustang out of all the drove remained standing quietly; the Indian made up to him, threw the lasso, but the mustang dodged his head between his fore legs, and escaped the noose, but did not attempt to escape. The Indian then rode up to him, and the horse very patiently submitted while he put a bridle on him, and secured him. When I approached, I immediately recognised in the captive the pestilent little animal that had shammed sickness and escaped from me the day before; and when he caught my eye he cast down his head and looked rather sheepish, as if he were sensible and ashamed of the dirty trick he had played me. I expressed my astonishment to the Indian chief at the mustang's allowing himself to be captured without an effort to escape; and he told me, that they are generally hurled to the ground with such violence when first taken with the lasso, that they remember it ever after, and that the sight of it will subdue them to submission, though they may have run wild for years. Just so with an office holder, who, being kicked out, turns patriot—shake a commission at him, and the fire of his patriotism usually escapes in smoke.

We travelled all day, and toward evening we came across a small drove of buffalos; and it was a beautiful sight to behold with what skill the Indians hunted down this noble game. There are no horsemen who ride more gracefully than the Cumanches; and they sit so closely, and hold such absolute control over the horse, that he seems to be part of their own person. I had the good fortune to bring down a young heifer, and as it was the only beef that we killed, the chief again complimented me as being a brave hunter; and while they were preparing the heifer for our supper I related to him many of my hunting exploits, at which he manifested pleasure and much astonishment for an Indian. He again urged upon me to become one of the tribe.

We made a hearty supper, hobbled our mustangs, which we turned into the prairie to graze, and then encamped for the night. I awoke about two hours before daybreak, and looking over the tract of country through which we had travelled, the sky was as bright and clear as if the sun had already risen. I watched it for some time without being able to account for it, and asked my friend, the chief, to explain, who told me that the prairie was on fire, and that it must have caught when we cooked our dinner. I have seen hundreds of acres of mountain timber on fire in my time, but this is the first time that I ever saw a prairie burning.

Nothing of interest occurred until we reached the Colorado, and were following the river to the place where it crosses the road to Bexar,[2] which place the Indians promised to conduct me to. We saw a light column of smoke ascending in the clear sky, and hastened toward it. It proceeded from a small cluster of trees near the river. When we came within five hundred yards of it, the warriors extended their line around the object, and the chief and myself cautiously approached it. When we came within eyeshot, what was my astonishment to discover a solitary man seated on the ground near the fire, so intent upon some pursuit that he did not perceive our approach. We drew nigh to him, and still he was unconscious of our approach. It was poor Thimblerig practising his game of thimbles upon the crown of his white Vicksburger. This is what I call the ruling passion most amazing strong. The chief shouted the war whoop, and suddenly the warriors came rushing in from all quarters, preceded by the old squaw trumpeters squalling like mad. The conjurer sprang to his feet, and was ready to sink into the earth when he beheld the ferocious looking fellows that surrounded him. I stepped up, took him by the hand, and quieted his fears. I told the chief that he was a friend of mine, and I was very glad to have found him, for I was afraid that he had perished. I now thanked him for his kindness in guiding me over the prairies, and gave him a large Bowie knife,[3] which he said he would keep for the sake of the brave hunter. The whole squadron then wheeled off, and I saw them no more. I have met with many polite men in my time, but no one who possessed in a greater degree what may be called true spontaneous politeness than this Cumanche chief, always excepting Philip

Hone, Esq.,[4] of New York, whom I look upon as the politest man I ever did see; for when he asked me to take a drink at his own side-board he turned his back upon me, that I mightn't be ashamed to fill as much as I wanted. That was what I call doing the fair thing.

Thimblerig was delighted at meeting me again, but it was some time before he recovered sufficiently from the cold sweat into which the sudden appearance of the Indians had thrown him to recount his adventures to me. He said that he felt rather down-hearted when he found himself abandoned both by the Bee hunter and myself, and he knew not which course to pursue; but after thinking about the matter for two hours, he had made up his mind to retrace the road we had travelled over, and had mounted his mustang for that purpose, when he spied the Bee hunter laden with honey. The mystery of his abrupt departure was now fully accounted for; he had spied a solitary bee shaping its course to its hive, and at the moment he couldn't control the ruling passion, but followed the bee without reflecting for a moment upon the difficulties and dangers that his thoughtlessness might occasion his friends.

I now asked him what had become of the Bee hunter, and he said that he had gone out in pursuit of game for their supper, and he expected that he would return shortly, as he had been absent at least an hour. While we were still speaking our friend appeared, bending under the weight of a wild turkey. He manifested great joy at meeting with me so unexpectedly; and desiring the conjurer to pluck the feathers off the bird, which he cheerfully undertook, for he said he had been accustomed to plucking pigeons,[5] we set about preparing our supper.

The position we occupied was directly on the route leading to Bexar, and at the crossings of the Colorado. We were about to commence our supper, for the turkey was done in beautiful style, when the sound of a horse neighing startled us. We looked over the prairie, and beheld two men approaching on horseback, and both armed with rifles and knives. The Bee hunter said that it was time for us to be on our guard, for we should meet, perhaps, more enemies than friends as soon as we crossed the river, and the new-comers were making directly for the spot we occupied; but, as they were only two, it occasioned no uneasiness.

As they drew nigh we recognised the strangers; they turned out to be the old pirate and the Indian hunter who had lodged with us a few nights before. We hailed them, and on seeing us they alighted and asked permission to join our party, which we gladly agreed to, as our journey was becoming rather more perilous every mile we advanced. They partook of our turkey, and as they had some small cakes of bread, which they threw into the general stock, we made a hearty supper; and, after a battle song from the Bee hunter, we prepared to rest for the night.

Early next morning we crossed the river, and pushed forward for the fortress of Alamo. The old pirate was still as taciturn as ever, but his companion was talkative and in good spirits. I asked him where he had procured their mustangs, and he said that he had found them hobbled in Burnet's Grant[6] just at a time that he felt very tired; and as he believed that no one would lay claim to them at Bexar, he couldn't resist mounting one, and persuading his friend to mount the other.

Nothing of interest occurred until we came within about twenty miles of San Antonio. We were in the open prairie, and beheld a band of about fifteen or twenty armed men approaching us at full speed. "Look out for squalls," said the old pirate, who had not spoken for an hour; "they are a scouting party of Mexicans." "And are three or four times our number," said Thimblerig. "No matter," replied the old man; "they are convicts, jail birds, and cowardly ruffians, no doubt, who would tremble at a loud word as much as a mustang at the sight of the lasso.— Let us spread ourselves, dismount, and trust to our arms."

We followed his orders, and stood beside our horses, which served to protect our persons, and we awaited the approach of the enemy. When they perceived this movement of ours, they checked their speed, appeared to consult together for a few minutes, then spread their line, and came within rifle shot of us. The leader called out to us in Spanish, but as I did not understand him, I asked the old man what it was, who said he called upon us to surrender.

"There will be a brush with those blackguards," continued

the pirate. "Now each of you single out your man for the first fire, and they are greater fools than I take them for if they give us a chance at a second.—Colonel, as you are a good shot, just settle the business for that talking fellow with the red feather; he's worth any three of the party."

"Surrender, or we fire," shouted the fellow with the red feather in Spanish.

"Fire, and be d——d," returned the pirate, at the top of his voice, in plain English.

And sure enough they took his advice, for the next minute we were saluted with a discharge of musketry, the report of which was so loud that we were convinced they all had fired. Before the smoke had cleared away we had each selected our man, fired, and I never did see such a scattering among their ranks as followed. We beheld several mustangs running wild without their riders over the prairie, and the balance of the company were already retreating at a more rapid gait than they approached. We hastily mounted, and commenced pursuit, which we kept up until we beheld the independent flag flying from the battlements of the fortress of Alamo,[7] our place of destination. The fugitives succeeded in evading our pursuit, and we rode up to the gates of the fortress, announced to the sentinel who we were, and the gates were thrown open; and we entered amid shouts of welcome bestowed upon us by the patriots.

CHAPTER XII.

The fortress of Alamo is at the town of Bexar, on the San Antonio river, which flows through the town. Bexar is about one hundred and forty miles from the coast, and contains upward of twelve hundred citizens, all native Mexicans, with the exception of a few American families who have settled there. Besides these there is a garrison of soldiers, and trading pedlars of every description, who resort to it from the borders of the Rio Grande, as their nearest depôt of American goods. A military outpost was established at this spot by the Spanish government in 1718. In 1731 the town was settled by emigrants sent out from the Canary Islands by the King of Spain. It became a flourishing settlement, and so continued until the revolution in 1812,[1] since which period the Cumanche and other Indians have greatly harassed the inhabitants, producing much individual suffering, and totally destroying, for a season at least, the prospects of the town. Its site is one of the most beautiful in the western world. The air is salubrious, the water delightful, especially when mixed with a little of the ardent, and the health of the citizens is proverbial. The soil around it is highly fertile, and well calculated for cotton and grain.

The gallant young Colonel Travis,[2] who commands the Texian forces in the fortress of Alamo, received me like a man; and though he can barely muster one hundred and fifty efficient men, should Santa Anna[3] make an attack upon us, with the whole host of ruffians that the Mexican prisons can disgorge, he will have snakes to eat before he gets over the wall, I tell you. But one spirit appears to animate the little band of patriots— and that is liberty, or death. To worship God according to the dictates of their own conscience, and govern themselves as freemen should be governed.

All the world knows, by this time, that the town of Bexar, or, as some call it, San Antonio, was captured from the Mexicans by General Burlison,[4] on the 10th day of December, 1835, after a severe struggle of five days and five nights, during which he sustained a loss of four men only, but the brave old Colonel Milam[5] was among them. There were seventeen hundred men in the town, and the Texian force consisted of but two hundred and sixteen. The Mexicans had walled up the streets leading from the public square, intending to make a desperate resistance: the Texians however made an entrance, and valiantly drove them from house to house, until General Cos[6] retreated to the castle of Alamo, without the city, and there hoisted the white flag, and sent out the terms of capitulation, which were as follows:

General Cos is to retire within six days, with his officers, arms, and private property, on parole of honour. He is not to oppose the re-establishment of the constitution of 1824.

The infantry, and the cavalry, the remnant of Morale's[7] battalion, and the convicts, to return, taking with them ten rounds of cartridge for safety against the Indians.

All public property, money, arms, and ammunition, to be delivered to General Burlison, of the Texian army,—with some other stipulations in relation to the sick and wounded, private property, and prisoners of war. The Texians would not have aceeded to them, preferring to storm him in his stronghold, but at this critical juncture they hadn't a single round of ammunition left, having fought from the 5th to the 9th of the month, General Ugartechea[8] had arrived but the day before with three hundred troops, and the four hundred convicts mentioned above, making a reinforcement of seven hundred men; but such rubbish was no great obstacle to the march of freedom. The Mexicans lost about three hundred men during the siege, and the Texians had only four killed, and twenty wounded. The articles of capitulation being signed, we marched into the town, took possession of the fortress, hoisted the independent flag, and told the late proprietors to pack up their moveables and clear out in the snapping of a trigger, as we did not think our pockets quite safe with so many jail birds around us. And this is the way the Alamo came into our possession; but the way we shall maintain our possession of it will be a subject for the future historian to record, or my name's not Crockett.—I wish I may be shot if I don't go ahead to the last.

I found Colonel Bowie,[9] of Louisiana, in the fortress, a man celebrated for having been in more desperate personal conflicts than any other in the country, and whose name has been given to a knife of a peculiar construction, which is now in general use in the south-west. I was introduced to him by Colonel Travis, and he gave me a friendly welcome, and appeared to be mightily pleased that I had arrived safe. While we were conversing he had occasion to draw his famous knife to cut a strap, and I wish I may be shot if the bare sight of it wasn't enough to give a man of a squeamish stomach the cholic, specially before breakfast. He saw I was admiring it, and said he, "Colonel, you might tickle a fellow's ribs a long time with this little instrument before you'd make him laugh; and many a time have I seen a man puke at the idea of the point touching the pit of his stomach."

My companions, the Bee hunter and the conjurer, joined us, and the colonel appeared to know them both very well. He had a high opinion of the Bee hunter, for turning to me, he said, "Colonel, you could not have had a braver, better, or more pleasant fellow for a companion than honest Ned here. With fifteen hundred such men I would undertake to march to the city of Mexico, and occupy the seat of Santa Anna myself before three months should elapse."

The colonel's life has been marked by constant peril and deeds of daring. A few years ago he went on a hunting excursion into the prairies of Texas with nine companions. They were attacked by a roving party of Cumanches, about two hundred strong, and such was the science of the colonel in this sort of wild warfare, that after killing a considerable number of the enemy, he fairly frightened the remainder from the field of action, and they fled in utter dismay. The fight took place among the high grass in the open prairie. He ordered his men to dis-

mount from their horses and scatter; to take deliberate aim before they fired, but as soon as they had discharged their rifles,
to fall flat on the ground and crawl away from the spot, and re-
load their pieces. By this scheme they not only escaped the fire
of the Indians, but by suddenly discharging their guns from another quarter, they created the impression that their party was
a numerous one; and the Indians, finding that they were fighting against an invisible enemy, after losing about thirty of their
men, took to flight, believing themselves lucky in having escaped with no greater loss. But one of the colonel's party was
slightly wounded, and that was owing to his remaining to re-
load his rifle without having first shifted his position.

Santa Anna, it is said, roars like an angry lion at the disgraceful defeat that his brother-in-law, General Cos, lately met
with at this place. It is rumoured that he has recruited a large
force, and commenced his march to San Louis de Potosi, and
he is determined to carry on a war of extermination. He is liberal in applying his epithets to our countrymen in Texas, and
denounces them as a set of perfidious wretches, whom the com-
passion of the generous Mexicans has permitted to take refuge
in their country; and who, like the serpent in the fable, no
sooner warmed themselves than they stung their benefactors.
This is a good joke.—By what title does Mexico lay claim to all
the territory which belonged to Spain in North America? Each
province or state of New Spain contended separately or jointly,
just as it happened, for their independence, as we did, and were
not united under a general government representing the whole
of the Spanish possessions, which was only done afterward by
mutual agreement or federation. Let it be remembered that the
Spanish authorities were first expelled from Texas by the American settlers, who, from the treachery of their Mexican associates, were unable to retain it; but the second time they were
more successful. They certainly had as good a right to the soil
thus conquered by them, as the inhabitants of other provinces
who succeeded against Spain. The Mexicans talk of the ingratitude of the Americans: the truth is, that the ingratitude has
been on the other side. What was the war of Texas, in 1813,
when the revolutionary spark was almost extinguished in Mex-

ico? What was the expedition of Mina,[10] and his three hundred American Spartans, who perished heroically in the very heart of Mexico, in the vain attempt to resuscitate and keep alive the spark of independence which has at this time kindled such an ungrateful blaze? If a just estimate could be made of the lives and the treasures contributed by American enterprise in that cause, it would appear incredible. How did the Mexicans obtain their independence at last? Was it by their own virtue and courage? No, it was by the treachery of one of the king's generals, who established himself by successful treason, and they have been in constant commotion ever since, which proves they are unfit to govern themselves, much less a free and enlightened people at a distance of twelve hundred miles from them.

The Mexican government, by its colonization laws, invited and induced the Anglo-American population of Texas to colonize its wilderness, under the pledged faith of a written constitution, that they should continue to enjoy that constitutional liberty and republican government to which they had been habituated in the land of their birth, the United States of America. In this expectation they have been cruelly disappointed, as the Mexican nation has acquiesced in the late changes made in the government by Santa Anna; who, having overturned the constitution of this country, now offers the settlers the cruel alternative, either to abandon their homes, acquired by so many privations, or submit to the most intolerable of all tyranny, the combined depotism of the sword and the priesthood.

But Santa Anna charges the Americans with ingratitude! This is something like Satan reviling sin. I have gathered some particulars of the life of this moral personage from a gentleman at present in the Alamo, and who is intimately acquainted with him, which I will copy into my book exactly as he wrote it.

Santa Anna is about forty-two years of age, and was born in the city of Vera Cruz. His father was a Spaniard, of old Spain, of respectable standing, though poor; his mother was a Mexican. He received a common education, and at the age of thirteen or fourteen was taken into the military family of the then Intendant of Vera Cruz, General Davila, who took a great fancy to him, and brought him up. He remained with General

Davila until about the year 1820. While with Davila he was made a major, and when installed he took the honours very coolly, and on some of his friends congratulating him, he said, "If you were to make me a god, I should desire to be something greater." This trait, developed at so early a period of his life, indicated the existence of that vaulting ambition which has ever since characterized his life.

After serving the Spanish royal cause until 1821, he left Vera Cruz, turned against his old master and benefactor, and placed himself at the head of some irregular troops which he raised on the seacoast near Vera Cruz, and which are called Jarochos in their language, and which were denominated by him his Cossacks, as they are all mounted and armed with spears. With this rude cavalry he besieged Vera Cruz, drove Davila into the castle of San Juan d'Ulloa, and after having been repulsed again entered at a subsequent period, and got entire possession of the city, expelling therefrom the old Spanish troops, and reducing the power of the mother country in Mexico to the walls of the castle.

Subsequent to this, Davila is said to have obtained an interview with Santa Anna, and told him he was destined to act a prominent part in the history of his country. "And now," says he, "I will give you some advice: always go with the strongest party." He always acted up to this motto until he raised the *grito*, (or cry,) in other words, took up the cudgels for the friars and church. He then overturned the federal government, and established a central despotism, of which the priests and the military were the two privileged orders. His life has been, from the first, of the most romantic kind; constantly in revolutions, constantly victorious.

His manners are extremely affable; he is full of anecdote and humour, and makes himself exceedingly fascinating and agreeable to all who come into his company; he is about five feet ten, rather spare, has a moderately high forehead, with black hair, short black whiskers, without mustachios, and an eye large, black, and expressive of a lurking devil in his look; he is a man of genteel and dignified deportment, but of a disposition perfectly heartless. He married a Spanish lady of property, a native of Alvarado, and through that marriage obtained the first part of his estate, called Manga de Clavo, six leagues from Vera Cruz. He has three fine children, yet quite young.

The following striking anecdote of Santa Anna illustrates his peculiar quickness and management: During the revolution of 1829, while he was shut up in Oxaca, and surrounded by the government troops, and reduced to the utmost straits for the want of money and provisions, having a very small force, there had been, in consequence of the siege and firing every day through the streets, no mass for several weeks. He had no money, and hit upon the following expedient to get it: he took possession of one of the convents, got hold of the wardrobe of the friars, dressed his officers and some of his soldiers in it, and early in the morning had the bells rung for the mass. The people, delighted at having again an opportunity of adoring the Supreme Being, flocked to the church where he was; and after the house was pretty well filled, his friars showed their side-arms and bayonets from beneath their cowls, and closed the doors upon the assembled multitude. At this unexpected de-nouement there was a tremendous shrieking, when one of his officers ascended the pulpit, and told the people that he wanted ten thousand dollars, and must have it. He finally succeeded in getting about thirty-six hundred dollars, when he dismissed the congregation.

As a sample of Santa Anna's pious whims we relate the following:

In the same campaign of Oxaca, Santa Anna and his officers were there besieged by Rincon, who commanded the government troops. Santa Anna was in a convent surrounded by a small breastwork. Some of the officers one night, to amuse themselves, took the wooden saints out of the church and placed them as sentries, dressed in uniforms, on the breast-work. Rincon, alarmed on the morning at this apparent bold-ness, began to fire away at the wooden images, supposing them to be flesh and blood; and it was not until some of the officers who were not in the secret had implored Santa Anna to prevent this desecration that the firing ceased.

Many similar facts are related of him. He is, in fact, all things to all men; and yet, after his treachery to Davila, he has the impudence to talk about ingratitude. He never was out of Mexico. If I only live to tree him,[11] and take him prisoner, I shall ask for no more glory in this life.

CHAPTER XIII.

I write this on the nineteenth of February, 1836, at San Antonio. We are all in high spirits, though we are rather short of provisions, for men who have appetites that could digest any thing but oppression; but no matter, we have a prospect of soon getting our bellies full of fighting, and that is victuals and drink to a true patriot any day. We had a little sort of convivial party last evening: just about a dozen of us set to work, most patriotically, to see whether we could not get rid of that curse of the land, whisky, and we made considerable progress; but my poor friend, Thimblerig, got sewed up just about as tight as the eyelethole in a lady's corset, and a little tighter too, I reckon; for when we went to bed he called for a boot-jack, which was brought to him, and he bent down on his hands and knees, and very gravely pulled off his hat with it, for the darned critter was so thoroughly swiped that he didn't know his head from his heels. But this wasn't all the folly he committed: he pulled off his coat and laid it on the bed, and then hung himself over the back of a chair; and I wish I may be shot if he didn't go to sleep in that position, thinking every thing had been done according to Gunter's late scale.[1] Seeing the poor fellow completely used up, I carried him to bed, though he did belong to the Temperance society; and he knew nothing about what had occurred until I told him next morning. The Bee hunter didn't join us in this blow-out. Indeed, he will seldom drink more than just enough to prevent his being called a total abstinence man. But then he is the most jovial fellow for a water drinker I ever did see.

This morning I saw a caravan of about fifty mules passing by

Bexar, and bound for Santa Fè. They were loaded with different articles to such a degree that it was astonishing how they could travel at all, and they were nearly worn out by their labours. They were without bridle or halter, and yet proceeded with perfect regularity in a single line; and the owners of the caravan rode their mustangs with their enormous spurs, weighing at least a pound a piece, with rowels an inch and a half in length, and lever bits of the harshest description, able to break the jaws of their animals under a very gentle pressure. The men were dressed in the costume of Mexicans. Colonel Travis sent out a guard to see that they were not laden with munitions of war for the enemy. I went out with the party. The poor mules were bending under a burden of more than three hundred pounds, without including the panniers, which were bound so tight as almost to stop the breath of the poor animal. Each of the sorrowful line came up, spontaneously, in turn to have his girth unbound and his load removed. They seemed scarcely able to keep upon their feet, and as they successively obtained relief, one after another heaved a long and deep sigh, which it was painful to hear, because it proved that the poor brutes had been worked beyond their strength. What a world of misery man inflicts upon the rest of creation in his brief passage through life!

Finding that the caravan contained nothing intended for the enemy, we assisted the owners to replace the heavy burdens on the backs of the patient but dejected mules, and allowed them to pursue their weary and lonely way. For full two hours we could see them slowly winding along the narrow path, a faint line that ran like a thread through the extended prairie; and finally they were whittled down to the little end of nothing in the distance, and were blotted out from the horizon.

The caravan had no sooner disappeared than one of the hunters, who had been absent several days, came in. He was one of those gentlemen who don't pride themselves much upon their costume, and reminded me of a covey who came into a tavern in New York when I was last in that city. He was dressed in five jackets, all of which failed to conceal his raggedness, and as he bolted in, he exclaimed,

"Worse than I look, by ——. But no matter, I've let myself for fourteen dollars a month, and find my own prog and lodging."

"To do what?" demanded the barkeeper.

"To stand at the corner for a paper-mill sign—'cash for rags'—that's all. I'm about to enter upon the stationery business, you see." He tossed off his grog, and bustled out to begin his day's work.

But to return to the hunter. He stated that he had met some Indians on the banks of the Rio Frio, who informed him that Santa Anna, with a large force, had already crossed the Neuces, and might be expected to arrive before San Antonio in a few days. We immediately set about preparing to give him a warm reception, for we are all well aware, if our little band is overwhelmed by numbers, there is little mercy to be expected from the cowardly Mexicans—it is war to the knife.

I jocosely asked the ragged hunter, who was a smart, active young fellow, of the steamboat and alligator breed,[2] whether he was a rhinoceros or a hyena, as he was so eager for a fight with the invaders. "Neither the one, nor t'other, Colonel," says he, "but a whole menagerie in myself. I'm shaggy as a bear, wolfish about the head, active as a cougar, and can grin like a hyena, until the bark will curl off a gum log. There's a sprinkling of all sorts in me, from the lion down to the skunk; and before the war is over you'll pronounce me an entire zoological institute, or I miss a figure in my calculation. I promise to swallow Santa Anna without gagging, if you will only skewer back his ears, and grease his head a little."

He told me that he was one in the fatal expedition fitted out from New Orleans, in November last, to join the contemplated attack upon Tampico[3] by Mehia and Peraza. They were, in all, about one hundred and thirty men, who embarked as emigrants to Texas; and the terms agreed upon were, that it was optional whether the party took up arms in defence of Texas, or not, on landing. They were at full liberty to act as they pleased. But the truth was, Tampico was their destination, and an attack on that city the covet design, which was not made known before land was in sight. The emigrants were landed, some fifty, who doubtless had a previous understanding, joined the standard of General Mehia, and the following day a formidable fort surrendered without an attack.

The whole party were now tendered arms and ammunition, which even those who had been decoyed accepted; and, the line being formed, they commenced the attack upon the city. The hunter continued: "On the 15th of November our little army, consisting of one hundred and fifty men, marched into Tampico, garrisoned by two thousand Mexicans, who were drawn up in battle array in the public square of the city. We charged them at the point of the bayonet, and although they so greatly outnumbered us, *in two minutes* we completely routed them; and they fled, taking refuge on the house tops, from which they poured a destructive fire upon our gallant little band. We fought them until daylight, when we found our number decreased to fifty or sixty broken down and disheartened men. Without ammunition, and deserted by the officers, twenty-eight immediately surrendered. But a few of us cut our way through, and fortunately escaped to the mouth of the river, where we got on board a vessel and sailed for Texas.

"The twenty-eight prisoners wished to be considered as prisoners of war; they made known the manner in which they had been deceived, but they were tried by a court-martial of Mexican soldiers, and condemned to be shot on the 14th day of December, 1835, which sentence was carried into execution."

After receiving this account from my new friend, the old pirate and the Indian hunter came up, and they went off to liquor together, and I went to see a wild Mexican hog, which one of the hunters had brought in. These animals have become scarce, which circumstance is not to be deplored, for their flesh is of little value; and there will still be hogs enough left in Mexico, from all I can learn, even though these should be extirpated.

February 22. The Mexicans, about sixteen hundred strong, with their President Santa Anna at their head, aided by Generals Almonte, Cos, Sesma,[4] and Castrillon, are within two leagues of Bexar. General Cos, it seems, has already forgot his parole of honour, and has come back to retreive the credit he lost in this place in December last. If he is captured a second time, I don't think he can have the impudence to ask to go at large again without giving better bail than on the former occasion. Some of the scouts came in, and bring reports that Santa Anna has been endeavouring to excite the Indians to hostilities against the Texians, but so far without effect. The Cumanches, in particular, entertain such hatred for the Mexicans, and at the same time hold them in such contempt, that they would rather turn their tomahawks against them, and drive them from the land, than lend a helping hand. We are up and doing, and as lively as Dutch cheese in the dog-days. The two hunters that I have already introduced to the reader left the town, this afternoon, for the purpose of reconnoitring.

February 23. Early this morning the enemy came in sight, marching in regular order, and displaying their strength to the greatest advantage, in order to strike us with terror. But that was no go; they'll find that they have to do with men who will never lay down their arms as long as they can stand on their legs. We held a short council of war, and, finding that we should be completely surrounded, and overwhelmed by numbers, if we remained in the town, we concluded to withdraw to the fortress of Alamo, and defend it to the last extremity. We accordingly filed off, in good order, having some days before placed all the surplus provisions, arms, and ammunition in the fortress. We have had a large national flag[5] made; it is composed of thirteen stripes, red and white, alternately, on a blue ground with a large white star, of five points, in the centre, and between the points the letters TEXAS. As soon as all our little band, about one hundred and fifty in number, had entered and secured the fortress in the best possible manner, we set about raising our flag on the battlements; on which occasion there was no one more active than my young friend, the Bee hunter. He had been all along sprightly, cheerful, and spirited, but now, notwithstanding the control that he usually maintained over himself, it was with difficulty that he kept his enthusiasm within bounds. As soon as we commenced raising the flag he burst forth, in a clear, full tone of voice, that made the blood tingle in the veins of all who heard him:—

"Up with your banner, Freedom,
Thy champions cling to thee;
They'll follow where'er you lead 'em,
To death, or victory;—
Up with your banner, Freedom.

Tyrants and slaves are rushing
To tread thee in the dust;
Their blood will soon be gushing,
And stain our knives with rust;—
But not thy banner, Freedom.

While stars and stripes are flying,
Our blood we'll freely shed;
No groan will 'scape the dying,
Seeing thee o'er his head:—
Up with your banner, Freedom."

This song was followed by three cheers from all within the fortress, and the drums and trumpets commenced playing. The enemy marched into Bexar, and took possession of the town, a blood-red flag flying at their head, to indicate that we need not expect quarters if we should fall into their clutches. In the afternoon a messenger was sent from the enemy to Colonel Travis, demanding an unconditional and absolute surrender of the garrison, threatening to put every man to the sword in case of refusal. The only answer he received was a cannon shot, so the messenger left us with a flea in his ear, and the Mexicans commenced firing grenades at us, but without doing any mischief. At night Colonel Travis sent an express to Colonel Fanning,[6] at Goliad, about three or four days' march from this place, to let him know that we are besieged. The old pirate volunteered to go on this expedition, and accordingly left the fort after night fall.

February 24. Very early this morning the enemy commenced a new battery on the banks of the river, about three hundred and fifty yards from the fort, and by afternoon they amused themselves by firing at us from that quarter. Our Indian scout came in this evening, and with him a reinforcement of thirty men from Gonzales, who are just in the nick of time to reap a harvest of glory; but there is some prospect of sweating blood before we gather it in. An accident happened to my friend Thimblerig this afternoon. He was intent on his eternal game of thimbles, in a somewhat exposed position, while the enemy were bombarding us from the new redoubt. A three ounce ball glanced from the parapet and struck him on the breast, inflicting a painful but not dangerous wound. I extracted the ball, which was of lead, and recommended to him to drill a hole through it, and carry it for a watch seal. "No," he replied, with energy, "may I be shot six times if I do; that would be making a bauble for an idle boast. No, Colonel, lead is getting scarce, and I'll lend it out at compound interest.—Curse the thimbles!" he muttered, and went his way, and I saw no more of him that evening.

February 25. The firing commenced early this morning, but the Mexicans are poor engineers, for we haven't lost a single man, and our outworks have sustained no injury. Our sharp shooters have brought down a considerable number of stragglers at a long shot. I got up before the peep of day, hearing an occasional discharge of a rifle just over the place where I was sleeping, and I was somewhat amazed to see Thimblerig mounted alone on the battlement, no one being on duty at the time but the sentries. "What are you doing there?" says I. "Paying my debts," says he, "interest and all." "And how do you make out?" says I. "I've nearly got through," says he; "stop a moment, Colonel, and I'll close the account." He clapped his rifle to his shoulder, and blazed away, then jumped down from his perch, and said, "That account's settled; them chaps will let me play out my game in quiet next time." I looked over the wall, and saw four Mexicans lying dead on the plain. I asked him to explain what he meant by paying his debts, and he told me that he had run the grape shot into four rifle balls, and that he had taken an early stand to have a chance of picking off stragglers. "Now, Colonel, let's go take our bitters," said he; and so we did. The enemy have been busy during the night, and have thrown up two batteries on the opposite side of the river. The battalion of Matamoros is posted there, and cavalry occupy the hills to the east and on the road to Gonzales. They are determined to surround us, and cut us off from reinforcement, or the possibility of escape by a sortie.—Well, there's one thing they cannot prevent: we'll still go ahead, and sell our lives at a high price.

February 26. Colonel Bowie has been taken sick from over exertion and exposure. He did not leave his bed to-day until twelve o'clock. He is worth a dozen common men in a situation like ours. The Bee hunter keeps the whole garrison in good heart with his songs and his jests, and his daring and determined spirit. He is about the quickest on the trigger, and the best rifle shot we have in the fort. I have already seen him bring down eleven of the enemy, and at such a distance that we all thought it would be waste of ammunition to attempt it. His gun is first-rate, quite equal to my Betsey, though she has not quite as many trinkets about her. This day a small party sallied out of the fort for wood and water, and had a slight skirmish with three times their number from the division under General Sesma. The Bee hunter headed them, and beat the enemy off, after killing three. On opening his Bible at night, of which he always reads a portion before going to rest, he found a musket ball in the middle of it. "See here, Colonel," said he, "how they have treated the valued present of my dear little Kate of Nacogdoches." "It has saved your life," said I. "True," replied he, more seriously than usual, "and I am not the first sinner whose life has been saved by this book." He prepared for bed, and before retiring he prayed, and returned thanks for his providential escape; and I heard the name of Catherine mingled in his prayer.

February 27. The cannonading began early this morning, and ten bombs were thrown into the fort, but fortunately exploded without doing any mischief. So far it has been a sort of tempest in a teapot; not unlike a pitched battle in the Hall of Congress, where the parties array their forces, make fearful demonstrations on both sides, then fire away with loud sounding speeches, which contain about as much meaning as the report of a howitzer charged with a blank cartridge. Provisions are becoming scarce, and the enemy are endeavouring to cut off our water. If they attempt to stop our grog in that manner, let them look out, for we shall become too wrathy for our shirts to hold us. We are not prepared to submit to an excise of that nature, and they'll find it out. This discovery has created considerable excitement in the fort.

February 28. Last night our hunters brought in some corn and hogs, and had a brush with a scout from the enemy beyond gun-shot of the fort. They put the scout to flight, and got in without injury. They bring accounts that the settlers are flying in all quarters, in dismay, leaving their possessions to the mercy of the ruthless invader, who is literally engaged in a war of extermination, more brutal than the untutored savage of the desert could be guilty of. Slaughter is indiscriminate, sparing neither sex, age, nor condition. Buildings have been burnt down, farms laid waste, and Santa Anna appears determined to verify his threat, and convert the blooming paradise into a howling wilderness. For just one fair crack at that rascal, even at a hundred yards distance, I would bargain to break my Betsey, and never pull trigger again. My name's not Crockett if I wouldn't get glory enough to appease my stomach for the remainder of my life. The scouts report that a settler, by the name of Johnson, flying with his wife and three little children, when they reached the Colorado, left his family on the shore, and waded into the river to see whether it would be safe to ford with his wagon. When about the middle of the river he was seized by an alligator, and, after a struggle, was dragged under the water, and perished. The helpless woman and her babes were discovered, gazing in agony on the spot, by other fugitives who happily passed that way, and relieved them. Those who fight the battles experience but a small part of the privation, suffering, and anguish that follow in the train of ruthless war. The cannonading continued, at intervals, throughout the day, and all hands were kept up to their work. The enemy, somewhat imboldened, draws nigher to the fort. So much the better.—There was a move in General Sesma's division toward evening.

February 29. Before daybreak we saw General Sesma leave his camp with a large body of cavalry and infantry, and move off in the direction of Goliad. We think that he must have received news of Colonel Fanning's coming to our relief. We are all in high spirits at the prospect of being able to give the rascals a fair shake on the plain. This business of being shut up makes a man wolfish.—I had a little sport this morning before breakfast. The enemy had planted a piece of ordinance within gun-shot of the fort during the night, and the first thing in the morning they commenced a brisk cannonade, point-blank, against the spot where I was snoring. I turned out pretty smart, and mounted the rampart. The gun was charged again, a fellow stepped forth to touch her off, but before he could apply the match I let him have it, and he keeled over. A second stepped up, snatched the match from the hand of the dying man, but Thimblerig, who had followed me, handed me his rifle, and the next instant the Mexican was stretched on the earth beside the first. A third came up to the cannon, my companion handed me another gun, and I fixed him off in like manner. A fourth, then a fifth, seized the match, who both met with the same fate, and then the whole party gave it up as a bad job, and hurried off to the camp, leaving the cannon ready charged where they had planted it. I came down, took my bitters, and went to breakfast. Thimblerig told me that the place from which I had been firing was one of the snuggest stands in the whole fort, for he never failed picking off two or three stragglers before breakfast, when perched up there. And I recollect, now, having seen him there, ever since he was wounded, the first thing in the morning, and the last at night,—and at times thoughtlessly playing at his eternal game.

March 1. The enemy's forces have been increasing in numbers daily, notwithstanding they have already lost about three hundred men in the several assaults they have made upon us. I neglected to mention in the proper place, that when the enemy came in sight we had but three bushels of corn in the garrison, but have since found eighty bushels in a deserted house. Colonel Bowie's illness still continues, but he manages to crawl from his bed every day, that his comrades may see him. His presence alone is a tower of strength.—The enemy becomes more daring as his numbers increase.

March 2. This day the delegates meet in general convention, at the town of Washington, to frame our Declaration of Independence. That the sacred instrument may never be trampled on by the children of those who have freely shed their blood to establish it, is the sincere wish of David Crockett. Universal independence is an almighty idea, far too extensive for some brains to comprehend. It is a beautiful seed that germinates rapidly, and brings forth a large and vigorous tree, but like the deadly Upas,[7] we sometimes find the smaller plants wither and die in its shades. Its blooming branches spread far and wide, offering a perch of safety to all alike, but even among its protecting branches we find the eagle, the kite, and the owl preying upon the helpless dove and sparrow. Beneath its shade myriads congregate in goodly fellowship, but the lamb and the fawn find but frail security from the lion and the jackal, though the tree of independence waves over them. Some imagine independence to be a natural charter, to exercise without restraint, and to their fullest extent, all the energies, both physical and mental, with which they have been endowed; and for their individual aggrandizement alone, without regard to the rights of others, provided they extend to all the same privilege and freedom of action. Such independence is the worst of tyranny.

March 3. We have given over all hopes of receiving assistance from Goliad or Refugio. Colonel Travis harangued the garrison, and concluded by exhorting them, in case the enemy should carry the fort, to fight to the last gasp, and render their victory even more serious to them than to us. This was followed by three cheers.

March 4. Shells have been falling into the fort like hail during the day, but without effect. About dusk, in the evening, we observed a man running toward the fort, pursued by about a dozen Mexican cavalry. The Bee hunter immediately knew him to be the old pirate who had gone to Goliad, and, calling to the two hunters, he sallied out of the fort to the relief of the old man, who was hard pressed. I followed close after. Before we reached the spot the Mexicans were close on the heel of the old man, who stopped suddenly, turned short upon his pursuers, discharged his rifle, and one of the enemy fell from his horse.

The chase was renewed, but finding that he would be over-taken and cut to pieces, he now turned again, and, to the amazement of the enemy, became the assailant in his turn. He clubbed his gun, and dashed among them like a wounded tiger, and they fled like sparrows. By this time we reached the spot, and, in the ardour of the moment, followed some distance be-fore we saw that our retreat to the fort was cut off by another detachment of cavalry. Nothing was to be done but to fight our way through. We were all of the same mind. "Go ahead!" cried I, and they shouted, "Go ahead, Colonel!" We dashed among them, and a bloody conflict ensued. They were about twenty in number, and they stood their ground. After the fight had con-tinued about five minutes, a detachment was seen issuing from the fort to our relief, and the Mexicans scampered off, leaving eight of their comrades dead upon the field. But we did not es-cape unscathed, for both the pirate and the Bee hunter were mortally wounded, and I received a sabre cut across the fore-head. The old man died, without speaking, as soon as we en-tered the fort. We bore my young friend to his bed, dressed his wounds, and I watched beside him. He lay, without complaint or manifesting pain, until about midnight, when he spoke, and I asked him if he wanted any thing. "Nothing," he replied, but drew a sigh that seemed to rend his heart, as he added, "Poor Kate of Nacogdoches!" His eyes were filled with tears, as he continued, "Her words were prophetic, Colonel;" and then he sang, in a low voice that resembled the sweet notes of his own devoted Kate,

> *"But toom cam' the saddle, all bluidy to see,*
> *And hame cam' the steed, but hame never cam' he."*

He spoke no more, and, a few minutes after, died. Poor Kate, who will tell this to thee!

March 5. Pop, pop, pop! Bom, bom, bom! throughout the day.—No time for memorandums now.—Go ahead!—Liberty and independence for ever!

[*Here ends Col. Crockett's manuscript.*]

CHAPTER XIV.

The hand is cold that wrote the foregoing pages, and it devolves upon another to record the subsequent events. Before daybreak, on the 6th of March, the Alamo was assaulted by the whole force of the Mexican army, commanded by Santa Anna in person. The battle was desperate until daylight, when only six men belonging to the Texian garrison were found alive. They were instantly surrounded, and ordered, by General Castrillon, to surrender, which they did, under a promise of his protection, finding that resistance any longer would be madness. Colonel Crockett was of the number. He stood alone in an angle of the fort, the barrel of his shattered rifle in his right hand, in his left his huge Bowie knife dripping blood. There was a frightful gash across his forehead, while around him there was a complete barrier of about twenty Mexicans, lying pell-mell, dead, and dying. At his feet lay the dead body of that well known character, designated in the Colonel's narrative by the assumed name of Thimblerig, his knife driven to the haft in the throat of a Mexican, and his left hand clenched in his hair. Poor fellow, I knew him well, at a time when he was possessed of many virtues, but of late years the weeds had choked up the flowers; however, Colonel Crockett had succeeded in awakening in his bosom a sense of better things, and the poor fellow was grateful to the last, and stood beside his friend throughout the desperate havoc.

General Castrillon was brave and not cruel, and disposed to save the prisoners. He marched them up to that part of the fort where stood Santa Anna and his murderous crew. The steady, fearless step, and undaunted tread of Colonel Crockett on this occasion, together with the bold demeanour of the hardy veteran, had a powerful effect on all present. Nothing daunted, he marched up boldly in front of Santa Anna, and looked him sternly in the face, while Castrillon addressed "his excellency,"—"Sir, here are six prisoners I have taken alive; how shall I dispose of them?" Santa Anna looked at Castrillon fiercely, flew into a violent rage, and replied, "Have I not told you before how to dispose of them? Why do you bring them to me?" At the same time his brave officers plunged their swords into the bosoms of their defenceless prisoners. Colonel Crockett, seeing the set of treachery, instantly sprang like a tiger at the ruffian chief, but before he could reach him a dozen swords were sheathed in his indomitable heart; and he fell, and died without a groan, a frown on his brow, and a smile of scorn and defiance on his lips. Castrillon rushed from the scene, apparently horror-struck, sought his quarters, and did not leave them for several days, and hardly spoke to Santa Anna after.

The conduct of Colonel Bowie was characteristic to the last. When the fort was carried he was sick in bed. He had also one of the murderous butcher knives which bears his name. Lying in bed he discharged his pistols and gun, and with each discharge brought down an enemy. So intimidated were the Mexicans by this act of desperate and cool bravery, that they dared not approach him, but shot him from the door; and as the cowards approached his bed, over the dead bodies of their companions, the dying Bowie, nerving himself for a last blow, plunged his knife into the heart of his nearest foe at the same instant that he expired.

The gallant Colonel Travis fought as if determined to verify his prediction, that he would make a victory more serious than a defeat to the enemy. He fell from the rampart, mortally wounded, into the fort; and his musket fell forward among the foe, who were scaling the wall. After a few minutes he recovered sufficiently to sit up, when the Mexican officer who led that party attempted to cut his head off with his sabre. The dying hero, with a death grasp, drew his sword and plunged it into the body of his antagonist, and both together sank into the arms of death. General Cos, who had commanded this fortress while in the possession of the Mexicans, and from whom it was captured, on entering the fort after the battle, ordered the servant of Colonel Travis to point out the body of his master; he did so, when Cos drew his sword, waved it triumphantly over the corpse, and then mangled the face and limbs with the malignant feelings of a Cumanche savage. One woman, Mrs. Dickinson, and a negro of Col. Travis, were the only persons whose lives were spared. The bodies of the slain were then thrown into a mass in the centre of the Alamo, and burned. The loss of the Mexicans in storming the place was not less than eight hundred killed and mortally wounded, making their losses since the first assault more than fifteen hundred. This immense slaughter, by so small a number, can only be accounted for by the fact of the Texians having five or six guns to each man in the fort. Immediately after the capture Santa Anna sent Mrs. Dickinson and the servant to General Houston,[1] accompanied by a Mexican with a flag, offering the Texians peace and general amnesty, if they would lay down their arms, and submit to his government. General Houston's reply was, "True, sir, you have succeeded in killing some of our brave men, but the Texians are not yet conquered." He sent him a copy of the Declaration of Independence recently agreed on at New Washington.

After the capture of San Antonio, Santa Anna had made a feint on Gonzales, where General Houston was with a very inferior force, which induced the latter to fall back on the Colorado, under the belief that the whole Mexican army was marching to attack him. A similar feint was also made by the Mexican General on Bastrop, a town on the Colorado, northeast of San Antonio. Gonzales lies east of that place. Having, in both instances, effected his object, Santa Anna concentrated his forces, and marched directly for La Bahia, or Goliad, which is situated about ninety miles south-east of San Antonio, on the Colorado. The fort at Goliad is of great strength, and was defended by Colonel Fanning with a small force of volunteers. About the middle of March, orders were received from General Houston directing the blowing up and evacuation of the fort, and that Colonel Fanning should concentrate with him on the

Colorado. On the 18th of March the Mexicans were discovered, in considerable force, in the neighbourhood of Goliad, and through the day there was some skirmishing with the advance parties. On the 19th the fort was set on fire, and its wooden defences destroyed; but the wall was left entire, and Colonel Fanning took up his line of march. His force, at that time, was reduced to two hundred and sixty, rank and file. With this force and several field pieces he set out to cross an open country, and endeavour to effect a junction with General Houston. On the evening of the first day of their march, the enemy made their appearance in the rear, about three miles distant. Colonel Fanning halted, and opened his artillery on them, instead of hastening forward to avail himself of the shelter of a wood, some distance ahead. The enemy manifesting a disposition to cut him off from the woods, he again put his forces in motion, but it was now too late. He not only lost the shelter of the timber, which would have ensured his safety against the enemy's horse, but the assistance of his advanced guard, which was cut off from him by this manœuvre of the enemy. The absence of the advanced guard reduced his forces to two hundred and thirty-three, rank and file, to which the enemy opposed five hundred cavalry and two hundred infantry. The action commenced about five o'clock, and continued until nearly dark. The enemy was repulsed with great loss in every charge, and never was able to penetrate nearer to Fanning's force than sixty-five or one hundred yards; and finally, about dark, drew off his forces to a secure distance, leaving only a few to succour the wounded, who were not molested. Fanning's loss was five killed and twelve wounded, two mortally. The enemy acknowledged the loss of one hundred and ninety-two killed, and a large number wounded. So soon as the Mexicans withdrew, Fanning commenced throwing up intrenchments, at which his men were employed during the whole night.

About sunrise on the 20th, the enemy again advanced on Fanning, and fired their cannon four times over him; a large reinforcement of Mexicans was plainly to be seen, three miles distant. At this moment a white flag, attended by a small party, was seen advancing from the enemy, which was met by a similar one from Fanning, under Major Wallace. The enemy demanded the surrender of Fanning and his forces, and promised, in the most sacred manner, that they should retain all their private property: that they might return, by the first opportunity, as prisoners of war, to the United States, or remain until they were regularly exchanged; and that they should be treated in the most humane manner while retained in confinement. With these specious promises he was induced to trust to the honour of the butchers of the Alamo, and accept of the terms of capitulation.

As soon as the necessary arrangements could be made the prisoners were marched, under a strong guard, to Goliad, and huddled together, officers and men, into a church within the fort at Goliad. The enemy having succeeded in capturing other small parties, the number of prisoners amounted to four hundred, and were all crowded together in the church, and compelled to sit or lie constantly. The only accommodation afforded was a few benches for the officers. They were retained in this situation for three days, and during this period received only a small ration of raw beef, not exceeding half a pound each. On the fourth day they were marched out into the open air, and limits prescribed them, over which they were not to pass. For four days longer they were kept in this situation, during which they were allowed only two rations similar to the first; and, but for the pecan nuts purchased from the Mexican soldiers, and a small quantity of jerked beef procured in the same manner, they must have suffered immensely. On the eighth day representations were made to the prisoners, that it would be necessary to remove them out of the fort, as they were about to drive in beeves to slaughter, in order to prepare rations for their removal to Matagorda, where they were to take shipping for New Orleans. They were accordingly marched out, in parties of one hundred each, and, in single file, were led along a high brush fence; when, at the distance of two hundred yards, they were ordered to face about, and the cocking of the guns gave the first intimation of the fate that awaited them. At the first fire nearly all fell mortally wounded. A few escaped by falling at the flash, and as soon as the firing ceased, they leaped up, and sprung over the fence, and succeeded in reaching the woods, where they eluded their pursuers. The Mexicans proceeded to despatch with their bayonets any who showed signs of life after the firing, and they then stripped and burnt the bodies. The authorities of Texas bestowed solemn obsequies upon their mutilated and blackened limbs, on the 4th of June, after their murderers had sank unto death on the plains of San Jacinto, under the appalling words, "Remember La Bahia!"

But this succession of barbarities, so far from intimidating, served to rouse the energies of the oppressed. The vainglorious Spaniard, elated with his success, without adverting to the fact that he had never been victorious without having at least from five to ten of his mercenaries opposed to one of his foes, now ventured to cross the Colorado, believing that victory was perched upon his standard, and would not leave it until Texas should be subdued.

His track was marked by death and desolation. Fire, famine, and the sword were in his train, and neither sex nor age was received as a plea for mercy. The hoary head of the grandsire, the flaxen curls of the babe, and the dishevelled tresses of the affrighted mother, were alike stained with gore. Farm houses were consumed by fire, the crops destroyed in the ground; and the settlers fled in dismay, feeling that the worst of scourges had been let loose upon them. The plains were strewed with thousands of the unburied slaughtered; and the air was fetid with corruption and decay. The merciless tyrant saw all this, and his heart expanded with joy, as he moved on, like Attila, and beheld the terror and wretchedness of those he came to annihilate, rather than to scourge into subjection. But his was a temporary triumph. He crossed the Colorado full of hope of carrying his demoniac intentions into execution, but shame, confusion, and defeat awaited his coming.

About the 18th of April the tyrant, with one division of his troops, marched in the direction of Lynch's ferry, on the San Jacinto, burning Harrisburgh as he passed down. The Texian forces under General Houston were ordered to be in readiness, and on the morning of the 19th they took up their line of march in pursuit of him, and found him encamped on the banks of the San Jacinto. About nine o'clock on the morning of the 21st the Mexicans were reinforced by five hundred choice troops, under command of General Cos, increasing their effective force to upward of fifteen hundred men, while the aggregate force of the Texians, for the field, numbered seven hundred and eighty-three. General Houston ordered the bridge on the only road communicating with the Brazos, distant from the encampment, to be destroyed, thus cutting off all possibility of escape. The Texian army was ordered to parade their respective commands, which they did with alacrity and spirit, and were anxious for the conflict; the disparity in numbers only seemed to increase their enthusiasm and confidence. Houston, having the enemy thus snugly hemmed in, and his little army drawn up in order of battle, addressed them, in person, briefly, and concluded by saying, "Fellow soldiers, there is the enemy before you; do you wish to fight?" "We do!" was the universal response. "Well, then," he continued, "remember it is for liberty, or death!—Remember the Alamo! Remember Goliad!" The soldiers shouted, "We shall remember!"—"Then go ahead!" From General Houston's official account it appears that the war-cry was, "Remember the Alamo." The attack was furious, and lasted about eighteen minutes from the time of close action until the Texians were in possession of the enemy's camp. Our riflemen, not having the advantage of bayonets, used their pieces as clubs, breaking many of them at the breach. The rout commenced at half-past four o'clock, and continued until twilight. In the battle our loss was two killed and twenty-three wounded, six of whom mortally. The enemy's loss was six hundred and thirty killed, and seven hundred and thirty were taken prisoners, among whom were Generals Santa Anna and Cos, who were captured a day or two after the battle. About six hundred muskets and three hundred sabres were collected: several hundred mules and horses were taken, and near twelve hundred dollars in specie.

We learn, from other sources, that General Cos, when taken, was pale and greatly agitated; but Almonte displayed, as he had during the fight, great coolness and courage. Santa Anna fled among the earliest who retreated. His horse bogged down in the prairie, near the Brazos timber; he then made for the timber on foot. His pursuers, in the eagerness of the chase, dashed into the same bog, and continued the pursuit on foot, following the trail of the fugitive, which was very plain on account of the recent rains, until they reached the timber, where it was lost. The pursuers then spread themselves, and searched the woods for a long time in vain, when it occurred to Arnold Hunter that the chase might, like a hard pressed bear, have taken a tree. The tree tops were then examined, when, lo! the game was discovered snugly ensconced in the forks of a large live oak. The captors did not know who the prisoner was until they reached the camp, when the Mexican soldiers exclaimed, "El General, El General Santa Anna!" When conducted to General Houston he offered to evacuate Texas, and acknowledge its independence, on condition that his life and liberty should be granted to him, and a safe escort to Mexico.

The enemy passed La Bahia and Bexar, blowing up the Alamo; spiking, and throwing the cannon in the river, in his retreat. The Cumanche Indians commenced depredating in the rear of the Mexican army, as they advanced from Bexar upon the settlements. All their horses and mules, of which they had many, as well as much baggage, were taken by the Indians. At every step they met with trouble, and are hurrying with all possible despatch toward the interior.

The fate of poor Fanning, who was not killed in the indiscriminate massacre of his troops, has since been ascertained. He was condemned to be shot. When he found that was determined on, and was ordered out for execution, he handed his watch to an officer, as compensation to have him buried, deliberately tied a handkerchief over his eyes, begged them not to shoot him in the head, bared his breast, and requested to be shot there. He was shot in the head, and never buried!

Such are the monsters that freemen have had to contend with, to maintain their freedom; true, the struggle is not yet over, but nothing can impede the onward march, and Texas must take her stand among independent nations.

THE END

APPENDIX

DEATH OF COL. CROCKETT

The following account of Crockett's death at the Alamo was published in *Davy Crockett's Almanack for 1837*, the cover of which was decorated with a woodcut depicting Crockett in the likeness of James H. Hackett as Nimrod Wildfire in James Kirke Paulding's play, *The Lion of the West*, wearing fringed and fur-lined buckskins, a hat made from a wildcat skin, and carrying a Kentucky rifle. The cover also contains Crockett's famous slogan, "Go Ahead!," and the words "O Kentucky: The Hunters of Kentucky!!!" from Samuel Woodworth's popular song celebrating Jackson's victory over the British in New Orleans. Supposedly printed in Nashville, Tennessee, at a time when no publishers were located in that frontier town, these decorative matters illustrate the cultural mix out of which the mythic Davy Crockett emerged. They were the work not of the western "folk" to which they were credited by Constance Rourke, Walter Blair, Franklin J. Meine, and Richard M. Dorson, but were the creation of eastern writers and artists.

It should be noted that what follows avoids the slangy, "vernacular" manner we associate with the Crockett almanacs, used for humorous purposes and not inevitable in the earliest examples of the publication. Clearly, the martyrdom of Crockett was considered a serious matter and therefore deserved a formal style. As indicated in the Introduction, the account of Crockett's death published in the almanac was the one that endured, though Smith's version has lately had scholarly validation.

BATTLE OF SAN ANTONIO DE BEXAR, HEROISM AND DEATH OF COL. CROCKETT

The ancient town of Bexar, the spot where the last scene in the life of Col. Crockett was acted, is situated on the San Antonio river, which flows through it. This place is in latitude 29° 25,' 140 miles from the coast. A military outpost was established at this spot by the Spanish government in 1718. This fort is separated from the town, which is chiefly inhabited by native Mexicans. Col. Travis with a small but heroic band occupied the forts. They were chiefly volunteers from the United States; among them were Col. Bowie, Col. Crockett, Mr. Benton, and many other brave officers. On the 23 Feb. 1836, the advance guard of the Mexican army entered the town, commanded by Gen. Santa Anna. They could not be prevented, as the Texans were only 150 strong. Santa Anna instantly sent a summons to the fort commanding them to surrender at discretion, calling them foreign rebels. This insolent message was answered by a cannon shot, when the Mexicans commenced a bombardment, from a five inch howitzer, which together with a heavy cannonade, was kept up incessantly. Expresses were instantly sent to Col. Fanning of Goliad and to the people of Gonzales and San Phillipe, for men. The next day some two or three hundred men crossed the river below the fort and under cover of the houses came up until within point blank shot, when the Texans opened a heavy fire of grape and cannister on them, together with small arms, which made them halt and take shelter in the houses, about one hundred yards distance from the fort. The action continued to rage about two hours, the enemy keeping up a continual bombardment. The loss of the besiegers was very great, while not a man in the fort was killed, though two or three were wounded by splinters of rock. Lieutenant Simmons of cavalry, and Capt. Carey and Dickerson of artillery, rendered great service; and Col. Crockett was seen at all points, and in the most exposed places, encouraging the men to do their duty. A sortie was made from the fort, led by Col. Crockett, in which he was attacked single handed by six Mexicans.

One he shot with his rifle and two with pistols, and with one blow of his sword severed the head from a fourth. He received a musket ball in his thigh, but was luckily supported by his friend Benton, who shot one of them and the other took to his heels. The wound was only a flesh one, and although it bled profusely, the surgeon staunched it. The Mexicans kept up a vigorous siege for several days, in which their loss was tremendous, the riflemen always killing their man at each discharge; generally putting a ball through the head. At length after withstanding repeated attacks for two weeks, with a continual bombardment, the last assault was made on the morning of the 6th of March, by the whole Mexican army, led by Santa Anna in person, consisting of 3000 men, and the place after a most bloody defence was carried about sunrise, after seven hours hard fighting. The whole garrison were put to death, except a woman and the negro servant of Col. Travis, and the wounded, together with seven men who asked for quarter. The rest all fought like bloodhounds; and Col. Crockett's body was found in an angle of two buildings with his big dagger in his hand, and around him were lying seventeen dead Mexicans, eleven of whom had come by their deaths by his dagger, and the others by his rifle and four pistols, which laid beside him. In the dark he had a decided advantage over them, as they could not get behind him, and he stabbed them as they passed by in the charge. He had received two musket balls in his body, both of which were mortal. A smile of scorn played on his features. Col. Bowie was murdered in his bed, and Col. Travis shot himself to prevent falling into the enemy's hands. Lieut. Dickerson tied his child to his back and jumped off a house, and thus killed himself. In the siege of Bexar the Mexicans lost 3000 men. This great slaughter is ascribed to the fact of each man in the fort having eight guns. The flag used by the Mexicans was a blood red one, instead of the old tri-colored one. The bodies of the slain were taken and thrown in a heap in the centre of the fort and burnt. When the body of Crockett was brought along, the Mexican general Cos said, So brave a man ought not to be burnt like a dog; but after a little hesitation he said, Never mind, throw him on. Thus perished Crockett, in a noble cause.

Fear was a word he knew not the definition of. It was calculated that during the siege he killed no less than 85 men, and wounded 120 besides, as he was one of the best rifle shooters of the west, and he had four rifles, with two men to load constantly, and he fired as fast as they could load, nearly always hitting his man; but the distance was so great that he could not put the ball through a mortal place every time.

Explanatory Notes

1. *Printed by T. K. & P. G. Collins.* The publishers were in reality Carey and Hart of Philadelphia. The four lines of poetry on the title page, credited to "The Author" (i.e., Richard Penn Smith masquerading as Crockett), are printed here as found in the first edition, including the mysterious phrase, "shoulder *flook,*" which has no obvious meaning. However, "Cut stick" may be found in Eric Partridge's *Dictionary of the Underworld* (1961 edition) as a slang term for "depart," so perhaps Smith's obscure language has some recondite meaning. The editorial staff at Penguin Group (USA) would welcome enlightenment on this matter.

2. *the Bee hunter.* This sentimental creation was undoubtedly adapted from Paul Hover, a bee-hunter who figures importantly in Fenimore Cooper's *The Prairie* (1827), the third published of the *Leatherstocking Tales.*

3. *Austin.* Stephen F. Austin (1793–1836) was the son of Moses Austin (1761–1821) and the heir to a grant of 66,000 acres of land in Texas, then under Mexican control. Attempting to fulfill the proviso that the land be colonized by three hundred families, in 1822 Austin set up a trading center that became the town bearing his name. He was in effect the ruler and chief *empresario* (colonial leader) of Texas, which greatly prospered under his leadership. Although opposed to the idea of Texas independence, in 1833 he traveled to Mexico City to negotiate the separation of Texas from the state of Coahuila, which was regarded by the Mexican government as a veiled attempt to annex Texas to the United States. Austin was jailed without trial until his release in 1835, when he returned to Texas and joined the revolution against Mexico. In 1836 he was defeated in the presidential election held in the now-independent republic of Texas by Sam Hous-

ton, but having successfully obtained U.S. support for Texan independence, he served as the president's secretary of state until his death.

4. *General Castrillon.* D. Manuel Fernandez Castrillon was in command of one of four "columns" under the command of General Santa Anna organized to attack the Alamo. In one version of Crockett's death (included in Smith's narrative) he is credited with having asked Santa Anna that the brave American not be executed. Castrillon was later killed in the decisive battle of San Jacinto. The story of the twice-recovered diary is of course a fiction.

5. *Charles T. Beale / Alex J. Dumas.* These are fictitious names, part of Smith's complex hoax. As an author familiar with French drama, Smith undoubtedly knew of Alexandre Dumas (*père*), well known in France by 1836 as a writer of melodramatic historical plays, and by 1844 famous in America as the author of *The Three Musketeers* and *The Count of Monte Cristo.* But knowing that Dumas's name would mean nothing to his probable audience, Smith was having a little joke, suggesting the sophistication and subtlety of the hoaxer.

CHAPTER I.

1. *go ahead.* The first allusion in Smith's narrative to Crockett's famous motto, "Be sure you are right, then go ahead," but by no means the last.

2. *Major Jack Downing.* Satiric persona invented by the Maine newspaper publisher Seba Smith (1792–1868) and later taken over by the anti-Jacksonian journalist Charles A. Davis. (See Introduction.)

3. *Post Office . . . public lands.* Policy matters on which Crockett differed with the Jackson administration. (See Introduction.)

4. *Little Flying Dutchman.* Derogatory reference to the ancestry, physical stature, and character of Martin Van Buren (1782–1862), a powerful Democratic politician. Former senator from New York and governor of that state, he was Jackson's secretary of state before becoming, in 1833, his vice president. Elected president in 1836 (after Crockett's death), defeated in the election of 1840 by the Whig candidate, William Henry Harrison, his antislavery sentiments eventually led to Van Buren's departure from the Democratic party.

5. *"the greatest and the best."* Sarcastic reference to President Andrew Jackson.

6. *"the Government."* Epithet frequently used by Crockett for President Jackson, a reference to his absolute power, evinced by his removal of government funds ("deposites") from Biddle's National Bank. (See Introduction.)

7. *Adam Huntsman.* Tennessee lawyer and democratic politician, who under the pen name "Black Hawk" published a satiric, pseudo-biblical "Chronicles" in 1833 that impugned Crockett's motives regarding the Land Bill. He defeated Crockett in the congressional election of 1835. (See Shackford, 139–40.)

8. *the Hero.* Andrew Jackson, also called "the monster" below.

9. *Sam Patch.* Native of Pawtucket, R.I. (c. 1807–1827), who gained notoriety by leaping into rivers from great heights until his death from same. (See Introduction.)

10. *Job Snelling.* The cunning Yankee was by 1836 becoming a comic stereotype, thanks in part to sketches like this, inspired by similar anecdotes in Matthew St. Clair Clarke's *Life and Adventures of Colonel David Crockett of West Tennessee* (1833).

CHAPTER II.

1. *governor Carroll.* William Carroll (1788–1844), Democratic politician and hero of the War of 1812, was governor of Tennessee, 1821–1827 and 1829–1835, and a prominent supporter of Andrew Jackson. The substance of the pages that follow was taken, often verbatim, from a letter from Crockett to Carey and Hart written after his defeat in the election of 1835. (See Shackford, 205–06.)

2. *Governor Poindexter.* George Poindexter (1779–1835) was a prominent Mississippi Democratic politician who was briefly governor of his state (1820–1821), hence his title here, but was more importantly a U.S. senator from 1830 to 1835, and like Crockett a frequent critic of President Jackson.

3. *Globe.* The Washington *Daily Globe* was edited by Francis P. Blair (1791–1876) from 1830–1845, and was a stalwart Democratic organ, founded by President Jackson. Blair originated the phrase "the democracy" in reference to Jackson's administration. (Cf. Crockett's "the Government.")

4. *Fitzgerald.* William Fitzgerald defeated Crockett in the congressional election of 1831.

5. *Grundy.* Felix Grundy (1777–1840) was a distinguished lawyer and Democratic politician from Tennessee. Serving in the U.S.

Congress from 1811 to 1815, he was by 1836 a U.S. senator who was often at odds with President Jackson but a party loyalist nonetheless. Still, he was hardly "the General's pet."

6. *show them the White feather.* The presence of a white feather in the tail of a fighting cock (cf. "game cock" above) was taken as a sign of inferior breeding and therefore indicated a lack of courage.

7. *"occupation's gone."* Othello, III, 3, line 357.

8. *Webster, Clay, and myself.* Smith here is placing Crockett in distinguished company. Daniel Webster (1782–1852) and Henry Clay (1777–1852) were the most powerful Whigs of their day. They were frequently thought of (by themselves as well as others) as potential presidential candidates, and Clay was nominated by the anti-Jackson party as its candidate in 1831, but was badly beaten in the election of 1832. He thenceforth became a ferocious senatorial adversary of Jackson's policies, mounting attacks tantamount to harassment and taking positions pretty much echoed by Colonel Crockett.

9. *Flemish account.* One showing a deficit.

10. *M'Adamized road.* A pavement made up of crushed stone rolled over with great pressure, hence smooth, the invention of J. L. McAdam (1756–1836). Perhaps also a punning reference to Crockett's opponent in the election of 1835, Adam Huntsman.

11. *Peleg Longfellow.* The reference would seem to be to Henry Wadsworth Longfellow (1807–1882), who within a decade would emerge as America's most popular poet, but who in 1836 was (like Alexandre Dumas) an unknown quantity in the United States, having just returned from Germany to assume a professorship of modern literature at Harvard. The reference is even more intriguing if one realizes that Longfellow's maternal grandfather was Peleg Wadsworth (1748–1829), a brigadier general in the American Revolution.

12. *carrier's address.* Generally a poem printed on a single sheet of paper, called a "broadside," which was purportedly addressed by a newsboy ("carrier") to his customers at Christmastime in hopes of receiving a cash present. These ephemeral productions were hardly prestigious works, though they are interesting aspects of American popular culture. As an aspiring poet, Smith was familiar with such matters (and perhaps knew of Longfellow's early work for magazines as well). What follows next is clearly a demonstration of his own talents and should have tipped off the reader early on that the *Exploits* were spurious, for Colonel Crockett never revealed a talent or taste for poetry.

CHAPTER III.

1. *promised . . . freedom.* As Shackford tells us, at the start of his trip to Texas Crockett was concerned only with locating a promising site for his new farm, planning to be joined there by his family as soon as he was established.

2. *tortled.* Adapted from "tortile," an adjective meaning twisted or winding, suggesting here a circuitous hence slow passage.

3. *Biddle.* Nicholas Biddle (1786–1844), here joined to Webster and Clay as a prominent Whig, was an accomplished scholar and statesman who in 1822 became president of the second National Bank of the United States, and was the target of the Jackson administration's attack on that institution. (See Introduction.)

4. *Betsey.* Smith is confused here. Named for his wife, Elizabeth, Crockett's favorite rifle, described by Clarke's *Life* in 1833, was not the one given him by the "Young Whigs" of Philadelphia on Independence Day in 1834, which was left at home when he departed for Texas. (cf. note to p. 27, below)

5. *came to a clearing.* The anecdote that follows was taken from a sketch in A. B. Longstreet's *Georgia Scenes* (1835). Titled "Georgia Theatrics," it was according to James D. Hart's *Oxford Companion to American Literature* (1941 ed.) "used in Crockett's *Autobiography*," when it is presumably this book that was meant.

6. *some things can be done as well as others.* Another reference to Sam Patch's boast.

7. *Benton.* Thomas Hart Benton (1782–1858) was a prominent Missouri statesman; elected as a Democrat to the U.S. Senate in 1820, he remained in that body for thirty years. In the 1830s he was a spokesman in the Senate for Jackson's administration and supported the president's attack on the National Bank. He was nicknamed "Old Bullion" because of his ardent support of hard (gold and silver) currency, to which further mention is made below.

8. *Isaac Hill.* Hill (1789–1851), another supporter of Jackson, was a Democratic senator from New Hampshire from 1831 to 1836, when he became governor of that state until 1839.

9. *Dick Johnson.* Richard M. Johnson (1780–1850) was a Democrat from Kentucky, a hero of the War of 1812 (credited with killing Tecumseh), and a member of Congress who was a close friend of President Jackson. He supported his positions even when disagreeing with them—as in the president's attack on the bank. He was rewarded by Jackson by being chosen as Van Buren's running

mate in the election of 1837. The "wool grower" tag is a reference to the fact that Johnson, who never married, had two children by Julia Chinn, a mulatto he inherited from his father's
estate; after her death he consorted, sequentially, with two mulatto ("high yellow") sisters.

10. *Lieut. Randolph.* In 1833, while reading a newspaper aboard a
steamboat bound for Fredricksburg, Virginia, the president was
suddenly struck in the face by Robert B. Randolph, a former navy
lieutenant who had been dismissed from the service for theft, on
Jackson's orders. Trapped between a table and his chair, Jackson
could not rise to defend himself. Randolph was arrested and
brought to trial, but the general (by then returned to private life)
asked Van Buren to pardon his assailant. This was the first time
in U.S. history that a president had been physically attacked and
the incident suggested the vast changes affecting the republic at
large. (See Remini, 252–53.)

11. *slang-whang.* Colloquial, often abusive speechifying. (See also
p. 48.)

CHAPTER IV.

1. *took a horn.* Probably colloquial but perhaps a literal reference to
a drinking horn.

2. *Dick Johnson . . . darkie.* See note to page 21, above.

3. *forgave Colonel Benton.* Refers to a violent brawl in 1813 involving Thomas Hart Benton, his brother, Jesse, and General
Jackson, which left the Hero of New Orleans badly wounded and
the Benton brothers in danger of their lives in Nashville, from
which they soon departed. In 1823, when Benton (then a resident
of Missouri) and Jackson served together in the U.S. Senate, they
resolved their past differences with a handshake. (See Remini,
69–71.)

4. *When it came to my turn.* In Fenimore Cooper's *The Pathfinder,*
Leatherstocking actually succeeds in firing a bullet so that it lands
on top of one previously fired at a target. Cooper borrowed the
feat from Sir Walter Scott's *Ivanhoe,* where an arrow splits another already in the bullseye. By contrast, Crockett's trick is a
variation of the shell game, in which the gambler palms a pea so
that the shell selected by the unsuspecting dupe is shown to be
empty. (See below, p. 43.) But the resemblance between the two
episodes is suggestive. Notably, Mark Twain included the un-

likely display of Leatherstocking's marksmanship in "Fenimore Cooper's Literary Offenses."

5. *And this is fame!* "Such is fame" was the epitaph on Sam Patch's wooden grave marker. The reference here, however, is to the dubious medium by which the landlord "handed his name to posterity," the "lasting columns" of a local newspaper, suggesting that fame is a sometime thing. As I have already suggested, Crockett's "fame," like that of Sam Patch, was the kind of notoriety associated with temporal celebrity. Smith, a former editor himself, is suggesting that newspapers serve the moment only and are of the essence of ephemerality. The same holds for the almanacs that helped create "Davy" Crockett.

6. *heir presumptive.* Martin Van Buren. In a democratic society there is no "heir presumptive," so this is another jibe at "King Andrew."

7. *"the times that tried men's souls."* Echoes the famous words that open Thomas Paine's *The American Crisis,* the first number of which was published in December 1776, when the fortunes of the new nation were bleak. Paine's pamphlet was intended to arouse enthusiasm for the Revolution and so impressed George Washington that he had it read to his troops. But here Paine's stirring words are so much generated by self-serving politicians, an expression of Crockett's bitterness regarding Jacksonian democracy.

8. *nem.con.* Abbreviation for *nemine contradicente,* Latin for "no one contradicting," a parliamentary usage meaning "passed unanimously."

9. *half horse half alligator breed.* A humorous epithet of obscure origins used to describe the wilder elements of the western population; usually found along rivers, specifically the Mississippi, these roughnecks were in essence amphibious, hence the implication. The expression was made popular by Samuel Woodworth's poem (as set to music), "The Hunters of Kentucky" (1818), celebrating the victory by frontiersmen over the British at New Orleans, and appears as well in Paulding's play inspired by Crockett, *The Lion of the West.*

CHAPTER V.

1. *all bountiful Providence.* This sermonette by the "parson" contains pious sentiments seldom if ever expressed by the "real" David Crockett, and like the character of the "old gentleman" are

intended to increase the sentimental burden of the narrative, one more indication of the increasing imposition of Smith's sensibility on the story.

2. *Temperance society*. The enthusiasm for total abstinence from "spirituous" drink was widespread in the 1830s, thanks to the missionary activities of the American Temperance Society. Crockett was inclined otherwise, as evidenced by his willingness to distribute liquor to voters and his fondness for taking a "horn" or two on social occasions. The parson's joining him in taking a drink is evidence that he is no narrow-minded killjoy, that despite his piousness he is a regular fellow.

3. *cutest clerk*. Not a reference to the person's physical attractiveness but a common abbreviation for "acute," meaning sharply intelligent, even cunning.

4. *following conversation*. What follows is a demonstration of the stereotyped Yankee's garrulous curiosity, which inspires the westerner's stereotyped taciturnity.

5. *slapsus slinkum*. Malapropism for *lapsus linguae,* meaning a slip of the tongue. The mistake indicates the pretentiousness of the ignorant Yankee (cf. "detentive" above where "retentive" is meant).

CHAPTER VI.

1. *blackleg*. A swindler.

2. *thimblerig*. A game in which three downturned small cups (thimbles) are used, under one of which a pea is placed. The gambler swiftly switches the cups about on a table or board, then asks the player to choose the one containing the pea. If the player chooses the right one, the gambler palms the pea as he lifts the cup. Also called a "shell game," it is here used to discount the reputation of Martin Van Buren, accused of swindling the American people.

3. *"whole hog."* To go the whole way. The thimblerigger later becomes drunk, and his claim of being a temperance man is intended to convince Crockett that he is highly moral and honest.

4. *Lynched*. The world is capitalized here because it was derived from the name of Charles Lynch (1736–1796), a justice of the peace in Virginia who permitted the suspension of due process by mobs seeking to punish accused Tories during the Revolution. The practice spread to the frontier, where formal legal systems were weak and slow to act, and juries often returned judgments deemed insufficiently severe by the populace. Thimblerig later

(pp. 55–57) renders an account of one such episode in Natchez. During Reconstruction, lynching was used in the South as an instrument to repress the civil rights of African Americans, while at the same time it was being practiced in the cattle country of the far West as a response to lawlessness, especially rustling.

In the 1830s and 1840s, abolitionists who expressed anti-slavery opinions in the deep South could expect rough treatment by mobs, explaining Crockett's equivocation in that regard. One solution to the slavery problem was put forward by the American Colonization Society, which recommended that freed slaves be sent to Africa, where they could serve as missionaries. This resulted in the creation of the country of Liberia. But ultra-abolitionists like William Lloyd Garrison were adamantly opposed to this rival movement, which they saw as a very imperfect solution to the problem. And in the deep South, as Crockett's demurrer suggests, slavery was not regarded as a problem but a solution. The historic David Crockett owned a few slaves but while siding with the Cherokees against Jackson's removal bill, which he regarded as unjust, seems to have had no opinions on the slavery issue.

5. *Judge White.* Hugh Lawson White (1773–1841), a jurist, banker, and Democratic senator from Tennessee (1825–1840). He backed Jackson's Indian removal policy, but eventually broke with the president and became the Whig candidate in the presidential campaign of 1836 against Van Buren with John Tyler as his running mate.

6. *Old Tippecanoe.* Refers to William Henry Harrison, yet another veteran-hero of frontier battles in the War of 1812 (though the one for which he was named occurred in 1811, against the confederated tribes led by Tecumseh). Nominated by the Anti-Masonic party for president in 1835, he made such a surprising showing in 1836 that he was chosen by the Whigs (over Henry Clay) as their candidate in 1840. Armed with a log cabin as a symbol and the slogan "Tippecanoe and [John] Tyler too," and dispensing large quantities of hard cider, the Whigs handily defeated Van Buren, characterized as a tool of eastern elites.

7. *blunt.* Slang for money, presumably in reference to coins, which have a round edge, hence blunt.

8. *He talked loud.* We hear more about this loud-mouthed Democrat later (pp. 61–66).

9. *Mr. Clinton.* DeWitt Clinton (1769–1828), famous for his support of the Erie Canal while governor of New York (1817–1823 and 1825–1828), had a very complex political record, typical of

the tangled loyalties during a period when the Jefferson Republicans were in power and the Federalist party was in decline. Nominally a Republican, Clinton (then mayor of New York City) allowed himself to be considered for nomination by the Federalists as their presidential candidate for the election of 1812, on the basis of his opposition to the war with Great Britain, even though he had already been nominated by the Republicans of the state legislature in Albany. Clinton ran against James Madison and lost, and by changing parties he lost his credibility and was removed in 1815 as New York's mayor.

Van Buren, a Republican who by 1812 had already gained a well-warranted reputation for political shiftiness, backed Clinton. He further demonstrated his hostility to President Madison's policies in 1813 when, as a member of the New York state legislature, he voted for Rufus King (1755–1827) for the U.S. Senate. King was a Federalist who was also opposed to the war with Great Britain—as were many New Yorkers—because of its negative impact on international trade. In 1836, these actions were hauled up by the Whigs (many of whom were former Federalists who had opposed the War of 1812) as evidence that Van Buren was a sunshine patriot opposed to the nation's best interests, which Smith's Crockett identifies with the war against Great Britain. But as this same speech reveals, his hostility to Van Buren was chiefly based on the New York senator's opposition to measures favored by western residents.

10. *wrote his life.* The foregoing attack on Van Buren sums up the materials and tone of the biography of the vice president written over Crockett's name in 1835. (See Introduction.)

CHAPTER VII.

1. *frog in the fable.* Aesop's fable about a frog, who, hearing an admiring description of a large bull, attempts to swell up to comparable size and explodes.

2. *Johnson's wife.* See note to p. 21, above. "Figuring" suggests "making a figure," that is, to become prominent in Washington society.

3. *"pump upon me."* That is, to be held under a pump and doused with water. See p. 66 below for a dramatic example of this punishment.

4. *Natchez under the hill.* Located on low ground and providing a landing place on the Mississippi, this was a community notorious in its day for gambling dens, saloons, and bawdy houses, catering to the crews of river craft.

5. *leg bail.* Leaving town so as to avoid being arrested.

6. *"yellow boys . . . Benton's mintage."* "Yellow boys" is slang for gold coins, hence the reference to Benton, but here it is mulatto children that are meant. (See Introduction and p. 62 below.)

7. *"Lynchers."* See note to page 45, above.

CHAPTER VIII.

1. *The evening preceding . . . put in circulation.* This anecdote is intended to be humorous, but is akin to Mark Twain's remark about the woman who was relieved when her child was born white, being both misogynistic and miscegenational. As we have already learned, the gentleman duped into passing the woman off as his wife, presumably in hopes of sexual favors, is a Jacksonian Democrat.

2. *a tall figure.* We are introduced here to Edward, the Bee hunter, who will accompany Crockett and Thimblerig to the Alamo. Unlike the rascally but humorous gambler, he is a stalwart frontiersman, and with his love of song, a romantic creation, as opposed to the picaresque Thimblerig. Expressing the poetic sensibility of Smith, he was undoubtedly borrowed from Cooper's Paul Hover in *The Prairie* (see Introduction). A courageous, forthright representative of the common man, he faces down the blustering, bullying Jacksonian, and in effect is a cosmeticized Crockett.

3. *cucumber blooded.* Cf. "cool as a cucumber."

4. *honey trees are abundant in Texas.* In his last surviving letter home, Crockett describes the Red River region as the place where he hopes to settle, having fertile soil, good hunting, "and bees and honey plenty" (Shackford, 214–15).

CHAPTER IX.

1. *heard the Woods sing.* I have not been able to identify this reference. There was a well-known minstrel company organized by Henry Wood in the 1840s, advertised as "Woods Minstrels," but such groups did not exist in 1836.

2. *Jim Crow.* Refers to the entertainer, Thomas Rice (1808–1860), credited with fathering the American minstrel show. In Louisville, Kentucky, in 1828, Rice introduced a song of this title to which he added a grotesque dance keyed by the words "Ebery time I wheel about I jump Jim Crow." By 1836, Rice and his song had become universally acclaimed, and he had performed in New York, Boston, Washington, and Philadelphia, most often between the acts of comic dramas. As with "Crockett's" allusions to Sam Patch, Smith's tribute to Rice is an example of the extent to which he was aware of the popular culture of his day.

3. *"Andrew Tumlinson."* What follows is an incident typical of the Indian-hater type, yet another aspect of frontier myth, and the subject of Robert M. Bird's sensational novel, *Nick of the Woods* (1837). As Richard Slotkin tells us, James Hall's *Sketches of History, Life, and Manners in the West,* published in 1835, gives an account of Colonel John Moredock, a "classic sketch of the 'Indian Hater' . . . [and] a well-known and frequently reprinted piece of Frontier history and legend" (*Fatal Environment,* pp. 129–30). Here again, we find Smith working into his narrative folkloric aspects of western life, in effect bolstering Crockett's mythic status.

4. *Caddo.* Member of a confederated tribe of Native Americans, found throughout southern Louisiana and Texas. They were not a particularly warlike people, so that the behavior of the Caddo in question, if the anecdote is true, was not typical.

5. *"What did he do that made him leave home?"* During the early days of Texas settlement, as the Bee hunter suggests, it was considered rude—even fatal—to ask this question, given the often unsavory backgrounds of people who had left the East for that region in the hope of beginning their lives anew.

6. *Vicksburg hat.* The description defines the article in question. Mitford M. Mathews, in his *Dictionary of Americanisms on Historical Principals* (1951), quotes a similar passage (p. 133) in this book as his only source.

7. *lazo.* More properly "lasso," as on p. 92 following.

8. *"grin down."* So ferocious was Crockett's grin in the mythic version that it had the power to destroy as well as kill. Shackford quotes an anecdote credited to Matthew St. Clair Clarke, author of the *Life* of Crockett, in which the redoubtable colonel, during a visit to a zoo, threatens to grin two hyenas to death and declares himself willing to take on a lion (Shackford, 259–60). In Clarke's *Life* the hyenas became wildcats, and Crockett tells the story of his attempt to "grin" a raccoon out of a tree, but the object in

question turns out to be a great knot in a limb that loses its bark from the intensity of his effort. This is the sort of thing that inspired the almanac version of "Davy" Crockett.

CHAPTER X.

1. *ruling passion.* An overwhelming desire for a particular activity that cannot be controlled, this was an eighteenth-century concept associated with the poetry of Alexander Pope: "The ruling passion, be it what it will, / The ruling passion conquers reason still" (*Moral Essays,* Epistle I). Crockett's love of hunting may be attributed in part to the need of keeping his family in food, but certainly his autobiography is filled with stories about the many bears and deer he has killed. There is no account of a buffalo hunt on his trip through Texas in the slim factual record, but what follows on pp. 83–84 is an acceptable transliteration of Crockett's stories of bear hunting, including his encounter with one resembling a very large black bull.

2. *dressed in a sailor's round jacket.* Another fictional invention, the pirate who joins Crockett's party helps round out the cast of American types. In the almanacs, Crockett will be given a boon companion, Ben Hardin, an old salt who seems out of place on the Mississippi River.

3. *Lafitte.* Jean Lafitte (c. 1780–c. 1826), French-born freebooter who headed a gang of pirates operating out of Barataria Bay in Louisiana and who assisted the Americans in defeating the British at the Battle of New Orleans. Lafitte subsequently moved his operation to Galveston, then still under Spanish rule.

4. *hunter belonging to a settler.* This is the only mention in Smith's narrative of slavery in Texas. In fact, in order to bypass the Mexican law against slavery, American settlers freed their human property, then immediately converted them to indentured servants.

5. *Post office accounts.* See Introduction.

6. *Benton's mint drops.* Another slighting reference to the senator's preference for hard currency, with a pun on "mint."

7. *John Gilpin's celebrated ride.* In William Cowper's comic poem, first published in 1785, a linen-draper takes an involuntary gallop on a borrowed horse from London to Ware and back again: "Now let us sing—Long live the king, / And Gilpin long live he; / And when he next doth ride abroad, / May I be there to see!"

8. *"race is not always . . ."* Ecclesiastes 9:11.

CHAPTER XI.

1. *fifty mounted Cumanches*. Shackford (p. 215) tells us when Crockett was on the trail in Texas, heading toward the southwest, he was warned that the Comanches were on the warpath, and changed his route accordingly. Smith, however, adds further color to his narrative by including this Cooper-like episode.

2. *Bexar*. The full name of San Antonio was San Antonio de Bexar (Spanish: "Bejar"). See p. 98, below.

3. *Bowie knife*. First fashioned by the brother of Colonel James Bowie, another of the Alamo heroes, these awesome weapons were called "Arkansaw tooth-picks."

4. *Philip Hone, Esq*. Hone (1780–1851) was a wealthy and affable Whig activist and mayor of New York City (1825), but is chiefly known for his extensive secret diary covering the years 1828 to 1851.

5. *Plucking pigeons*. That is, the gambler is skilled at skinning suckers.

6. *Burnet's Grant*. Large tract of land settled by the American *empresario* David G. Burnet under the terms of the Mexican colonization law of 1825. It lay to the northeast of San Antonio and was bisected by the Trinity River. It is details like this that gave credibility to Smith's narrative.

7. *fortress of Alamo*. The modern-day Alamo is represented by the mission chapel built in 1756 that by 1836 had fallen into ruins, thanks in no small part to the damage caused by the American rebels the year before. At the time of the attack by the Mexican army the fort itself was of considerable size, surrounded by a thick wall (hastily repaired in anticipation of the Mexican attack) and barrack buildings, and the chapel occupied a only a small space in the southeast corner. The "independent flag" is another of Smith's embellishments. According to Albert Nofi, "there may have been at least four flags in use at the Alamo," none of which was the one bearing the familiar lone star (p. 110, below), another matter that "remains unresolved" (Nofi, 129).

CHAPTER XII.

1. *revolution in 1812*. Refers to the start of the long struggle for Mexican independence from Spain.

2. *Colonel Travis*. William B. Travis (1809–1836) was a native of South Carolina practicing law in Texas when, opposing Mexican

rule, in 1835 he led a company of volunteers and successfully attacked the fort at Anahuac, recently garrisoned by the Mexican government as a gesture of its authority over increasingly restive settlers. Though many Americans in Texas disavowed this action, it in effect was the start of the revolution against Mexican rule. Once the revolution proper began, Travis was commissioned lieutenant-colonel of cavalry and ordered to assume joint command of the fort with Colonel James Bowie. Twenty-seven years old at the time, Travis was a handsome, charismatic leader, who apparently deserved Smith's epithet, "gallant."

3. *Santa Anna.* Antonio López de Santa Anna (1794–1876), a career soldier and politician, was born in Vera Cruz, the province that he governed after Mexico overturned Spanish rule in 1821. He was instrumental in making his country a federal republic, but in 1832, having led a successful revolt against President Bustamante, Santa Anna abolished the federal constitution and declared himself dictator. Although he commenced his political career as a liberal, he now pursued a reactionary policy, including the establishment of Mexican garrisons in Texas, a step that only strengthened the colonists' resolve to gain full independence. (See Smith's account, pp. 101–105 below).

Following the surrender of the fort at Anahuac and the fall of the garrison at San Antonio (see next note), Santa Anna led a large army north with the intent of quelling the American revolt. Victorious at the Alamo and Goliad, he was defeated by Sam Houston at the battle for San Jacinto, and though his conduct of the campaign warranted his execution, Santa Anna was set free on the condition that, as dictator of Mexico, he would use his influence to guarantee Texan independence. During this period, he traveled to Washington and paid a visit to Andrew Jackson, who was impressed by the bearing, dress, and suave manner of his fellow general-president. Santa Anna was likewise impressed by Jackson, but proved to be a slippery negotiator regarding the extension of the U.S. border to include what had been Mexican territory. Despite his dictatorial status, the general deferred to the power of the Mexican congress, which, after Santa Anna's return (facilitated by a U.S. warship), refused the surrender of Texas on any terms. (See Remini, 312–13.)

For a time Santa Anna retreated to his Santa Cruz estate, but when the province was attacked by the French in 1838, he was instrumental in its defense, exhibiting (as always) great courage and suffering the loss of a leg. In 1844 he once again became dictator of Mexico, was overthrown in 1845, and sought refuge in Cuba until 1846. He was then recalled to command the forces defending Mexico against the invading American army, hostilities attending the formal annexation by the United States of Texas, still regarded by the Mexican government as its property. He was defeated at the Battle of Buena Vista in 1847 by General Zachary Taylor (1784–1850), resulting in a return to exile for Santa Anna and the successful candidacy for president of Taylor in 1848, in the grand Whig tradition of nominating old generals for that office.

In 1853 Santa Anna was brought back to Mexico and was given the title Serene Highness, signaling his appointment as president for life, an office that ended in 1855, though Santa Anna lived on for another twenty years, seeking through various means to regain power, whether legitimately or by revolution. Eventually he was able to return to Mexico, having been granted amnesty on the grounds that he was too old to pose a threat to the then and future governments. He died in obscurity in 1876.

A thorough account of Santa Anna's political and military career would occupy several more pages, for he seems to have combined the political agility of Van Buren with the autocratic personality and military bravado of Andrew Jackson, to which must be added an extra measure of arrogance and pride. Though Santa Anna was fully justified in his invasion of Texas, which was still Mexican territory, his merciless cruelty at the Alamo and Goliad served to arouse the patriotism of all Americans, eventually contributing to his defeat and capture at the battle of San Jacinto. Whatever the consequences of his several adventures and administrations for Mexico, it must be said that he had a powerful influence on Texan and U.S. affairs, though much different from that which he intended. Certainly it can be said that without Santa Anna there would never have been a mythic Davy Crockett. For a succinct account of the Mexican general's own "legend," including the inspiration for the minstrel song, "The Yellow Rose of Texas," see Nofi, 160–65.

4. *General Burlison*. Edward Burleson (1798–1851) was a native of North Carolina who as the text states was the victorious commander of the attack on San Antonio in 1835; he subsequently fought at the battle for San Jacinto, became a state senator in 1836, and was elected vice president of the Texas republic in 1841.

5. *Colonel Milam*. Benjamin F. Milam (1791–1835), Texas pioneer and surveyor, led the successful attack on the Mexican garrison at

Goliad a week after the revolution had begun. Later, he figured in the week-long siege of the garrison at San Antonio that ended with the surrender of the Mexican defenders. "Old Ben," age forty-four, died in the battle and is honored with a square named after him and a larger-than-life-size statue placed therein.

6. *General Cos.* Martin Perfect de Cos, having fought for Mexican independence, and having married Santa Anna's sister, was advanced to the rank of brigadier general and assigned the military and political command of Texas, a rank and responsibility "for which he was wholly unsuited" (Nofi, 28). General Cos, despite the terms of surrender, participated in the siege of the Alamo, commanding the First Column of Santa Anna's army.

7. *Morales.* Like General Cos, Colonel Juan Morales, commander of the San Luis Potosi Battalion, participated in Santa Anna's attack on the Alamo.

8. *General Ugartechea.* Domingo de Ugartechea was in command of the Mexicans at Fort Velasco, and having refused to allow the Texan rebels free passage on the Brazos River with artillery for the siege of Anahuac, was himself attacked shortly thereafter and after eleven hours of fighting surrendered his garrison.

9. *Colonel Bowie.* James Bowie (1796–1836), one of the three immortals associated with the defense of the Alamo, is perhaps best remembered for the large knife of his brother's invention. Born in Tennessee, raised in Louisiana, Bowie settled in San Antonio in 1828, becoming a citizen of Mexico, a Roman Catholic, and the husband of Maria de Veramendi, daughter of a prominent Mexican family. He had already made a fortune in the slave trade, had a dubious reputation for crooked land deals, and after the death of his wife, in 1832, he allied himself with the revolutionary element. In 1836, he was in joint command with Travis of the American garrison at the Alamo, but by the time of the Mexican attack, was bedridden with typhoid fever. According to the legend propagated by Smith's account (among others), the colonel was armed with loaded pistols, firing them at the soldiers as they came through the door before being killed, but by all dependable accounts, he was already near death before Santa Anna's men arrived.

10. *Mina.* In 1816, Francisco Xavier Mina joined Don Luis Aury, another soldier of fortune and filibuster, at Galveston, which was being used by Aury as a base for ships attacking the Spanish merchant fleet. Seeking to gain advantage during Mexico's ongoing war of independence from Spain, they planned an invasion of the

Mexican coast, but the two leaders quarreled, and Aury pulled out, leaving Mina and his men to their fate.

11. *only live to tree him.* It is language like this that validates Slotkin's thesis that frontier hunters (as in Woodworth's song) were nascent soldiers waiting for the right occasion. But as Smith's narrative tells us, after his defeat at San Jacinto, Santa Anna fled, and being pursued, was found to "like a hard pressed bear have taken [to] a tree" (p. 125), explaining the words put into Crockett's mouth before the event.

CHAPTER XIII.

1. *Gunter's . . . scale.* Edmund Gunter (1581–1626), English mathematician and inventor. Gunter's scale was an instrument used for purposes of navigation and trigonometric calculations, hence a byword for exactness.

2. *the steamboat and alligator breed.* What follows is a typical frontier boast, associated with Crockett himself in Clarke's *Life,* Paulding's play, and the almanac anecdotes. Mark Twain renders a luxuriant example in the raftsmen episode taken from the manuscript of *The Adventures of Huckleberry Finn* and published in *Life on the Mississippi* (1883).

3. *Tampico.* The reference is to an attempt by Spain to regain control of Mexico in 1829. Though the soldier's story does not mention it, the invasion was successfully repulsed by Santa Anna. The point of the story is to emphasize the barbarity with which prisoners of war were handled by Mexican authorities.

4. *General Sesma.* Joaquin Ramirez y Sesma was in command of the Mexican cavalry.

5. *national flag.* See the note to p. 97.

6. *Colonel Fanning.* James Walker Fannin [sic] (1804–1836), a native of Georgia, briefly attended West Point, and by 1834 had settled in Texas with his wife and two children. Prospering in slave smuggling and land speculation, he naturally was drawn to the revolutionary faction, and participated in a number of early battles of the war, culminating in the attack on San Antonio in December, 1835. He was then placed in charge of a force gathering in Goliad with the intention of invading Mexico, an event that never came off but which was responsible for Fannin's failure to commit any of the four-hundred-odd men under his command for

the relief of the garrison at San Antonio. (His eventual fate is recounted on p. 125, below, the massacre at Goliad serving as a powerful motive for revenge against Santa Anna, second only to the fate of the Alamo.

7. *Upas. Antiaris toxicaria,* a large tree native to Java, the sap of which was used to poison arrows, but which was not so deadly as to kill anything within range of its branches, a fable promulgated by Erasmus Darwin's "Loves of the Plants" (1789).

CHAPTER XIV.

1. *General Houston.* Samuel ("Sam") Houston (1793–1863) was born in Virginia but raised in Tennessee, in Cherokee country. He served under Jackson in the Creek War, was wounded, and having served as a Democratic representative to Congress (1823–1827), he was in 1827 elected governor of Tennessee. When his wife left him for unknown reasons, he resigned his office and went to live with the Cherokees as an adopted member of the tribe, whose removal he opposed but not to the point of breaking with Jackson. In 1835, he became identified with the Texan revolution and commanded the rebel army. His Fabian strategy was unpopular, but Houston's reputation was redeemed after his victory over Santa Anna at San Jacinto. As president of the Republic of Texas, he negotiated the recognition by the United States of the new republic in 1836 and, though not in favor of annexation, did not oppose it. He represented the state as U.S. senator from 1846–1859, when he was elected governor of Texas. An ardent Unionist, he refused to swear allegiance to the Confederacy, and resigned his office, still believing that Texas was an independent nation.

FOR THE BEST IN PAPERBACKS, LOOK FOR THE

In every corner of the world, on every subject under the sun, Penguin represents quality and variety—the very best in publishing today.

For complete information about books available from Penguin—including Penguin Classics, Penguin Compass, and Puffins—and how to order them, write to us at the appropriate address below. Please note that for copyright reasons the selection of books varies from country to country.

In the United States: Please write to *Penguin Group (USA), P.O. Box 12289 Dept. B, Newark, New Jersey 07101-5289* or call 1-800-788-6262.

In the United Kingdom: Please write to *Dept. EP, Penguin Books Ltd, Bath Road, Harmondsworth, West Drayton, Middlesex UB7 0DA.*

In Canada: Please write to *Penguin Books Canada Ltd, 10 Alcorn Avenue, Suite 300, Toronto, Ontario M4V 3B2.*

In Australia: Please write to *Penguin Books Australia Ltd, P.O. Box 257, Ringwood, Victoria 3134.*

In New Zealand: Please write to *Penguin Books (NZ) Ltd, Private Bag 102902, North Shore Mail Centre, Auckland 10.*

In India: Please write to *Penguin Books India Pvt Ltd, 11 Panchsheel Shopping Centre, Panchsheel Park, New Delhi 110 017.*

In the Netherlands: Please write to *Penguin Books Netherlands bv, Postbus 3507, NL-1001 AH Amsterdam.*

In Germany: Please write to *Penguin Books Deutschland GmbH, Metzlerstrasse 26, 60594 Frankfurt am Main.*

In Spain: Please write to *Penguin Books S. A., Bravo Murillo 19, 1° B, 28015 Madrid.*

In Italy: Please write to *Penguin Italia s.r.l., Via Benedetto Croce 2, 20094 Corsico, Milano.*

In France: Please write to *Penguin France, Le Carré Wilson, 62 rue Benjamin Baillaud, 31500 Toulouse.*

In Japan: Please write to *Penguin Books Japan Ltd, Kaneko Building, 2-3-25 Koraku, Bunkyo-Ku, Tokyo 112.*

In South Africa: Please write to *Penguin Books South Africa (Pty) Ltd, Private Bag X14, Parkview, 2122 Johannesburg.*